737-0178

WHEN THE LAW LETS KILLERS GO FREE

"Judge Lengel climbed back on the bench, looked down at the District Attorney and said, 'Do I understand the People wish to make a statement at this time?'

"And the District Attorney, his face red, stands up and says something like, 'Judge Lengel, confronted by Your Honor's rulings, the People find it impossible to make a *prima facie* case. Therefore, we consent to this indictment being dismissed.'

"I jumped up and shouted, 'You can't do that!'

"Judge Lengel only rapped his gavel and said, 'Clear the courtroom.'

"It was all over. Just like that. And that black bastard and his white lawyer walk out. He's free. And laughing.

"Nedda broke down and cried. If she hadn't been there, I would have cried."

OUTRAGE

BY HENRY DENKER

AVON
PUBLISHERS OF BARD, CAMELOT, DISCUS AND FLARE BOOKS

AVON BOOKS
A division of
The Hearst Corporation
959 Eighth Avenue
New York, New York 10019

The William Morrow and Company, Inc. edition contains
the following Library of Congress Cataloging in Publica-
tion Data:

Denker, Henry.
   Outrage, a novel.

   I. Title.
PS3507.E547509   813'.54   81-22551
                                     AACR2

First Avon Printing, May, 1983

Though *Outrage* is a fictional creation, all legal references and quotations contained therein are authentic.

To my wife, Edith

OUTRAGE

DENNIS RIORDAN WAS extremely nervous. He had never before bought a gun. Never before planned to commit murder.

He stared into the shop window amazed at the display of long-barreled .45's, short, stubby-nosed, nickel-plated .38's, flat, black .32's, automatics. Back in New York, places that sold guns did not display them so openly.

He wished he had learned more about the most effective handgun to kill a man. But he had not dared ask, for fear of betraying his plan. He would have to rely on what he had learned from watching television shows and movies. A .38 or a .45, either weapon should do it.

He entered the store, his hands sweaty and clenched to hide their trembling. The young clerk behind the counter interrupted arranging a new shipment of pistols on the top shelf of the display case.

"Yes, sir? Help you, sir?"

Dennis Riordan was sixty-six. He was of medium height and had a compact build, with sparse, graying hair and a ruddy, freckled face. He wet his lips and said, "I'd like to see something in a . . . a thirty-eight."

Then, because he thought some special reason might be required in this state, he added, "For home protection.

11

Too many break-ins in our neighborhood the last few months."

"I know how it is," the clerk said. "My wife'd never be without one."

The clerk picked a weapon out of the case, a short-nosed, nickel-plated .38, and handed it to him. Riordan realized it was the first time in his life he had ever handled a weapon specifically intended to kill a human being.

As he examined it, surprised at its weight, he asked, "A woman could manage this all right? I mean, it's mainly for my wife. She being home alone all the time I'm at work."

"Oh, sure," the clerk said. "Of course, a twenty-two would be lighter. But a thirty-eight will really do the job."

"That's what I want. Something that will really do the job," Dennis Riordan said. He examined the gun in the manner in which he thought someone buying a gun should. It still felt cold and too heavy. However, he would not have to carry it long or use it more than once.

"I guess my wife can handle it," Riordan said. "And I'll need some ammo." He tried to say it casually, a word he had picked up from police and detective television shows.

"You got it," the clerk said, reaching into the cabinet behind him to produce a small, heavy box. "Four dozen. That should keep you. Unless you figure to invade some foreign country."

Riordan hoped he had laughed easily enough at the young man's weak joke.

"Then we're all set. Except, of course, for the form," the clerk said.

"Form?" Riordan was startled.

"Got to fill this out with every sale. But I don't think you'll have any trouble," the clerk said, then asked the questions provided on the paper. "You swear you have never been convicted of a crime punishable by imprisonment for more than one year?"

"I have never been convicted of any crime."

"You a fugitive from justice?"

"No, sir!"

"Ever been committed to a mental institution?"

"No."

"Are you in any way unsuited to bear arms?"

"No, sir."

"Now, I'll need some positive identification. Driver's license is best. But I'll take anything with your signature and your picture on it."

Since his driver's license would betray that he was from out of state, Riordan countered, "I got cards with my signature on them. But nothing with a picture."

The clerk hesitated for a moment, a most uneasy moment for Dennis Riordan, then said, "You don't look dangerous to me, Pop. Just your signature will do."

Riordan produced two charge cards with signatures on them, his Social Security card and his Medicare card.

The clerk made note of them, turned the form around and asked Riordan to sign. As he did, the clerk picked up the Medicare card. "I'd never have guessed. You don't look old enough for Medicare."

"Thanks to working. Retire early, you die young. You want to keep your health and live to be a hundred, keep right on working, son."

"At the rate I get paid, I don't have much choice," the clerk joked as he entered the sale of the weapon and its number in his official ledger. "That'll be $163.77, including the ammunition and a box of blanks."

"Blanks?"

"Mister, you've never handled a gun before, have you?"

Riordan paused, then confessed, "No."

"Then take this box of blanks. Use them for practice. A shooting range is the best place. But down in your cellar will do. Provided you protect your ears. Get used to the feel of it. And let your wife get used to it, too."

This last remark relieved Riordan's mind. The clerk had not suspected that Mrs. Riordan was dead, or the real purpose for which he had purchased the weapon.

"Good idea," Riordan agreed. "I'll take both boxes." He pushed nine twenty-dollar bills across the counter.

As the clerk handed him his change, Dennis Riordan thanked him, slipped the gun into his pocket and took his two boxes of bullets. He left the store saying to himself, "Nedda, I'm sorry I had to lie about you. But if you were alive today, you'd agree I have to do what I'm going to do."

2

FOR THE SECOND TIME Dennis Riordan circled the block between 117th and 118th Streets on Lenox Avenue, a neighborhood of sleazy bars with dirty neon signs and tenements built almost a century ago. Some had been abandoned, their windows shattered. In some doorways derelicts slept, victims of whatever drug they had been able to procure. Riordan's faded green Dodge was nondescript enough not to attract attention in this rundown area. But he was keenly aware that he was a white man in a totally black neighborhood. He could not keep circling the block without becoming the object of suspicion. If luck was with him, this time would be enough. If not, he would come back tomorrow, and the next day and for as many days as necessary. For he had arranged to work the night shift at the warehouse in order to have his days free for this mission.

He was making the downtown leg of his route when he spotted his man. Riordan focused sharply to make absolutely sure. He could never mistake that face. Ever since it happened, it was burned indelibly into his memory. He had spent nights brooding over it, burning at the injustice this man had so ruthlessly inflicted on him and his family. The man was laughing now just as he had been the last time Dennis Riordan had seen him.

No question, that was the face, that was the man. Tall, black, with the physique of a heavyweight boxer or an NFL tackle, he was coming out of the corner bar with another man, also black but much shorter, and he, too, was laughing.

Riordan double-parked and left the motor running. He slipped out, his sweaty hand gripping the nickel-plated .38 in his pocket. The man had his back to him.

Riordan called out, "Cletus Johnson!"

The big black man turned. Riordan produced his gun, pulled the trigger five times. The big man crumpled and fell to the sidewalk. His companion, who had ducked behind a brownstone stoop at the first shot, made no attempt to pursue Riordan, who calmly walked to his car, got in and drove away.

All during the time he had planned this killing, he had wondered how it would feel afterward. Would he suffer remorse or guilt? Now he knew. He felt no pangs of conscience, only freedom, relief from the constant need to hate that man. His gun hand, which had been sweaty before, was dry now. The constant ache in his chest was gone.

"I did it, Nedda, I did it!" he exulted.

3

SEVEN MINUTES LATER Dennis Riordan pulled up before the Twenty-sixth Police Precinct. A law-abiding citizen for all his sixty-six years, this time he deliberately chose to park in a zone clearly marked *No Parking.*

This would be only the second time in his life that Dennis Riordan had reason to enter a police station. The first time was when his son, Frank, then aged twelve, had been taken in for climbing a locked schoolyard fence to play basketball.

Now, Dennis Riordan, father, husband, for forty-one years conscientious employee of the Astoria Moving and Warehouse Company, vestryman of St. Malachy's Church, paused before the precinct house.

He had anticipated this moment from the inception of his plan. It felt far less terrifying than he had thought, far less onerous even than some confessions he had made at St. Malachy's. He became aware of the car keys in his broad, strong workman's hand. He realized he would never need those keys again. For an instant he felt inclined to toss them into the street. Instead, he shoved them into his pocket and continued to the door of the precinct.

He approached the desk and announced to the sergeant:

"I just killed a man on Lenox Avenue between a Hundred and Seventeenth and a Hundred and Eighteenth Street." He pulled out the nickel-plated .38, placed it on the desk. "I want to be booked and I want to be tried."

Suspecting he might be dealing with a psycho, Sergeant Abe Kalbfus flashed an eye signal to two uniformed patrolmen who were talking over cups of coffee. They quickly seized Riordan.

"Let go of me!" Riordan protested. "I won't try to escape. I just want to be booked and tried."

"Okay," Kalbfus ordered. "Nobody say a word. Not even you, Mister. Just hold still!" He picked up the phone, pressed down an intercom button. "Who's free in Homicide? Send him out!"

In moments Detective August Marchi emerged. He was a tall man in his early forties.

"What's up?" Marchi asked.

"Man claims to have committed a homicide. This is the weapon."

Marchi reached out gingerly to touch the nose of the .38, only enough to turn it about so he could sniff the muzzle.

"I'd say the man might be right. Give me an envelope."

The sergeant handed Marchi a transparent plastic envelope. Marchi pulled a ballpoint pen out of his pocket, delicately inserted it into the end of the barrel and lifted the gun. As he slipped it into the plastic envelope, the desk phone rang. The sergeant answered, "Twenty-sixth desk. Kalbfus. A homicide? Lenox Avenue and a Hundred and Seventeenth Street? Okay, we'll alert the Medical Examiner."

He hung up, turned to Marchi, who said, "I guess the man is really telling the truth."

Riordan interrupted. "You're wasting time. I want to make a full confession. I want to be booked and tried."

Marchi glanced at Kalbfus, then at Riordan. "Mister, it is not that simple. First, you are not to say another word. Except if I ask you, do you want some coffee? you can say yes or no. Otherwise, nothing! Now, go along." He gestured to the two officers, who led Riordan off to a small interrogation room.

Marchi reached for the desk phone, dialed and asked, "D.A. please?" When he was put through, he said, "Would you send one of your bright young men up to the Twenty-sixth? We got a confession in a homicide. Half an hour? No more than that. You know how these kooks are. One minute they're hot to trot, insisting they want to confess. Half an hour later they never even heard of the victim. So rush. This could be the strangest one yet."

Dennis Riordan and Detective August Marchi had been sitting staring at each other for more than half an hour. To Dennis Riordan the small, bare room with its faded yellow walls seemed to have grown smaller, more confining. Confessing was not so simple as he had expected. Every time he started to speak, Marchi would stop him. "Not a word! Nothing, Mr. Riordan. Not yet!"

"But all I want to do is confess."

"Not in this city, you don't. We have to wait for the D.A. So just sit quiet and wait. The man should be here any minute."

Meantime there were sounds at the door. They did not trouble Riordan because he had no idea what they were. They comforted Marchi because he knew it was Rosenthal, the television technician, setting up the video camera to make a record of what would transpire in this room in the next several hours.

Finally, the door opened. A young black man, wearing

heavy-framed glasses and carrying an attaché case, leaned in to ask, "Detective Marchi?"

"That's me," Marchi said, rising.

The young black man held out his hand to the detective. "Lester Crewe." As they shook hands, he asked, "This the man?" Marchi nodded. "Okay," the young District Attorney said.

He stared at Dennis Riordan, who stared back. Crewe could tell from the surprise in Dennis Riordan's frank blue eyes that he had not expected a black district attorney. Lester Crewe was past resenting that. It was one of the burdens that went with his job.

Crewe wore heavy-framed glasses for two reasons. In his high school days, being tall, muscular and well-coordinated, he was being primed for a basketball scholarship, when he was severely elbowed in the eye while going up for a rebound. This had left him with a permanent visual impairment which cut short his athletic career. He also felt that glasses, particularly with imposing, heavy black frames, endowed him with the look of a serious and intelligent young man.

Actually, he had no need for such props since he had graduated in the top 10 percent of his class at New York Law School and had passed the bar examination the first time he took it. But he labored under the stigma that he had received his appointment not on the basis of his ability but because a highly political district attorney was under pressure to phase in minority attorneys to placate the black community, which had begun to vote in substantial numbers.

Lester Crewe was determined to obliterate that slander on his reputation. He was efficient in pursuit of his duties and had earned a reputation for being as zealous in his prosecution of black defendants as whites.

An attractive young man, and vigorous, there had

been talk lately that he might be nominated to run for state assemblyman as the first step in a promising political career. But he refused to live in a black neighborhood merely to exploit its support. He and his wife, Hortense, felt that for the sake of their two young daughters, it was far more important to live close to an excellent grade school in a white neighborhood, even though Hortense herself was assigned to teaching in an all-black school up in Harlem.

Lester Crewe always carried himself with what seemed cool composure and total security, but in moments of tension he betrayed himself by constantly readjusting his glasses, setting them firmly in place on his slender nose.

Crewe made that gesture now as he scanned the room, then said to Dennis Riordan, "Would you please sit here? Under this wall clock." As Riordan complied, Crewe continued, "Mr. Riordan, I want you to understand that everything that happens in this room from now on is going to be recorded on television tape and may be used against you later."

Crewe turned toward the door. "Ready out there?" Once Rosenthal gave the word, Crewe ordered, "Start rolling!"

In a legal and precise manner, Lester Crewe commenced. "You understand, sir, that what you will say from now on will be taped for a permanent record? There is a television camera affixed to that door. Sir?"

Riordan nodded, as if eager to get on with it.

"Your name?"

"Dennis Riordan."

"Address?"

"Seventeen-oh-nine, Twenty-fourth Street, Astoria, Queens."

"Occupation?"

"Clerk. In a warehouse."

Because of Riordan's suspiciously calm demeanor Crewe leaned a bit closer. In a voice lower than normal and more like a psychiatrist than a prosecutor, he asked, "Now, sir, do you understand that you have a right to make no statement at all?"

"Yes, but I want to."

"That's not the point, as long as you understand you don't have to."

"Okay! I don't have to! I understand!"

"Before you make any statement, you may call an attorney. Or if you haven't got one, I'll see that you get one."

"I don't want an attorney. I just want to make my statement."

"You understand that anything you say may be held against you?"

"I hope that it will!"

Crewe glanced at Marchi to share his uneasy feeling with the veteran detective. Of all the confessions Crewe had ever taken, this was the strangest. Never had he come across a murderer so calm, so insistent on confessing.

"So we get it clear. You refuse to call an attorney. You don't want us to provide one. And you insist on making a statement. Is that correct?"

Riordan nodded brusquely, impatient now.

"Please answer in words, Mr. Riordan," Crewe insisted.

"I know my rights. I don't want an attorney. And I want to make a confession!" Riordan maintained.

"You make this statement free of any compulsion and of your own volition?" Crewe asked pointedly. For, under certain circumstances, no confession was sometimes better for the prosecution than a confession that later could be attacked and thrown out.

"I make this statement freely," Riordan said, staring at the door and into the camera.

Crewe glanced at Marchi, who stared back as suspicious of Riordan's motives as was the young District Attorney. Were they being set up for some new legal defense of which this confession was only the first step?

"All right, then," Crewe finally said. He drew a pad out of his attaché case, prepared to make his own written comments on Riordan's statement. He adjusted his glasses and said, "Proceed, Mr. Riordan!"

"My name is Dennis Riordan. I live alone, my wife having died two months ago. And my daughter having been murdered ten months before that."

Crewe and Marchi exchanged surprised and puzzled glances.

"I work at the Long Island warehouse of a moving and storage company. I'm a checker. Used to work outside on the dock until loading and unloading became too heavy.

"I've lived at my present address for thirty-one years. Own the place. Free and clear. Nedda and me burned the mortgage nine years ago. We had three children. Boy, Dennis Junior. Who became a priest and is serving in South America now. Another son, Frank, died in Viet Nam. And my daughter, Agnes . . ."

Riordan's lips began to tremble. For the first time he doubted his ability to complete his confession, but he managed to regain control.

"And my daughter, Agnes . . . who was . . . one night she was on her way home . . . you see, she worked in a law firm down on Wall Street. Legal secretary. And very good. So good that the firm sent her to law school at night to become a lawyer. Which she was doing, when it happened. When . . . it was this one night . . ."

Riordan hesitated, as if in the emotion of the memory

he had lost all sense of continuity. So Crewe suggested softly, "Take your time, Mr. Riordan, no need to rush."

"Somehow if I don't get it all out at once, I . . ."

"Just take your time."

"You see, she was going to this law school at night in a building down near the Brooklyn Bridge."

"Yes, I know. I went there myself," Crewe said gently, to urge him along.

"Well then, you know night classes don't get out until after nine. So it was dark. She was going across City Hall Park to get to the subway entrance when he grabbed her. This big . . ." Riordan faltered before saying aggressively to Crewe, ". . . this big black man! He came up behind her. Grabbed her. Put his big black hand over her mouth. That's why nobody heard her scream. He dragged her off under a tree and then he . . ."

Riordan turned away from Crewe, away from Marchi, away from the camera, as if it were his own shame he was confessing.

"He . . . he did terrible things to her. After he robbed her, he . . . he ripped off her clothes . . . and . . . I mean, this was a fine girl, a religious girl, a decent girl . . . and he did things to her. Rape. And more. Then, for no reason . . . no reason at all . . . I mean, what was he afraid of, that she would identify him? Aggie was too shy a girl ever to make such a terrible thing public. She would have suffered in silence. Why did he have to kill her? Why?"

He was finally able to face the camera again.

"He took whatever money she had and threw away her purse with some cards in it. That's how I got called the next morning to come down to identify her body. One morning she left my house, she was my daughter and I was so proud of her. And the next morning, a body I had to go and identify.

Riordan covered his face with his hands.

"Mr. Riordan, would you like some coffee?" Lester Crewe asked.

Riordan shook his head but did not bare his face. "I'm all right, all right," he kept repeating.

Crewe looked at the television technician through the one-way panel in the door to indicate he should keep the camera rolling.

Finally, Riordan resumed.

"I went to that place, expecting it was going to be like in the movies or on television where they bring you into a large room with lots of bodies under sheets and they lift the sheet for you to see. Not like that at all. They take you into a small room. There's a big glass panel in the wall and they raise the body up from below. Just one body. There I was, looking at Aggie. Her hair was all rumpled so I wanted to reach out and straighten it since she was always so neat. But I couldn't. There was that glass panel.

"I looked and I said, 'Aggie, darling, I'll make sure that they find him. I take a holy oath on it. I'll keep after the police until they make him pay!'

"Turned out I didn't have to keep after the police. They'd picked him up. That same night. They wasn't sure it was him. Not till I was called to identify the jewelry they found on him. Agnes's watch. And a gold chain with a cross. Which her brother, Dennis, gave her on her confirmation. The watch was the one Nedda and I gave her last Christmas.

"Once I identified those things the police was sure they had their man. Evidently he knew it wouldn't do no good to deny it. Because after they read him his rights and all, like you just did with me, he made a full confession. Nedda and I, we said 'Thank God, now that animal will pay for what he did to our Aggie.'

"They indicted him fast enough. And I asked this detective on the case, his name was Bridger . . ."

"Harry Bridger . . . nice man," Marchi said.

"Yes, he is," Riordan said. "Kept us advised every step of the way. Then one day he calls and says there's going to be a hearing before a judge. So I take the day off from work, I was on the day shift then, and me and Nedda, we go into Manhattan to the court there. We meet Bridger, who looks very nervous. I don't know why, they had that bastard's confession. And I could identify the jewelry that tied him right to Aggie's murder. So what was there to worry about?

"We go into the courtroom. Wasn't any spectators there. I guess it not being a regular jury trial, nobody was interested. We wait. Then that bastard shows up with his lawyer."

Riordan turned on Crewe once more. "To make himself look respectable he got himself a white lawyer!"

Crewe did not respond, though a slight flush of resentment rose in his tan face.

"Then the young District Attorney comes in. Man named Kalich. The judge appears, very businesslike, as if he's in a hurry. He says, 'I know the contentions of the defense. The People ready?'

"So the young District Attorney calls this cop to the stand. Turns out to be the policeman who arrested that bastard the night he killed Agnes. The District Attorney starts asking him questions about how and why he made the arrest. All the time I'm sitting there, waiting my turn to get on the stand and identify Aggie's jewelry. That's what'll put that sonofabitch in jail for life! But they don't call me. They just keep asking the policeman questions. First the District Attorney. Then the defense lawyer. Why did he arrest him? How did he look? Questions like that.

"But I kept thinking, 'Just call me to the stand, Judge, swear me in, let me identify Aggie's jewelry. That'll prove it all!'

"Then they got to yelling at each other, both lawyers. Until this Judge Lengel, he bangs his gavel and says, 'Gentlemen, come into the robing room. Let's settle this!'

"Nedda and me, we didn't understand. So I glanced at Detective Bridger, who looked more worried than before. We could hear voices from the other room. There was a lot of shouting going on. Mostly by that young District Attorney, Kalich. Then it got quiet. Soon they came out. Judge Lengel climbed back on the bench, looked down at Kalich and said, 'Do I understand the People wish to make a statement at this time?'

"And the District Attorney, his face red, stands up and says something like, 'Judge Lengel, confronted by Your Honor's rulings, the People find it impossible to make a *prima facie* case. Therefore, we consent to this indictment being dismissed.'

"I jumped up and shouted, 'You can't do that!' Bridger tried to pull me down but I wouldn't let him. I cried out, 'Judge, I can identify Aggie's jewelry! He's the murderer! There's no doubt! No doubt in this world! Just put me on the stand! Ask me anything!'

"Judge Lengel only rapped his gavel and said, 'Clear the courtroom.'

"It was all over. Just like that. And that black bastard and his white lawyer walk out. He's free. And laughing. Like he was standing at Aggie's grave and laughing. I swung at him as he went by, but Bridger caught my arm. Then they were gone.

"Nedda broke down and cried. If she hadn't been there, I would have cried. I turned to Bridger and asked, 'How can a judge do that?'

"The young District Attorney came toward us, so I asked him, 'How can a judge do something like that?'

"And he says, 'You see, Mr. Riordan, when he killed your daughter, he was out on bail for another crime.'

" 'That's crazy!' I said. 'It doesn't make sense!'

" 'It doesn't make sense to prosecutors either,' Kalich said, 'but that's the law in this state.'

"I said, 'You mean to say the law lets a man like that go free! He'll do it again! You know that!'

" 'Yes, sure, I know that,' Kalich admitted, 'but I don't make the laws. The courts do.'

" 'And the courts let a man like that go free?' I asked. Kalich looked sick enough, but I kept on, 'What about Aggie's jewelry which they found on him? Why didn't you put me on the stand so I could testify?'

"And Kalich says, 'I couldn't. Judge Lengel ruled that out.'

"I was so mad I grabbed Kalich by the coat. 'What do you mean, Judge Lengel ruled that out? What is this? Russia? Where a man is prevented from getting on the witness stand and testifying to the truth? What kind of country has this become?'

"All Kalich could say was, 'I'm sorry, Mr. Riordan. I would have liked to do better for you. But my hands are tied.' Then he said something about a rule . . . I forget the word . . . the exact legal word . . .' "

Sympathetic to Riordan's painful confusion, Lester Crewe said, "Exclusionary rule?"

"Yeah, yeah, that's it," Riordan recalled. "He said under that rule I couldn't testify about the jewelry because of how the cop arrested that bastard."

"Not all evidence in the possession of the prosecutor or the police can be used in a criminal case," Crewe explained.

Impatient to get on with his confession, Riordan continued, "So I said, 'Forget the jewelry! He made a confession! He admitted the whole thing!'

" 'That was ruled out, too,' Kalich said, 'because of his being out on bail for a previous crime.'

" 'And if he hadn't been arrested and out on bail?' I asked.

" 'Then his confession would have been admissible,' Kalich said.'

Riordan turned to seek confirmation from the young, black District Attorney.

Crewe nodded. "That's true, Mr. Riordan. In this state, under certain circumstances, the confession of a man free on bail can be thrown out."

Riordan shook his head, as confused now as he was on that day in the courtroom when his daughter's murderer was set free. He stared down at his hands, then seemed to become aware again of the camera in the door. He looked straight into it as he continued, "I took Nedda home. From then on she started failing. The doctor said nothing was wrong. Just lost the will to live. So that bastard not only raped and killed my Aggie, he killed my Nedda, too.

"I made the vow at Nedda's grave. If the law wouldn't do anything about a man guilty of murder, a man who was out on bail when he killed Aggie, then I would do something about it.

"So three days ago I drove out of state to where I could buy myself a gun. That gun you have there, Detective. And today, just about an hour ago, I found Cletus Johnson, the man who killed my Aggie. And I shot him. Fired five times. If there's anything else you care to know, just ask."

He stared directly into the television camera as he demanded, "Now, I want to be tried!"

Crewe glanced at Marchi, then asked, "Anything else you'd like to say, Mr. Riordan?"

Riordan responded softly, "Yes. I'd like to talk to my priest."

"If I may suggest, Mr. Riordan, before a priest you need an attorney."

"I want to see my priest."

By the time Lester Crewe left the precinct house,
there were four television crews waiting. They besieged
him with microphones and hand-held cameras.

"We understand a white man has killed a black man
up here. Is that true?"

"Do you have any idea what his motive was?"

Lester Crewe adjusted his heavy-framed glasses and
said only, "There has been a homicide. And we have a
suspect in custody."

"We heard he came in to confess voluntarily. Is that
true?"

"No comment," Lester Crewe said, pushing his way
through the crowd of reporters.

With a case this solid, he was not going to do or say
anything that would jeopardize it. Though now he did
regret he had not insisted that Riordan have an attorney
before allowing him to confess.

Ironic, Crewe mused sadly, an experienced criminal
would have known how to protect himself. An innocent
like Dennis Riordan was a sitting duck.

Too bad, Lester Crew thought, but he had scrupulous-
ly done all that the law required of him.

4

BENJAMIN FRANKLIN GORDON ENTERED the small, drab
law office where he shared space with three other young
attorneys in an old building that overlooked the Supreme
Court, New York County.

The sole secretary, who served all four attorneys, was
on the phone, so she held out a meager batch of mail to
him. From the top envelope, Ben Gordon could tell they
were all solicitations. Once he had sent out announce-
ments that he had resigned from the District Attorney's
staff and was now engaged in the private practice of
criminal law, he had been deluged by a torrent of sales
literature offering stationery, electric typewriters, desks,
chairs, case books, legal forms and air conditioners.

The only thing that had not descended on him was a
demand for his legal services by clients whose fees would
enable him to pay for all those appurtenances of the well-
equipped law office. His resignation had been so precipitous that he had not had the opportunity to establish any
connections. And, though his former colleagues in the
District Attorney's office had promised to recommend
defendants to him, so far there had been very few.

He went into the small office he shared with Vince
Monelli, who this morning must be out pleading a client
in Criminal Court or else interviewing one on Riker's

31

Island. Ben sank into his creaky, second-hand swivel chair, flipped through the mail by simply scanning the return addresses. No need to read the contents. He tossed the unopened envelopes into the wastebasket and leaned back.

Only four years out of law school, he felt that he had already failed his professional ambitions. Yet, if he had to relive the past few months, he would have done exactly the same. It was a matter of principle. Arlene agreed with him at the time. But now, he wondered, with his dearth of clients and income, how did she feel? Not that she complained. She was willing to go on being their main support and never utter a word of recrimination. Sometimes Ben found himself hoping that she would say something more than "Ben, darling, it'll get better. Patience!"

Patience, he complained in bitter silence, twenty-eight, eager for legal combat, well-equipped by virtue of three years in the D.A.'s office, but aside from an arson case, a few prostitutes and some kids up for car theft, he was an underemployed young lawyer. Where were the cases he dreamed about, in which a crusading Ben Gordon would defend the rights of those unjustly accused or who suffered the prejudices of society? Even if that meant taking a case right up to the Supreme Court of the United States! Where, indeed, he pondered, as anger made his handsome, square-jawed face seem even stronger.

Today, as on most days in the past two months, Ben Gordon wondered if he had made a fatal career blunder by resigning so precipitously. Many times in recent weeks he had cause to relive that angry confrontation with his Chief, the District Attorney for New York County, who had assigned Ben Gordon to prosecute a policeman accused of shooting an unarmed suspect.

The policeman had pursued the youth at night, up a dark alley that became a dead end. As the suspect turned, something flashed. The officer assumed it was a gun. He fired, hitting the suspect twice, once in the head. The wound was fatal. No weapon was found on the dead black youth. The policeman was a white man.

To quell an incipient uprising in the black community, Ben Gordon had been given orders to go before the grand jury, present the case and demand an indictment charging Murder in the Second Degree, which could mean a minimum sentence of fifteen years to life. The policeman's attorney offered to submit his man to questioning before the grand jury. Ben had listened carefully to the testimony.

The officer had not been wearing his bulletproof vest on the night of the shooting. It was being cleaned. That fact, in conjunction with the killing of an officer in Brooklyn only two days before, had made the policeman quick to fire. But he did not intend to kill the suspect, only to prevent himself from being killed.

When Ben heard the officer's testimony, he did not urge an indictment for Murder Two. Instead he asked for a recess, tried to reach his Chief on the phone, and when he could not, decided on his own to ask for a charge of Manslaughter in the Second Degree, which, upon conviction, could lead to a light or even a suspended sentence.

When he returned to the office, his Chief was waiting for him, irate almost to the point of apoplexy as he commanded, "Gordon! Come in here!"

"Yes, sir?"

"Whatever you do, don't tell me that without my okay you lowered that charge from Murder Two to Manslaughter in the Second?"

"I tried to get you, you were out. So I decided to act on my own."

"Your own?" the District Attorney scoffed. "You don't have to contend with calls from the Mayor's office or with petitions and pickets from the black community. What right have you got to act on your own in matters like that? You don't get the heat. I do!"

"If I may, sir . . ."

"Yes, you 'may'!" his Chief replied sarcastically.

"In the first place, I don't think we could have made a case on Murder Two. In the second place, I'm convinced in that man's mind it was a matter of self-defense." Ben explained. "Feeling that way, it would have been dishonest of me to go for Murder Two."

"Damn it, Gordon, don't use words like 'dishonest' with me. I have principles, too. But I am also responsible for keeping this office running in face of crime waves, community pressure and political considerations. *I* know we couldn't get a conviction on Murder Two! But an indictment would at least keep the heat off this office. Then months from now, when things cool and some judge wants to reduce the charge, let *him* do it! But while I'm in command here, this office will not appear to be covering up for a cop!"

"Sorry, sir. I didn't honestly feel justified in putting this officer through a year of hell for political reasons," Ben insisted respectfully.

" 'Honesty' again?" his Chief challenged him. "I can see the pickets outside our office now!"

The irate man turned from his desk to stare out the window as if he actually expected to find protesters. Then, grumbling, he confessed the source of his consuming anger.

"Gordon, I've already had calls from three network stations and five independent channels for television interviews. Most of the reporters who called are black. They all want to know if it's possible to ever get a murder indictment of a white officer for killing a black man."

"What are we running here," Ben asked, "a prosecutor's office or a public relations agency?" The D.A. turned toward him angrily but Ben continued, "We've got to stop sacrificing individuals to achieve political objectives."

"Don't give me principles! You don't have to run for reelection, I do!" his Chief shouted.

In a surge of anger, Ben Gordon declared, "Sorry. I wasn't running for office. Just trying to do an honest job. But if you need a scapegoat, I'll resign! You can say you fired me for disobeying orders. That ought to satisfy them!"

"Yes!" the D.A. agreed immediately. "That would do it! Good idea! I accept your resignation!"

So, Benjamin Franklin Gordon, suddenly, and without forethought for his career, had resigned from the office of the District Attorney of New York County.

Thereafter he had considered, but only briefly, seeking a position in a large law firm. It would pay well but that would confine him to civil practice. He was devoted to criminal law, and there were no large offices engaged solely in doing that. So he decided to do what young assistant district attorneys usually do when they resign, he went into practice for himself, unfortunately with very meager results. In two months his total fees amounted to $1,750. He might have done better on welfare.

Ben's premature resignation had been the second unplanned reversal in his budding law career. The first had occurred when his uncle Harry died.

Uncle Harry had been his father's youngest brother. Of four sons in the Gordon family, two had completed college, but only one had gone on to law school. Uncle Harry. And only through the support of Ben's father, who worked as a cutter in the garment industry and lived frugally with his young wife. After Harry graduated law school and Ben was born, Harry insisted, "Morris, he's as much my responsibility as yours. That boy will go to a good college and a good law school and when he gets out, instead of having to scrounge for a start as I did, I'll take him into my office."

On the day his father died, Ben was only sixteen. While all the other relatives were consoling his mother, Harry took him aside.

"Kid, I want you to know I will make good on the promise I made your father. You will have money for school. And I already have space for you in my office. It's an exciting, challenging practice, criminal law. You have to be inventive, alert, especially when you're defending a man you know is guilty. You're not to judge him, only defend him. You have to fight for his rights. The law is there for the protection of your client. Learn to use it!

"But that will come later. In the meantime, work, study, get good grades. And the proudest day of my life will be when they paint *Benjamin F. Gordon* in gold on the door of my office and I can honestly say, 'Morris, I made good on my promise!'"

No one expected that one day, in his fifty-first year, during the trial of a particularly arduous case in Supreme Court, New York County, Criminal Term, Harry Gordon would suffer a massive stroke. He lingered in coma for three days, then died.

To Ben it felt as if he had lost a father for the second time. As for Harry's thriving office, the two young men who worked for him had appropriated all the clients between them. There was no longer an office of Harry Gordon, Counselor-at-Law. No door on which to proudly inscribe in gilt lettering *Benjamin F. Gordon*.

Without that opportunity, Ben Gordon had resolved to get his courtroom training in criminal law as many young lawyers did, in the District Attorney's office. Once he had earned a reputation as an effective trial lawyer, he would go out on his own, free to take those cases that appealed to his sense of justice. He was determined not to remain an employee of some large office or government agency where he would be forced to handle cases in which he had no particular interest, or with purposes which conflicted with his own principles.

If that meant weeks, now months, and possibly a few years of squeaky, second-hand swivel chairs, sharing a secretary, waiting days for that damned phone to ring, it was a price Ben Gordon was willing to pay. Though, on this particular day, he had to admit the price seemed very high indeed. He was looking over his sparsely marked calendar to see what few court appearances he had to make in the next several weeks, when his phone rang.

Grudgingly he lifted it, expecting to be greeted by another law-book salesman, but this time it was a stern, officious female voice.

"Mr. Gordon, don't you return phone calls?"

"What?" he asked, stunned. "Sorry. Say that again."

"Late yesterday afternoon I called you at Judge Aaron Klein's request. I said to call back before ten o'clock this morning."

"Sorry. I never got the message," Ben replied. "Besides, I don't have any matter before Judge Klein."

"He would like to see you in chambers at his lunch break. One o'clock!" It was an order, not an invitation.

"Yes, ma'am. One o'clock!"

Ben mused, what would Judge Klein want with him? He had never tried a case before him. How would Klein even know of his existence? Of course, it could be a matter of sheer chance. Like almost all young lawyers who left the D.A.'s office, Ben had registered with the 18B panel of lawyers who signified their availability for assignment to criminal cases in which the defendant had no attorney. The fee was modest for the time involved, limited at most to several thousand dollars. But it was one way to pay some bills and get added experience until more lucrative cases came along. But if his name had been picked from the 18B panel, how would a judge be involved?

At a quarter to one, Ben Gordon washed up, pulled his tie into place, combed his unruly black hair and set out for Judge Aaron Klein's chambers, a tall, almost handsome, quite serious and puzzled young man.

In his early days as a young lawyer, Aaron Klein had been an ardent member of the Liberal Party. Because of his short stature and his fiery advocacy, one newspaper had dubbed him the Gamecock of Liberalism. He had served well, donating his services in trials on issues of principle for which he received no fees, giving his time every election day to make sure that Liberal voters were not harassed at the polls and to see that the voting machines were not tampered with so that the Liberal Party received a fair count.

Since in those days the Liberals constituted a substantial swing vote in New York, the Boss of the Party was always given a certain number of positions to fill, including several judgeships. For his unselfish efforts, Aaron Klein was appointed to one of those.

He had embraced his judicial post with great enthusiasm and lofty ideals, not only because of the honor involved but in anticipation of bringing to the administration of justice a new and enlightened voice.

But that had been thirteen years ago. Now Judge Aaron Klein was a short, pudgy man of fifty-four, whose liberalism had gradually diminished and whose enthusiasm and lofty ideals had been eroded by the pressure of court calendars that were always behind, not by months but by years. Not justice, but quick justice, had become the need. His love of the law had decreased until his work became a duty to be carried out in the face of never-ending obstacles. Along with his youth, his early dreams and ideals had somehow slipped away.

He was now a middle-aged man, who took refuge in the cigars he loved to smoke and who looked forward to the end of the day, when he could go home and eat the substantial dinners his devoted wife, Berenice, prepared for him. Then he would pore over motion papers and briefs with which persistent lawyers burdened him. On nights when he was fortunate, there were no phone calls from overbearing lawyers seeking to influence his judgment or plead for special consideration. His one self-justification was that in his years on the bench, he had been reversed only three times by the judges in the Appellate Division.

For the rest, he looked forward to the end of his term, when he would resume the practice of law as counsel to some substantial firm, and receive three or four times as much money as he earned as a jurist. He would gladly forgo the honor and the title of judge so he could have time off and, with Berenice, go on trips whenever he felt like it, not when crowded court calendars allowed.

A man of fifty-four has no illusions left, and very few ambitions. Aaron Klein's main ambitions were reserved for his children. Sheldon was an assistant professor and a brilliant mathematician at MIT. His daughter, Melanie, who had been married seven years ago, had one child and had already been divorced. After that, she had entered law school at her father's expense.

But at least she had provided him with a grandchild, David. A delightful boy, and handsome, he was worth all the expense and trouble involved in Melanie's marriage and divorce. The boy was one of the few bright things in Aaron Klein's life, which consisted of routine day-to-day duties, in the course of which he tried to administer justice with some sense of fairness. Unfortunately, that was not always possible.

Now as he sat in his chambers, chewing on the soggy end of his cigar, Judge Klein studied young Ben Gordon.

"Gordon, you're a very nice-looking young man. Even more handsome than your uncle Harry. Ah, there was a man, your uncle Harry. He helped me a lot when I was starting out. First election day case I ever handled, I botched up. So I called your uncle Harry frantically, 'Help!' He came down, tried the case, won it, and we Liberals swept the district that year. 'We Liberals.' God, I'm talking ancient history. Well, let's get down to business. There is a rather unusual case on my calendar . . ."

Klein paused, then confessed, "Look, I might as well be honest with you. This is a very tough case. Two attorneys assigned to it have already quit. That's why, unofficially and off the record, I decided to see what I could do about getting this defendant an attorney. I sent for the 18B list. I spotted the name Gordon and said to myself, must be Harry Gordon's nephew. You know, he used to brag about you, even when you were a kid . . ."

Ben interrupted. "Judge Klein, if I'm here because you owe my uncle a favor, the answer is no thanks. I'm on my own now. And I intend to keep it that way!"

Klein smiled. "You're just about what I expected."

Puzzled, Ben stared across at the amused jurist.

"They said you were proud, quick-tempered, principled *and* stubborn."

"Who said?" Ben asked.

"The men at the D.A.'s office. Who else?" Klein responded.

"Oh, you knew about that," Ben said sheepishly.

"And so does half the legal community in this city," Klein said. "That's the reason you're here. Not any favors

I owe Harry. Because what I am going to hand you is no favor. It is a tough case. With a very difficult client. As I told you, two other men, highly qualified, have quit because this defendant does not want an attorney."

"He's going to defend himself," Ben said, "and you just want me to advise him so he doesn't make any legal mistakes that jeopardize his rights."

"No," Klein corrected him. "He does not want to defend himself either. He does not want to be defended at all."

"Then why not let him plead guilty?" Ben asked.

"Because, as a matter of personal principle, I do not accept guilty pleas when the charge is Murder Two."

"Murder Two!" Ben said.

"The man committed a deliberate murder. He wants to be tried and convicted. A man in that frame of mind desperately needs a young, tough lawyer. Young for endurance; tough because you'll have to battle your client as well as the D.A. Frankly, what you did before that grand jury is the real reason you're here now. I want to make sure this defendant gets the kind of principled defense the poor man is entitled to."

"Who is this 'poor man'?" Ben asked.

"Dennis Riordan," Klein said, studying Ben's face for his reaction.

"Riordan? Isn't he the man who . . . ?" Ben started to say.

"Yes," Klein interrupted. "He's the man who killed his daughter's murderer in cold blood. Now, Gordon, this is not the most promising case I've ever seen. Just from what I've heard from the D.A. and the two lawyers who asked to be removed, the case against him is solid. But it's exactly in solid cases like this that I like to make sure a defendant coming before me gets the fairest shake our system

has to offer. That's why I would like you to take it on. What
do you say?"

"Of course!" Ben agreed. "From what I've read, the
most natural thing in Riordan's case would be to plead
insanity. Or try to reduce the charge to Manslaughter in
the First, on the ground of extreme emotional disturbance."

"Gordon, once you said you'd take the case I was no
longer free to discuss it with you. I don't intend to prejudice my position as to future rulings I may have to make.
From this moment on, as far as I'm concerned, you are no
longer Harry Gordon's nephew. You are a name from the
18B panel. You take this assignment on that basis.
Agreed?"

"I understand, sir," Ben said.

"Then get over to Riker's Island and see your
new client. He has to plead to the indictment Tuesday
morning.

The first thing Ben Gordon did when he returned to
his office was seize his telephone and dial. It rang twice;
then he heard that cool, efficient voice respond, "Robbins.
Can I help you?"

"Yes, Robbins. This is Gordon. And you can help me
by explaining how a girl who can be as soft and sexy as you
are at night can be so businesslike and brisk at two o'clock
in the afternoon."

"Sorry, darling, but it's been a hectic day down here
on the Street. Energy stocks started to fall and it's panic
time," Arlene Robbins said apologetically.

"It's been a hectic day in the Halls of Justice, too," Ben
teased.

"Ben?" she asked impulsively, that single word con-
taining all her hopes for him, without permitting herself
to become too optimistic. For she knew how much it had

pained him during these past few months to admit his disappointments to her.

"It's finally happened."

"Tell me!" she insisted, more excited now.

"I've just been assigned to a case," he said, adding with considerable emphasis, "Murder Two!"

"Tremendous opportunity," Arlene said. "Congratulations!"

"Tremendous responsibility, too, so save the congratulations," Ben said. "Remember reading about a man named Riordan? Killed the rapist who murdered his daughter?"

"Is that your new client?" Arlene asked, her enthusiasm now somewhat diminished by her recollection of the event and the unquestionable guilt of the unfortunate man. "God, what can you do for him?"

"Offer him the Uncle Harry treatment. Every legal advantage it's possible to give him!" Ben said.

5

WHEN BEN OPENED the door of the small conference room in the Riker's Island prison, he was met with so heavy a stench of stale smoke it seemed to have physical presence. Many lawyers, many anxious prisoners had smoked many cigarettes in this room while plotting legal defenses and strategies. Ben looked around at the pale green walls, streaked from vain attempts to wash away the places where prisoners had scrawled their obscene opinions of society, the prison system and the world in general.

He dropped his briefcase onto the small, yellow pine table and slipped into the straight-backed chair, ready for his first interview with his new client. Aside from the indictment, a copy of which he took out of his briefcase, and a still photograph which Ben had seen in newspaper accounts of the crime, Dennis Riordan was a total stranger to him. To judge from his photograph, Riordan appeared nondescript. Among average men, he would be considered most average. While two psychiatrists whom Ben had consulted in preparation for this meeting would not venture a guess as to Riordan's mental condition, they did admit that what he had done was most *un*average. Ben considered that fact a clue to a potential defense in a case in which a defense seemed almost impossible.

He was taking his yellow legal pad out of his briefcase when the door opened. Ben Gordon turned to greet Dennis Riordan, who paused in the doorway.

Ben's first thought was, *The photograph was right.* Riordan was a man of average height, compact in build for a man in his sixties, with graying hair and that undistinguished face except around his jaw, where the line was firm and determined, and in the eyes which, though watery blue, were clear, sharply focused and defiantly suspicious. He stood his ground, staring at Ben.

"Kids," Riordan said. "These days kids out of high school are lawyers. Same as that young black D.A. who took my confession. Kids!"

"Mr. Riordan." Ben rose, gesturing to Riordan to join him at the small table.

Riordan hesitated, then entered, the guard locking the door behind him.

"Mr. Riordan, I've been appointed to be your new attorney."

"I wouldn't waste my own money on any lawyer. Whatever I have will go to my church, St. Malachy's. Over in Astoria."

Ben pointed to the chair facing him. "Won't you sit down?"

"I'd rather stand."

"This may take some time," Ben pointed out.

"Hope not," Riordan said. "I left a very interesting crossword puzzle, half done."

Ben controlled his growing irritation. "Mr. Riordan, under the old law this would be a clear case of Murder One. However, now, since Johnson wasn't a cop or correction officer, the indictment reads Murder Two. But Murder in the Second Degree is no trivial matter. If I'm going to defend you I'll need to know exactly what happened. Why you did what you did. What you thought at the time.

Everything. And I mean everything. You'll have to tell me things you've never told anyone else. And I'll keep them in the strictest confidence."

Riordan did not respond, only stared at the young attorney.

"Mr. Riordan?" Ben prodded.

"Everything you have to know is in my confession. Did they show it to you? The tape, I mean."

"Yes. But that's not enough. Right now, I want your innermost thoughts, your feelings. Your state of mind before you bought that gun, while you were buying it and on the drive back to New York. Especially your thoughts while you were tracking Cletus Johnson and at the moment you saw him, the moment you shot him," Ben said, acting on the advice of his psychiatric consultants.

Riordan seemed to brighten. "Oh, I get it. Okay. If that's what you want, start making notes." As Ben wrote, Riordan spoke hurriedly, "From the time Agnes got killed . . . raped and murdered . . . all I thought about was, get that bastard!"

"That's all you thought about," Ben said with emphasis.

"Day and night," Riordan continued. "Then when Johnson got off scot-free, I went out of my mind. If I didn't have to take care of Nedda . . . my wife . . . she began to waste away after that . . . if I hadn't had her to worry over, I'd have done it then. But I waited until she died. Then I had a double reason to get that bastard. So I began plotting and planning. Day and night. Couldn't sleep, couldn't eat for thinking about it."

"It became an obsession." Ben suggested the key word that had been recommended to him.

"Right! An obsession. I mean I went out of my mind from thinking about him being responsible for killing

Agnes, then going free. To me the only thing in this world was to kill that sonofabitch!"

"Right, right, got it," Ben said, eagerly taking notes. "Keep going, Mr. Riordan!"

"When I'd figured out how to do it, I asked for time off from the warehouse to go out of state to buy that gun. Then I changed to the night shift to have my days free to track that bastard. And I did. Found him. Shot him. Five times."

"The Medical Examiner's report said four times," Ben corrected him.

"Must have missed once. What difference, as long as the sonofabitch is dead," Riordan said.

"How did you *feel?* While you were shooting him, and after?" Ben asked.

"Strangest thing. While I was shooting him I didn't feel anything. Didn't know anything. My mind was a total blank," Riordan repeated.

"Good!" Ben said, seeing a credible defense in the making. "And after that?"

Riordan's intense expression changed to a faraway look. "After . . . that . . . I heard this voice . . ."

"Voice?" Ben seized on the word; this was more encouraging than he had anticipated.

"Yeah, this voice said to me, 'Dennis Riordan, my beloved son, well done!' "

" 'My beloved son,' " Ben repeated, then asked pointedly, "whose voice was it?"

"Who else would speak those words? God, of course," Riordan said solemnly.

Before Ben noted that, he made meticulously sure he had it right. "The voice of God praised you for killing Johnson?"

Riordan did not answer but asked, "You got that? All of it?"

"I sure do!" Ben confirmed enthusiastically.

"Okay, now tear it up!" Riordan ordered. Disbelieving, Ben stared at him. "I said, tear it up!"

"Mr. Riordan, this has the makings of a damn good defense!" Ben protested.

Riordan glared at him. "I figured that's what you came here for. An insanity plea. Right? Well, it is very important for the people to know that I was sane when I did it! Very sane! There was no voice of God. No obsession. Nothing but the will to do what needed doing. And I am still sane! So tear that up!"

"Mr. Riordan . . ." Ben started to protest.

"Tear it up!" Riordan said, his voice rising.

Ben glared at him. Riordan glared back until Ben finally relented, tore the yellow sheets in half and then tore them again. Riordan stretched out his hand. Ben surrendered the pieces. Riordan tore them again, and yet once more, then shoved the bits into his pocket.

"Now look, kid, I know you appointed lawyers don't get much money. So I don't want to waste your time. I want my trial. I want to be found guilty, as I should be. I don't want to be defended."

"Well, Mister, whether you like it or not, you are going to be defended. *By me!*"

Riordan studied him a moment, and Ben could not tell if the man was actually smiling condescendingly.

"Will you put me on the stand?"

"Depends." Ben refused to be pinned down.

"I want to tell everyone why I did it," Riordan insisted.

"That's the best reason in the world *not* to put you on. You see, Mr. Riordan, one of the key elements the prosecution must prove in Murder Two is intent to kill. If I put you on the stand and you admit that, that's the ball game!"

"It's in my confession," Riordan pointed out.

"I know. And I'll do my damnedest to have your

confession ruled out, but I don't have much hope. So I'll
have to devise some way to take the sting out of it. But
putting you on the stand is not that way," Ben said.

"I would like to testify," Riordan insisted.

"Mr. Riordan, you don't seem to understand what's
staring you in the face. Conviction means a minimum
sentence of fifteen years to life! That's probably longer
than you have to live."

"It's worth it, to let the people know," Riordan said.
"Now, I got the crossword puzzle to finish." He turned to
call the guard. "We're done in here. Take me back!"

The door was unlocked. Riordan was gone. Frustrated,
young Ben Gordon threw his blank yellow pad into his
briefcase.

In a darkened room in the District Attorney's office,
they had just run the television tape of Riordan's confession for the third time. Before the lights went up, Assistant District Attorney Lester Crewe asked, "Want to see
it again, Ben?"

"No thanks, Les," Ben Gordon said. "Just answer a few
questions for me."

"Without prejudicing the State's position," Crewe
pointed out.

"Or your own?" Ben challenged.

"What the hell does that mean?" the young black attorney demanded.

"Being called in to take Riordan's confession was a
matter of chance. You were the free man in the office at
that moment. But insisting on being assigned to prosecute
the case . . ."

"The man who takes the confession usually sees the
case through," Crewe reminded him.

"Usually. But not always. This time you insisted. Why?
So you can avenge yourself on Riordan for the racial atti-

tudes he expressed in his confession?" Ben was probing
for any clue to ruling out his client's devastating confession.

"I asked to be assigned to this case because I think
there is an important legal issue involved here. Does a
man have the right to take the law into his own hands?"

"Les, what if I ask you to take the stand at a suppression hearing and testify as to Riordan's mental condition
at the time he confessed? Do you think you could answer
truthfully?"

"Yes!" Crewe insisted.

"I hope so," Ben said with a faint smile.

"If you want to know what I'll say, I don't mind,"
Crewe volunteered.

"Don't prejudice your case," Ben taunted.

Crewe's tan face reflected his controlled anger, as he
replied precisely, "The man was in complete possession of
all his faculties. He was neither harassed nor coerced, was
perfectly calm and aware of his rights. He seemed to have
a compulsion to confess!"

"That's what you'll swear to?" Ben asked, concealing
his satisfaction with Crewe's answer.

Crewe nodded.

"Fair enough, Les, fair enough," Ben said.

6

". . . HE SEEMED TO HAVE a compulsion to confess . . ."

Ben Gordon repeated those words to himself while nervously running his fingers through his unruly black hair as he waited impatiently in the quiet anteroom of Dr. Ephraim Morton's office. He had selected Dr. Morton for two reasons. First, the psychiatrist was black. Second, he was highly respected for his psychiatric testimony which had been vital in court cases in which black children had won certain important rights. Since any jury selected in New York County was bound to be racially mixed, Ben wanted a black expert on his side to impress the black members of the jury and a famous one to impress the white members.

As for Riordan's refusal to cooperate in an insanity plea, Ben had wrestled with that, both legally and morally. Legally, in hours spent in the library, Ben had turned up no case in which a court held that a defendant's opinion of his own mental condition was germane to a legal finding of insanity. Morally, Ben felt eminently justified in seeking psychiatric advice. Riordan might be driven by the need to become a martyr, but as an aggressive, conscientious lawyer, Ben felt no duty to assist in that process. He had not been appointed to help Riordan martyr him-

self but to defend him. And defend him he would. even
at the risk of incurring Riordan's wrath. Ben could understand why Riordan's two previous attorneys had resigned,
but he had no intention of resigning or being replaced. He
would put his theory to Dr. Morton and be guided by his
expert advice.

Ben had finished explaining to Dr. Morton all the facts
in the case, stressing Lester Crewe's words, "He seemed
to have a compulsion to confess."

"Now," Ben continued, "taking Crewe's words, fitting
them with the words in Riordan's own confession and
what he said to me, wouldn't you say we had grounds for
claiming an obsessive-compulsive psychosis?"

"Well," the bearded black psychiatrist considered,
"one might arrive at that conclusion. A man driven by
revenge to perform an illegal act. The drive is the obsession; the act of killing, the compulsion."

"Exactly!" Ben said. "By his own admission, after his
wife was buried, that's all Riordan thought about. Kill that
man! Then he goes out and actually does it."

Morton rocked in his high-backed leather swivel chair
for a moment. "Gordon, you're kind of blurring the lines
now. Crewe's words, 'He seemed to have a compulsion to
confess,' do not have to do with an obsession about Johnson or a compulsion to kill him. They have to do only with
confessing. So, from a legal point of view, his compulsion
to confess is of no value because it comes *after* the crime.
You would have to establish an obsessive-compulsive state
of mind *before* the crime."

"Can't you say it's all part of one continuous state of
mind?" Ben asked.

"Claiming it is one thing. Proving it is another," Morton explained. "An obsessive-compulsive state of mind
relates to an obsession with a fancied or repugnant act,
such as killing a member of one's own family. Something

a person fears he might do, which creates such a state of severe anxiety that it finally explodes into violent action.

"In Riordan's case he was not dealing with some fancied act. Johnson had raped and killed his daughter. Fact, not fantasy. The law, through its machinations, had set the murderer free. No fantasy there. Riordan was dealing realistically with a real situation. Then he performed his own act of justice. In these times, I would not consider that the act of an irrational man," Morton concluded. "I'm afraid, Mr. Gordon, that I can't be of any help in your case."

"Would it do any good if you viewed Riordan's confession?"

"It wouldn't change my opinion. Mr. Gordon, I suggest you try some other psychiatrist. One with more . . . shall we say . . . flexibility in his standards."

On the following Tuesday morning, Dennis Riordan was brought over from Riker's Island to appear in court before Judge Aaron Klein to plead to the indictment charging him with Murder in the Second Degree.

With Ben Gordon alongside him, Dennis Riordan faced the bench as Judge Klein read the indictment then asked, "How do you plead?"

Riordan looked up at the judge. His blue eyes accusing, anger clear on his broad, ruddy face, Riordan responded, "How do I plead? How do *you* plead? You're a judge. Explain it to me. A man works hard all his life. For his wife, his kids. And he ends up with one son dead in a war. His daughter murdered. His wife dead from grief because nobody lifted a finger to see that justice was done! How do I plead? I want my trial!"

Patiently, Judge Klein listened to Riordan's tirade, then quietly said to the stenographer, "The defendant pleads not guilty!"

* * *

The chunky olive-skinned woman showed Ben Gordon into Father Nelson's study in the rectory of St. Malachy's, announcing him in English heavily accented by her native Puerto Rican.

"Father, I'm Ben Gordon, Dennis Riordan's lawyer."

A small, frail man, so bald his rosy scalp glistened as if it had been polished, Father Nelson smiled up at Ben, put aside the parish account books he had been working on and gestured him to a chair.

"A cup of tay?" the old man asked, his pronunciation of the word tea betraying that he had long ago come over from Ireland.

"No thank you, Father. I have permission from Mr. Riordan to ask you what transpired during his confession after he shot Johnson."

"I know. He told me when I went to visit him," the old priest said, then added, "pity. Man like Dennis in such a place."

"I was turned down on bail for his own safety," Ben explained. "Father, I need your help. He refuses to aid in his own defense. He is resigned to accepting whatever punishment the court hands out, just so long as he gets a full public trial."

"So I understand," Father Nelson said, shaking his head in despair. "I tried to advise him otherwise. I pointed out that our Lord Jesus found it in His heart to forgive sinners and thieves, so long as they repented."

"Father, that could be an important point. In his confession he did repent, didn't he?"

"No."

Taken aback, Ben asked, "Then what was his purpose in confessing?"

"Quite the reverse, I'm afraid," the priest said. "He wanted to know if there could be absolution for him, since he felt perfectly justified in what he did. He had no regrets, felt no repentance. The only thing he could promise was that he would never do such a thing again."

"And what did you tell him?"

"That every good Catholic knows, without repentance there can be no forgiveness."

Ben seized on the opportunity. "Father, in all your years of hearing confessions, has any parishioner ever come to you seeking absolution, yet refusing to repent?"

"No."

"You answered that pretty quickly."

"Because it's never happened," the old priest said. "They come distraught, tormented, weeping, guilty, ashamed, but I've never had one come unrepentant. Mind, I don't say they won't go out and do the same thing again. But at the moment at least they are penitent. They seek to be forgiven. And in order to deserve forgiveness, they must repent."

"So you would say that Riordan's conduct was strange, bizarre, highly unusual? As you admitted, unprecedented within your experience?" Ben persisted.

The priest leaned back in his chair, drummed his delicate pale fingers on the black leather arms.

"Young man, what are you really trying to accomplish here?"

"Without my client's cooperation, without a psychiatrist's opinion, it might help if I put you on the stand to testify that when you went to visit Riordan in jail, his conduct was the most unusual you have ever observed in a man who wanted to confess."

"So that if I swear his conduct was"—and here Father Nelson echoed Ben's words—"strange, bizarre, highly unusual, that might be a defense?"

"At least it would give me something to work with,"

Ben said. "I could enlarge on it, maybe use it in my summation."

"Surely there are enough psychiatric quacks around
who would cooperate," Father Nelson suggested.

"I can't rely on quacks. Because once I put the State
on notice that our defense will be insanity, they'll come
up with twenty good, reputable men who will destroy it.
That's why I would like someone like you to get on the
stand and testify to the man's state of mind."

"I'm not a psychiatric expert," the old priest pointed out.

"You know Dennis Riordan, have known him for
years, taken his confession for years. And, by your own
admission, this is the first time he has ever come to confess
and was unrepentant. Highly unusual, isn't it?"

"But far from insanity," Father Nelson reminded him.

"Father, just give me something to work with."

The priest lapsed into a thoughtful silence.

"Tell me, Mr. Gordon, if you put me on the stand and
I so testify, will I be cross-examined?"

"The prosecutor has that right. But out of deference
to your clerical status, there's a chance he might not."

"But if he does," the priest persisted, "and if he asks
me directly, was Dennis Riordan agitated at the time he
confessed? I will have to say no. And if he asks, did I
suspect his state of mind? I will have to say no. In other
words, son, I might do Dennis's case more harm than
good. Think about that."

Ben Gordon nodded, his black eyes focused and sharp
in his lean face.

"Mind, my boy, I'll do whatever I can to help Dennis.
But I don't want to hurt him. As it is, I think I may have
overstepped his wishes. He didn't want Father Dennis
. . ."

"His son?" Ben asked.

"Yes. He's serving with the Maryknolls in South America. He didn't want me to inform him of his father's situation. But I sent a note anyhow. I didn't feel that was part of the confidence of the confessional," the priest explained.

Ben nodded, encouraged that the presence in the courtroom of a son in priestly garb might have a beneficial effect on the jury.

Ben Gordon walked down Twenty-fourth Street in Astoria, Queens. A street of modest private homes with small but carefully tended lawns and shrubs, it was obviously a neighborhood that had a sense of pride. It was a quiet time of day because school was in session. Ben passed several young women rocking their infants in baby carriages while they gossiped. He was also aware of elderly faces that, from time to time, stared out of windows.

He sought the home of Dennis Riordan. He had insisted his client give him the keys so that he could look around. There might be some artifact there that would help Ben formulate his defense.

As he walked, he recalled a lecture in criminal practice which his uncle Harry had given while Ben was still in high school. Harry always invited him to attend such occasions.

"Gentlemen," Harry had begun, his twinkling eyes peering over his glasses at the seven young women in the class, "the secret of succeeding in the practice of criminal law is really quite simple.

"The burden of proof is always on the prosecution. For starters, before it can even get to the jury, the State has to prove a *prima facie* case. Which means it must prove every essential element of the crime. I've had more than a few cases dismissed on motion at the end of the State's case. But, of course, you can't count on that.

"What you *can* count on is this: The *State* has to prove 'beyond a reasonable doubt' that your client is guilty. Now, then, what is *your* obligation? The law does not require you to prove your client innocent. It merely asks that you establish in the minds of the jury a reasonable doubt.

"So you see, the odds are in your favor. You have only to find one loophole in the State's case, while the Prosecutor's case has to be virtually airtight. Now, with odds like that, all you have to do is be alert and sharp as a hawk, because sooner or later the prosecutor will make a mistake, ask the wrong question, introduce a witness you can break down. Once you do, you've established a reasonable doubt and your client is home free."

Harry had laughed and added, "One more piece of advice. Always get your fee in advance. Nothing will shorten the memory of a defendant quicker than the words, 'Not guilty!' "

Easy advice, Ben thought now, given with great relish and amusement by his uncle Harry. But what Harry did not explain that night was how to handle a case like Dennis Riordan's, in which there were no loopholes. The act, the weapon, the intent, the witnesses, the confession, all were unassailable. There was no doubt, reasonable or otherwise.

If only Uncle Harry were alive now.

Ben had arrived at 17–09 Twenty-fourth Street. It was a plain, neat, brown-trimmed, white stucco house. The lawn and garden, which Riordan must have tended with devotion, were beginning to betray the effects of his absence. Ben pushed open the gate and started up the short path to the front porch. He mounted the steps, approached the door, inserted Riordan's key.

To his surprise, he discovered he needed no key. The door gave way as soon as he touched the knob. He stepped inside. The condition of the living room shocked him. Two lamps had been ruthlessly overturned. The cabinet which must have housed Nedda Riordan's bric-a-brac collection was empty, its door ripped open so violently that it hung precariously by one twisted hinge. He crossed the hallway to the dining room. The sideboard had been forced open, silver drawers pulled out and emptied. Where a silver tray had left its footmarks, there was nothing. In haste, some looter had overturned the armchair at the head of the table, Riordan's chair.

Incensed, Ben inspected the rest of the house. He found the drawers in the bedroom dresser overturned, their contents dumped onto the floor in disorderly piles. The table which had supported a television set was bare, its antenna wires ripped away.

Animals, Ben Gordon said to himself, *the animals have invaded.* Having read in the newspapers that Riordan was in jail, they hadn't taken long to break in, enter and loot.

Out of respect for the decent people the Riordans obviously were, Ben Gordon set about restoring the drawers, putting back their contents as neatly as he could.

As he gathered up pieces of clothing, his fury mounted at the injustice of justice. The system had set Agnes Riordan's murderer free, causing Dennis Riordan to do what he did. Now, while that same system held Riordan for trial, it had left his home unprotected and prey to vandals who had violated it and stripped it bare.

Damn it, Ben resolved, there must be some measure of justice for a decent man like Dennis Riordan. And he would find it.

But among the effects that remained Ben found nothing to give him a positive lead to his defense strategy. There were only some family photographs in shattered frames. A very nice picture of Agnes, in cap and gown, when she graduated from high school. *Pretty girl,* Ben thought. A picture of Dennis Riordan Junior on the day he was ordained, and a photograph of young Frank, in battle gear, taken shortly before he was killed in Viet Nam.

In one hand Ben Gordon held the life history of Dennis Riordan. For the first time he could share Riordan's determination to have a trial, to show the system the havoc it had created and tolerated.

Yes, Ben determined, *let's have that trial!* But he knew that anger was neither a legal strategy nor a defense. It would take more, much more, and he was determined to see that Dennis Riordan would get it.

7

"ANY LUCK TODAY?" Arlene asked, as she prepared to serve Ben the new exotic veal dish she had discovered in Wednesday's "Living" section of *The New York Times*. It was one of those quick, sixty-minute, easy-to-prepare gourmet recipes the *Times* featured especially for working women who were ambitious enough to want careers yet devoted enough to excel at running a household.

Ben stood in the doorway of the small white kitchen, watching. He loved the way Arlene's long blond hair undulated gracefully with every movement of her head. He admired the way this very pretty and disarmingly intelligent young woman could rush home from her office on Wall Street, shed the jacket of her proper suit, slip on a kitchen apron over her bright silk blouse and in seconds transform herself from a very successful financial analyst into an efficient and competent cook.

He was so intent on admiring her that he failed to respond to her question.

"Ben? How did it go today?"

"No luck," he admitted grimly.

She set down the dish she had just created and waited for him to taste it. One bite, and he nodded. "Hey, not bad."

"Is that all?" Arlene asked, disappointed. "Do you

have any idea what veal costs these days? How I had to rush home from the office to make this supposedly simple sauce? And all you can say is, not bad?"

Though she was a hard-facts analyst in the stock market, Arlene was extremely sensitive about her housekeeping abilities. Guilty about not having responded more enthusiastically, Ben resorted to hyperbole. *"Brava!"* he cried. *"Bravissima!* Better?"

Tears welled up in Arlene's bright blue eyes. "Now you're being sarcastic. And you only do that when you're angry. Really angry."

"Angry? Me? Why? I am living with perhaps the most beautiful blonde in all New York. Who is an excellent cook. Cordon bleu. And a wonderful lover. Better than cordon bleu. And who, based on our comparative income figures, is supporting me."

"That'll change. Just be patient," she urged.

Because he thought that his anger had ruined the dinner she had worked over so diligently, he tried to joke. "One thing I must admit, the very idea of making love to a stock market analyst could make a man impotent."

"Is that your excuse for the last few days?" she asked softly. "Is that why we haven't made love?"

It was no longer a joke. Her words, her voice, the look in her eyes demanded an answer.

"It's this Riordan case. The more I dig into it the angrier I get. I've never seen a man who deserved a defense more. And I've never seen a case in which the facts were more damning."

"You can't arrive at a theory for your defense in just a few days. You've told me that your uncle Harry used to say, 'Every case is a war, so it should have a carefully planned strategy which includes attack as well as defense. Since on that strategy you win or lose, take your time. Don't grab the first likely defense and run with it.'"

Ben leaned back, smiling. "Darling, you have a mind like a computer. Everything I've ever told you about Uncle Harry you remember practically word for word."

Arlene smiled back sarcastically. "Darling, everything you've ever told me about your uncle Harry you've told me at least a hundred times, which may account for my excellent memory."

"I guess so. I'm sorry he never lived to see you. You two would have loved each other."

"Eat your veal," she said.

He was enjoying the veal and the white wine Arlene had brought home when she said, "Oh, by the way, she called me at the office again today."

In that household "she" referred to only one person, Ben's mother.

"What did she want?"

"She's noticed a big change since you went into private practice. You're impatient with her when she calls. Of course, as she has a habit of doing, she finally got around to topic A."

"Why don't we get married."

"She says she's embarrassed at Sisterhood meetings at the Temple. The other women brag about what their sons are doing."

"And since I left the D.A.'s office, she doesn't have much to brag about," Ben agreed.

"So," Arlene continued, "if she can't brag about you, she would at least like to brag about a daughter-in-law. And maybe soon, some grandchildren. She feels terrible. All the other women have pictures to show except her."

"Then why waste time eating? Let's go right to bed!" he said.

Arlene put down her fork, stared across the table at him in such a demanding way that he stopped eating. Then quite suddenly he confessed, "Wrong as it is for a doctor to become emotionally involved with a patient, it is even more dangerous for a lawyer to be too emotionally involved with a case. Calm, cool, shrewd and opportunistic, that's what a defense lawyer should be."

"Last time you were so personally involved was when you were still in the D.A.'s office and prosecuting that child pornographer," Arlene recalled.

"Whom the judge let off with a sixty-day sentence!" Ben exploded. He rose from table, went into the living room to stare out the large bay window that faced New York Harbor. When he heard her quietly enter the room behind him, he admitted, "Riordan is no longer just a client. I never met him until two weeks ago. I have seen him only four times. I have viewed his confession three times. The last time I saw it, it dawned on me.

"I closed my eyes as he talked, and suddenly it hit me. Change a few expressions. Change St. Malachy's to Temple Sinai, and he could be my father talking. He could be so many good men I've seen in my lifetime. Neighbors. Relatives. All of them unspectacular, but those men are our everyday heroes. The husbands, the fathers, the men who make our families what they are. Riordan lived for only one thing, his family. Lived for them, killed for them. And there are lots of fathers who would have done the same. I think even my father might have."

Ben turned to stare into Arlene's eyes and confessed, "Every time I visit him in that damned jail I want to put my arm around his shoulder and say, 'Pop, let's get out of here. A man like you doesn't belong in a place like this.' But that's where he's going to be. And worse, if they find him guilty."

"Will they?"

"The facts and the law are both against him," Ben had to admit. "It's hard to formulate a good defense with two strikes on you."

"He has one thing in his favor," Arlene said.

"What?"

"A lawyer who's angry and willing to fight."

"Angry may not be enough," Ben said. "Boy, how I wish Uncle Harry were alive now." Then, because he felt obligated to respect her culinary efforts, he said, "I . . . I want more of that veal. It's terrific."

"You don't want any more veal," she said. "You don't have the appetite for it. Coffee? A scotch?"

"Coffee."

As she turned to go, he caught her hand and pulled her back and embraced her. His face pressed against hers, he whispered, "Why do you put up with me? With my moods? Another woman would be in that kitchen in tears because I couldn't eat the dinner that she slaved over. You just take it in stride."

"Not in stride, Ben, not in stride," she said softly. "If it would do any good to cry, I would. If it would do any good to become furious, I would. But it wouldn't change you. You would still be concerned, intense, idealistic and maybe that's what I love about you."

She slipped out of his arms and went back to the kitchen to brew him some coffee. On her way, she paused to turn on the floor lamp and brighten the entire room with a warm glow. Ben looked around this room, which he had come to love in the two years he had lived here. It reflected Arlene's attitude toward life, bright, warm, affirmative. Who else, he wondered, would have taken this top floor of a shabby old brownstone house on Brooklyn Heights and made it into an apartment of such color and warmth? The light gold walls, the richly upholstered gold and white couch, the comfortable wing chair and, in the corner near the big bay window, an antique table of gold-embossed red leather that added just the right punctuation to this world of white and gold.

Through the large bay window, he could see the vast expanse of New York Harbor. In the distance, far to the right, the last glow of the setting sun was just disappearing over New Jersey. The lights on the bridges leading to Manhattan and Staten Island had just come on, lending pale green accents to dusk as it changed into night. Across the bay, Liberty stood astride her floodlit pedestal.

This was Arlene's private world, and she had consented to share it with him. He often thought, *I must be the luckiest man in the world. And the luckiest thing that ever happened to me during my time in the District Attorney's office was Arlene.*

He had met her while working up a prosecution in a case involving the theft of negotiable bonds from her office.

When first told that he would have to get all his information from a Miss Robbins, Ben Gordon was prepared to meet an overbearing, aggressive career woman. Arlene Robbins turned out to be not only beautiful but utterly feminine as well as efficient, informed and extremely helpful.

Under the guise of qualifying her as a possible witness, he had been able to ask some personal questions, the most important of which was, "Are you married?"

"No," she had said, smiling. "Are you?"

Ben had actually blushed. "Not married, not going steady, not even thinking of it."

"Now what did you want to know about those stolen securities?" Arlene directed the conversation back to business.

He had interviewed her several times after that and was always about to ask her to dinner, or lunch. Always he was inhibited by the fact that she was so beautiful. She must have a dozen such offers every week. Surely there was a special man in her life. So what could she possibly want with a young lawyer whose prospects at this stage were not exactly impressive.

The last day he had called her, he blurted out urgently, "I must see you!"

"Why? What happened?" she had asked, alarmed. "Did the case fall apart?"

"No, but I have to see you," he insisted. "Preferably away from your office."

"Lunch?" she suggested. "I'll put you on my expense account. I'll say you're a potential client."

"Lunch! Great!"

They met in a small, crowded restaurant in the financial district.

Twice Arlene asked, "What's so urgent?"

Twice he had ignored her question to talk of other things. When lunch was over he yanked the check from her hands, refusing to let her sign it. He paid the bill. They left and she asked again, "What's so urgent?"

"Let's walk," he said.

He steered her toward the East River, toward the strong smell of roasting coffee that infiltrates Wall Street on humid days. They reached the river and stood watching a flock of scavenger gulls attacking a departing garbage scow as it went out to sea. Suddenly he blurted out, "This is the last time I'm going to see you."

He glanced at her out of the corner of his eye to assess the impact of his sudden announcement. She seemed disappointed. "Are you off the case?"

"What I've dug up makes this crime interstate. So it's become a federal matter," Ben said. "We have to surrender jurisdiction."

"Oh, I see," she said.

For the first time he felt that he had touched her emotions. She seemed unhappy it had to end this way.

"That doesn't mean . . ." Ben said. "At least I hope that

doesn't mean that I can't . . ." He had difficulty saying it. Then he heard himself blurt out suddenly, "Would you like to get married?"

She had stared at him, trying to determine if he were serious. When she saw that he was, she said in a soft and kindly way, "Thanks. But no, I would not like to get married."

"Not to me," Ben concluded.

"Not to any man," she pointed out. "Actually, I've come to like you a lot. I think to myself, I could make something out of that young man. He would dress a little differently. And I'd send him to a hair stylist to get that head of unruly black hair styled into some semblance of shape."

"You thought all that about me?" he asked, flattered even by her criticisms.

"Yes."

"Well, I'm offering you the chance to do that," he urged. "Marry me and I'll do anything you say. Including getting my hair styled. Just marry me!"

"Sorry," she said.

"Why not?"

She did not answer that question.

"Then can I at least see you again?"

"Yes. But don't call me at the office. I have no time for that kind of thing." She gave him her phone number and the address of her flat in a brownstone over on Brooklyn Heights.

On their fourth date he stayed the night. Warm, passionate, she was as wonderful to make love to as she was to look at. In the middle of the night, when they were too spent to do anything but talk, he said, "Now you've got to marry me. If my mother ever found out what we've done, she'd insist," he joked.

Arlene did not joke when she said, "Please, Ben, don't ask me. Not till I bring it up. If I ever do."

He turned to face her. In the dark he could see her classic profile as if it were marble in moonlight. "I think I have a right to know. Especially now," he had said very softly.

She slipped out of bed, reached for her silk robe, wrapped it about her and left the bedroom. He found her staring out of the bay window at New York by night, peaceful, quiet, deceptive. He stood behind her, embracing her.

"Tell me," he urged in a whisper.

She did not respond at once. Then she started, as slow, as halting as a shy young girl, "You see, my mother ... no, that's wrong. My father is where it begins. He was a very attractive man. Still is, I guess."

"You don't know?"

"I haven't seen him in years. But he was handsome, with flair, style. Women loved him, especially my mother. He was her life. He had to travel on business very often. Each time he came home was a celebration for her and for me.

"Nobody ever suspected how much my mother lived only for him. She was so social and so active, in school and local functions. But she was filling up time, just waiting for Joe to come home from another business trip. She was a lovely woman. And so popular. Everyone loved her. Nobody as much as I. I worshiped her.

"Then came that evening. He arrived home from another trip. We had a wonderful dinner. But as the evening wore on, conversation between them started to lag until I felt I was in the way. So after dinner I went up to my room and tried to study. But I couldn't. I had this nervous feeling. So I sneaked out to the top of the stairs and overheard them. My mother said very little. And what she said she said through tears. She was pleading, begging. But my father was firm. Not loud, but very firm.

"Soon it became clear to me. He was leaving. Leaving her. Leaving us. We would never have to worry financially. But he was going out of her life. I wanted to rush down those stairs and say, 'You can't do that! Not to a woman who loves you the way Mother does!' Instead, I went back to my room and cried.

"Two days later when I came home from school, I called out to her. She didn't answer. I started up the stairs to her room. But I think I knew, because I went up very slowly.

"When I opened the door of her closet I found her, hanging from a hook, a nylon stocking around her throat."

At that moment, Ben had turned Arlene about, embraced her, pressed his face against hers and found it wet with tears.

"I made a promise that day. No man in this whole world is ever going to do that to me. I am never going to make any man the center of my life."

"That has nothing to do with us. All men are not like your father," Ben said. "My father was in love with my mother and faithful to her all his life."

Arlene had not answered, only continued weeping.

Thereafter she had consented to Ben's moving in. But his urgings of marriage always met with evasions.

That was how their life together had begun. And though she had never succeeded in having his hair styled, she came to love the unruly way it looked.

Now he was standing in that same bay window, looking out at that same view of New York Harbor.

This time it was Arlene who came up behind him, embraced him and asked, "What are you thinking?"

"Harry used to say every case has ragged edges. A witness who can be impeached, conflicting testimony, a faulty confession. There's always a loophole, an area of doubt. So keep picking away. Picking away was the term Harry used."

"So pick away," Arlene urged.

"That's not good enough this time. The prosecution's case is too solid."

"What about Riordan's reason?" Arlene asked.

"It's no legal justification in such a case."

"Insanity?"

"I can't get any reputable expert to testify."

"Crime of passion?" Arlene ventured.

"That doctrine isn't accepted by the New York courts."

"There must be something. And I know you'll find it," she insisted.

"We've got one thing going for us, public sympathy," Ben said.

"Then why not capitalize on that before sympathy turns to apathy?" Arlene asked.

"Arlene Robbins, you are a very bright girl. Do Messrs. Merrill, Lynch, Pierce, Fenner and Smith congratulate each other every morning on having the smartest and most beautiful stock market analyst in the world working for them?"

He kissed her, then held her tighter and kissed her again. This time it was a prelude to making love. She knew it and she was happy, because she could relieve him of his torment.

8

BEN GORDON HAD SERVED his notice of discovery on the
District Attorney's office, demanding access to all the evidence the prosecutor had in his possession, and also the
names of all witnesses Lester Crewe intended to call in
the course of the trial.

Ben found no surprises. There was the 38-caliber pistol, the slugs taken from Johnson's body, the Medical Examiner's findings, the photos of the body. The list of
witnesses was complete, from the clerk who sold Riordan
the pistol to the eyewitness to the killing to Lester Crewe
himself, who had taken Riordan's confession.

That was the most damning thing. Not only was that
confession replete with detail, but the television tape revealed a man in full possession of his faculties.

Despite the many hours Ben had spent in the law
library researching cases on evidence, he had not found
a single case in any jurisdiction that would permit him to
make a credible argument that Riordan's confession was
inadmissible. Lester Crewe, in his usual capable professional fashion, had handled that in a manner which made
it immune to attack. Les had not only observed the rule
in the Miranda case, in which the United States Supreme
Court had circumscribed the manner in which confes-

sions must be taken, he had done it so meticulously that any judge had to receive that confession in evidence.

The more research Ben did, the more convinced he became the best thing for Dennis Riordan would be an immediate trial, which would at least enable him to capitalize on jury sympathy. He called Lester Crewe, who expressed no reluctance to go to trial at once.

Secretly Les Crewe felt, the sooner the better, for he was troubled by Riordan's age. A man in his late sixties, enduring prison life, suffering the mental strain of an impending trial, could very possibly become ill. *Bad enough,* Les thought, *to have to prosecute a man of that age, but to have to prosecute an old man who came into the courtroom every day sick or perhaps even in a wheelchair.* Les did not like those odds. Nothing could suit him better than an immediate trial.

When Ben called Judge Klein's office, instead of setting a trial date by phone, Klein insisted he come in. While Ben waited outside Klein's private office, he could hear an attorney loudly haranguing the judge, who had obviously ruled against him in some case. Then Ben heard the jurist shout back at the attorney. Finally, the door opened and the furious, flushed attorney, still holding a set of blue-backed legal motion papers in his hand, emerged, pausing only long enough to shout back, "Believe me, Judge Klein, the Appellate Division will reverse you on this one!"

When Ben entered, Klein was starting to light up a fresh cigar. But the glisten of sweat on his face indicated his distress over the legal battle just concluded. Between puffs as he was trying to light up, Klein said, "You think that was something? You should have heard him on the phone last night. Tracked me down at my daughter's apartment. I was with my grandson. The boy's just started school this year and he was all excited telling me about the

museum trip they made. Then that damned call came in.
I was on the phone an hour and twelve minutes! By that
time, the boy was in bed and asleep."

Klein blew out the match, which was beginning to
scorch his fingers.

"Gordon, if they ever offer you a judgeship, turn it
down! It's no way to live."

He seemed to put that case behind him as he said, "So
you want to go to trial early. Okay. The trial I'm on now
ends this week. I have another one starting Monday.
Should go maybe two weeks, three at the most. I could fit
your case in, say, March twenty-seventh."

"March twenty-seventh would be fine," Ben said.
"That'll give me three weeks to prepare."

Klein exhaled a cloud of smoke, then said, "Now, Gordon, *you* do something for *me.*"

"If I can, Your Honor," Ben replied, puzzled.

Klein swung his swivel chair around so that he did not
face Ben but looked out the window at the imposing Federal Courthouse across the street. The matter seemed too
personal for Klein to discuss face-to-face.

"Every once in a while a case comes before me that
really troubles me. I mean, the kind of case that keeps me
awake nights. You see, I've always believed that it's as
much a judge's duty to achieve a measure of rough justice
as it is to preside punctiliously over a complicated trial. In
Civil Part, I try to work out settlements whenever I can.
In Criminal Part, I try to avoid lengthy trials that are
costly to the defendant and the State. This Riordan case
bothers me more than any case I can remember. Why put
an old man through such an ordeal? I would feel derelict
in my duty if I didn't try to work out some reasonable and
just solution. So, if you would talk to your man and he's
amenable, I think I could talk the D.A. into a plea. Say,
Manslaughter in the First."

"I don't think my client'll go for it," Ben warned.

"And I won't feel right unless you try. So, Gordon, for my sake, please?"

"I'll do my best. Otherwise, March twenty-seventh, Your Honor."

Ben Gordon waited in the small, shabby, stained-walled conference room on Riker's Island until they brought his client to him.

Dennis Riordan carried a book. The flexible black leather binding told Ben it was a Bible. Riordan had his finger in the place where his reading had been interrupted.

He refused Ben's invitation to sit down. Instead, the stocky man stood, strong hands clasped before him, holding his Bible.

"Yes, son?" he asked indulgently. "What is it this time?"

"We've got a break, an offer from the judge. He is willing to exert pressure on the District Attorney to reduce the charge."

"Can a judge do that?"

"During a trial a judge rules on lots of questions that could foul up the prosecution's case. And the D.A. is damned well aware of that. So he might go for a deal, if the judge insists," Ben explained.

"And if the D.A. goes for a deal?" Riordan asked, as if he might consider it.

"The way it works is this: The indictment now reads Murder Two, meaning with intent to cause death. That carries a sentence of at least fifteen years to life. The judge has no discretion about that minimum. But if they reduce the charge to Manslaughter One, because of extreme mental disturbance, the judge does have discretion. So if you plead guilty, you might have to serve maybe a year."

Riordan asked thoughtfully, "If I plead guilty . . . ?"

"It's all handled very simply," Ben started to explain eagerly.

"Wait a minute, kid, wait a minute!" Riordan interrupted. "I killed a man with what you fellows call intent to cause death. Yet now you would all be willing to call it manslaughter, not murder?"

"That's not exactly the way I would put it."

"But that's the truth of it, isn't it, son?"

"Yes," Ben admitted.

"That's really a fraud. I *did* intend to kill Johnson. So I should be *charged* with murder, *tried* for murder and *convicted* of murder. Else you fellows are just playing games, the kind of games that put men like Johnson back on the street to rob, rape and kill girls like my Aggie. Well, I am not going to play those games. I have my rights. I want to be tried for murder. I want everyone in this State to know that Dennis Riordan did what he had to do because the State wouldn't. Then maybe they'll change the system. Maybe that judge . . . what's his name?"

"Klein," Ben said.

"No, the other one, the one who let Johnson go, the one who said I couldn't testify, who said Johnson's confession was not admissible . . ."

"Judge Lengel."

"Yeah. Maybe next time he won't be so quick to let a guilty killer off scot-free!"

"Mr. Riordan," Ben began in a compassionate tone, "listen to me, please? I know how you feel, but . . ."

"Unless you lost your daughter and your wife, you couldn't know how I feel!" Riordan shouted back.

"Believe me, Mr. Riordan, I've seen plenty in my few years in the law. The system isn't perfect. It has its faults. But explain to me what good it will do for a man like you to spend the rest of his life in prison while the real deadly criminals walk the streets?"

"It will be a lesson, a sign to the rest of the people," Riordan insisted.

"The people'll forget. They always do."

"I don't care! So long as for one day they realize what justice has come to in this country."

"And in exchange for that day you're willing to spend the rest of your life in prison?"

"With Aggie gone, with Nedda gone, what life?" Riordan asked simply. He tightened his grip on his Bible, then in a voice softer and far more intimate than before, he admitted, "You see, it didn't come clear to me until after Nedda. I was so busy taking care of her, consoling her, doing for her, worrying about her that I never realized . . .

"Actually, it was out in the back garden I first understood. It was a habit, you see. Every evening after supper I always used to go out back, just before dark and work around. Pruning here, watering there, raking up where the earth got too packed down. It was a lovely garden. Not much in the way of vegetables. Ah, but the flowers. Nedda loved my flowers. And Aggie, she would take them to the office. Brightened up things, she'd say, gave a little life, a little perfume to that air-conditioned office where the air smelled like it came out of a plastic package. Aggie loved my roses most of all. Of course, after Nedda was gone . . . look, you don't want to hear this."

"Yes, yes, I do!" Ben said.

Riordan turned away, was silent for a time before he found the words.

"A man doesn't ask much out of life. Just a chance to do for his wife, for his kids . . . especially if they're good kids like mine. . . ."

He fell silent again. Ben prodded. "Mr. Riordan?"

"The . . . the neighbors, they were so kind after Nedda. Bringing food, worrying over me. I know they meant well, but to be honest, I couldn't wait for them to clear out. I wanted to be alone, in my own house, with my own memories. The first evening I was, I took up my life again. Made my own supper. Put the dishes in the washer, turned it on, like Nedda used to. Then I went out into the garden, like always. I was digging around one of the rose bushes when I realized. Crying. I was crying. I couldn't do that while Nedda was alive. I had to be brave for her. But without Nedda to take care of, I was able to realize how alone I was. For the first time in more than forty years.

"Memories came back in a rush. Jumbled. Out of order. Never again would young Frank come banging through the front door, toss his first baseman's mitt toward the hall closet and miss. He always missed. And Nedda'd pick up for him before I could bawl him out. Never again would I know young Dennis was up in his room, studying, the door always closed. He was the bright one, Dennis, the quiet one. Never again would Aggie wrap newspaper around a bunch of my roses to take to the office, and kiss me before she left. Never again would Nedda pack me a lunch, with things I didn't always fancy, but she'd say, 'Eat them, Dennis, they're good for you. . . .' Never again . . .

"Everything in life that I loved so, would be never again. Kneeling there in the earth, crying, I made up my mind. If the law couldn't stop an animal like Cletus Johnson from destroying a whole family, then *I* would stop him. But the important thing was to let the people know. To grab them and say, 'Listen to me! Yesterday it was Dennis Riordan's family. Tomorrow it's yours. Unless you do something. Stand up! Demand the right to live in safety. The right to raise a child and see her live. Not to have twenty-four years of love and care and raising get choked off in one minute of a dark night in some place that should be safe.

"So, you see, kid, I got to have a trial. Else what have I done? Killed one killer? There are too many more out there. The people have to be warned!"

There was nothing Ben could say.

"Look, son, don't torment yourself. I know what I'm doing."

Ben looked into Riordan's calm blue eyes, then finally said, smiling. "Mr. Riordan, do something for me?"

"Sure, kid. Anything but plead guilty to manslaughter," Riordan said, smiling now too.

"Don't call me 'son.' And in the courtroom, don't call me 'kid.' It doesn't look good."

"Counselor. How's that?"

"Better. Much better."

"Okay, kid."

Ben smiled. "I took the liberty of going back to your house and getting you some suitable clothes for the trial."

"You knew all along I wouldn't agree to a deal," Riordan said.

Ben nodded. "But I had to try."

"As long as you knew," Riordan said with some satisfaction.

"I got your dark gray suit, some white shirts and a plain dark tie. To make a good impression on the jury."

"Make a better impression if they knew that's the same suit I wore when I buried Aggie, and then Nedda," Riordan said grimly.

9

ON MONDAY MORNING several hundred prospective jurors crowded into the Central Jury Room on the fifteenth floor of the Criminal Courts Building at 100 Centre Street in lower Manhattan. It was a vast, high room with walls paneled in dark brown oak up to a height of seven feet, and above which the walls were painted a light, innocuous green. The room was filled with a disorderly array of chairs and benches, some of dark wood, some of cheap white plastic. Though the signs on the wall clearly instructed *No Smoking*, there were large, heavy concrete urns on the carpeted floor for the disposal of ashes and burned-out cigarettes.

Against one wall of the room was a huge three-sided walnut counter, covered in worn brown formica, on which stood a desk microphone. Behind the counter two clerks were ready to greet the jury candidates.

Each prospective juror presented a slip on which was noted name, address and occupation. Most surrendered their slips without the exchange of a word. A few, however, asked to be excused. The clerks pointed out, in a manner neither polite nor friendly, "Look! It says very clear on this slip, if you want to be excused, apply a week ago. We can't do anything for you today. So just give me your slip and take a seat!"

Within half an hour more than five hundred candidates had filed into the room. Each slip had been received, checked against the master attendance file and dropped into a vertical dark green metal drum. Among those hundreds were the twelve who would eventually sit in judgment on Dennis Riordan.

Shortly after ten o'clock the phone rang. A gossiping clerk interrupted himself to answer.

"Yeah? Fifty? You got 'em!"

He spun the metal drum vigorously, then flipped open the top, extracted a slip and announced the name into the microphone. The prospect came forward obediently. The clerk repeated the procedure in monotonous fashion until he announced, "Violet Tolliver!"

The instant he enunciated that name, he looked at the slip a second time to make sure. The entire room suddenly grew quiet as a tall, extremely attractive woman with beautifully styled, short, strawberry-blond hair and striking green eyes came forward. She moved with grace and confidence, and her subtly styled blue tweed Adolfo suit complimented her svelte figure, which, for a woman about to turn forty, made her seem years younger. All eyes turned to follow her as she approached the counter.

"Please wait here, Miss Tolliver," the clerk said, extremely deferential.

He continued to call out names until fifty prospects had assembled at the desk. He turned their slips over to a uniformed court attendant who led them from the Central Jury Room to the elevator. On the fourth floor he directed them into a courtroom. He indicated the spectators' benches, but before they could be seated, he commanded, "Raise your right hands!" He intoned, "Do you solemnly swear that you will truly answer the questions put to you touching upon your competency as an impartial juror between the People of the State of New York and Dennis Riordan, the defendant at the bar, so help you God?"

In various ways, by nods, by whispered "I do's," all fifty candidates assented. Though each was startled to realize that the case upon which they might sit involved a man they had read about in their newspapers or heard about on television. Suddenly the possibility seemed both fascinating and awesome.

Violet Tolliver was more concerned than all the others, for she held in her hand a list of reasons her attorney had prepared to ensure that she would be excused from serving as a juror on any case, excuses she had carefully rehearsed: harboring a prejudice against the defendant for any reason, inability to be fair and impartial due to the nature of the specific crime, prejudice due to general concern over lack of law and order.

"Be seated." The court attendant interrupted her thoughts. He went forward through the railing that separated the well of the courtroom from the spectators, handed the fifty slips to the court clerk, exchanged a few words and departed, leaving the jurors to stare at two young attorneys who were chatting at one end of the two counsel tables. One was a tall, young white man with unruly black hair, the other a light-skinned black man who had a nervous habit of adjusting his glasses.

The court clerk dropped the fifty slips into the drum on his desk. While he spun it, Violet Tolliver had a chance to observe the courtroom's windows, which were seven feet up from the floor. She assumed they were constructed that way to keep jurors and others involved in a trial from being distracted by outside views and noises. Below the windows the walls were paneled in dark cherry veneer reaching a floor of inlaid linoleum in two shades of what once must have been distinctly brown and tan.

Only behind the judge's bench did the paneling reach

the ceiling. And on it, in raised metal letters, were the words *In God We Trust.* To one side of the judge's bench a limp American flag hung slack against its pole. On the other side of the bench was the witness box, directly in front of which stood the court stenographer's desk. Against the near wall was the jury box with fourteen leather swivel chairs fixed to the floor. In the spectators' area, on each side of the center aisle, were six long oak benches. The fifty prospective jurors filled almost half of them.

Once the court clerk had spun the drum sufficiently, he reached in, extracted a slip and called out the name "Elihu Prouty!"

A black man, very thin, in his middle sixties and wearing steel-framed glasses, rose and started forward.

"Take Seat One in the jurors' box," the clerk ordered. He fished out a second slip. "Violet Tolliver!"

Only when she rose did he realize who she was. He stared in awe. Both attorneys ceased their conversation to watch as she moved past the railing and into the jury box to take the chair next to Elihu Prouty.

Not until she was seated did the clerk feel free to pick out another name.

"Walter Grove!"

A craggy-faced man in his middle forties, wearing a tweed jacket, plain gray slacks and a navy blue turtleneck sweater, untangled his unusually long legs, folded *The New York Times* and started toward the jury box. As he approached, he glanced at Violet Tolliver in such a way that she had the discomfiting feeling he was seeking to assert some claim to familiarity with her. Attractive, famed for her television commercials, she drew such unsolicited attention and resented it. Grove passed her, circled the jury box and took Seat 3 beside her.

Instinctively she drew aside slightly, inclining in Mr. Prouty's direction.

When all fourteen chairs in the jury box had been filled by twelve potential jurors and two alternates, the court clerk disappeared through the door behind the judge's bench. He reappeared several minutes later to call out, "All rise!"

The short, stout judge, attired in his black robe of office, entered. The other jurors did not recognize him, but Violet Tolliver did. He was Aaron Klein, who had been sitting in Jury Part only last week when she had come down to insist on being excused from serving. She reached into the jacket pocket of her Adolfo suit to clutch the list of excuses her attorney had provided. If Judge Klein was to preside over this case, she would need them.

Klein stared down at her from the bench, smiled, apparently gratified to find her ready to perform her civic duty.

"Ladies and gentlemen, for those of you who have never served on a jury before, let me explain that we are entering the judicial process known as the *voir dire*. The examination of potential jurors to select twelve jurors and two alternates who can hear the evidence and render a fair and impartial verdict. There are two grounds on which an attorney can challenge and disqualify a juror.

"First, for cause. Meaning that some answer a candidate has given indicates a bias that either attorney feels may prevent a fair and just verdict. Second, there is what we call a peremptory challenge. When, for no reason at all, the attorney decides he does not want you on his jury. Either for cause, or peremptorily, a juror may be excused and another picked to fill his place.

"This can be a long and tiresome procedure. But it is the best way we know to ensure a man a fair trial. Now,

I will ask the first questions and then turn you over to the tender mercies of the prosecutor.

"Ladies and gentlemen, this case has received considerable coverage on radio, television and in newspapers. Will you be able to ignore all that and base your verdict solely on the evidence presented during this trial, without regard to any preconceived ideas you may have had? If not, please raise your hand."

With all the business burdens pressing on her, demands for decisions on advertising, marketing and publicity which she alone had to make for Beauty-by-Tolliver, Ltd., the large cosmetics company she headed, Violet was prepared to ask to be excused, for this was one of the reasons on her list. But confronted by the gravity of this particular case, she hesitated. Besides, Judge Klein was looking directly at her.

No hand being raised in the jury box, the judge turned to those prospects in the spectators' area. "Any of you?" Two hands went up. Klein said, "Take your slips and report back to Central Jury for assignment to another case."

He addressed the jury box once more. "Would the race or color of a defendant in any way influence your judgment as to guilt or innocence?"

Again no juror raised his hand, either in the box or among the reserves.

Judge Klein went on. "Would the color of his victim in any way influence your judgment?" No hand being raised, Klein continued. "Is there anyone who feels unable to serve by virtue of problems of health that would interfere with the course of what may be a demanding trial?"

Again no hands.

"Now, ladies and gentlemen, I will read off to you a list of names. Persons who may be called as witnesses in this trial. If you know any of them personally, raise your hands. William Simmons? Wilbert Ward? Abe Kalbfus?

August Marchi? Allan Frost? Lester Crewe? Irving Rosenthal?"

When it was obvious that they knew none of the prosecutor's witnesses, Judge Klein turned to Lester Crewe.

"The People may continue."

Lester Crewe approached the jury box carrying the board on which the clerk had arranged the jurors' slips in the order in which they had filled their seats. He adjusted his glasses, peered at the jurors, then at their names on the board.

"Ladies and gentlemen, this is a case involving the charge of Murder in the Second Degree. Aside from killing a law-enforcement officer, which constitutes Murder in the First Degree, this is the most serious crime with which a person can be charged in New York State.

"If you are selected for this jury you will be called on to determine if a man is guilty of murder, conviction for which calls for a sentence of up to twenty-five years to life in prison. Would any of you shrink from exercising that responsibility if convinced by the evidence that man is guilty?"

Violet Tolliver realized she had another opportunity and she might have seized it had she not noticed Judge Klein staring at her over his reading glasses.

Crewe continued. "Would any of you refuse to give the same degree of credence to the testimony of a law-enforcement officer as to that of any other witness?"

Four hands went up in the jury box and eight more among the reserve jurors on the benches beyond the railing. Crewe glanced at Ben Gordon, who could not suppress a slight smile. Crewe looked to the bench.

Judge Klein grumbled, "You can thank television news and editorials for that! Excused!"

Four more names were selected from the drum to

replace the four who had left the jury box. After Crewe inserted the new names on the jury board, he asked, "Has any of you ever been the victim of a crime?"

Three hands went up in the jury box. *Three out of fourteen, about average,* Crewe thought sadly.

The procedure was long and painstaking, resuming after the lunch break and late into the afternoon. Twice Judge Klein leaned across his wide desk to ask Crewe, "How long is this going to go on?"

"Until I get a jury that is free of any taint of prejudice against the law and the police," Crewe announced.

Whereupon Ben Gordon said, "The prosecutor can one day retire on a fat pension. I'm only getting an assignment fee of a few thousand dollars. I can't make this one case my life's work."

Judge Klein smiled sardonically and turned his attention back to Crewe. "Look, we both know what the crucial questions are. Get to them. Now!"

Crewe turned to the jury box, adjusted his black-rimmed glasses and paused before he asked, "Has any woman here ever been the victim of a rape?"

There was a stunned silence. The unexpected question seemed almost irrelevant, until each juror recalled that connected with the murder charge under consideration was the rape of Agnes Riordan.

A young woman in the second row of the jury box timidly raised her hand to ask, "Does attempted rape apply?"

"Yes," Crewe said.

The attractive young woman nodded slightly.

"Excused," Crewe said. He glanced in Ben Gordon's direction. They both realized what such a woman on the jury would have meant to Dennis Riordan's cause.

Violet Tolliver debated answering that question. Once her first husband had tried violently to force her to have sex after their divorce. Whether that was considered attempted rape she did not know. But she would remain silent.

Now Crewe proceeded to open a new line of inquiry.

"Have any of you ever read about, listened to a radio broadcast, or seen a television newscast about a group called The Guardian Angels?"

For the first time, Ben Gordon rose to his feet. "Your Honor, there is no connection between The Guardian Angels and my client."

Crewe responded quickly, "The question of a private citizen taking the law into his own hands is at the heart of this case. The response of the jurors to my question is a clue to their state of mind and their ability to render a fair verdict."

Klein nodded thoughtfully throughout Crewe's argument, but then said, "I will sustain Mr. Gordon's objection."

Disappointed, Crewe proceeded more directly. "Does anyone in this jury box feel that a private citizen is ever justified in deciding on his own that another man is guilty of murder and carrying out the sentence of death?"

One man in the second row of the jury box raised his hand, blurting out, "The way crime is rampant in this city . . ."

Judge Klein interrupted with a sharp rap of his gavel. "No speeches! Just leave the jury box!"

One woman shyly raised her hand.

"Excused!" Crewe said, looking to the bench for approval, which he received.

At that point, Judge Klein addressed the potential jurors on the spectators' benches. "We'll save a lot of time if any of you feel the same way. Just raise your hands."

Two women and one man did and were excused.

As for Elihu Prouty, Violet Tolliver and Walter Grove,

the only three of the original fourteen who still remained in the jury box since early this morning, each had different and singular reactions to that question.

Elihu Prouty, a religious man, taking very literally the words "Vengeance is mine, saith the Lord," could honestly answer that he did not condone any man taking that right into his own hands.

Walter Grove had grown more interested in this case as jury selection wore on. At first, he had responded to his jury notice as a welcome break from the novel he was writing and which was frustrating him at the moment, but now, curious about his personal reaction to the circumstances in the Riordan case, he had decided to remain.

Violet Tolliver realized this was her last chance to avoid serving. But that part of her which was an outraged citizen decided to stay on that jury and render what help she could in the cause of Dennis Riordan. *If that constituted a prejudice, it was a justifiable prejudice*, she thought defiantly.

Once the excused jurors had been replaced and all those remaining responded favorably to his questions, Les Crewe turned to the bench and said, "The People accept this jury."

Klein looked down at Ben Gordon. "Counselor, you've been remarkably silent throughout this procedure. Are you satisfied with the jury? Or are you only giving your client a few thousand dollars' worth of defense?"

Ben smiled.

Klein prodded. "No questions? No challenges?"

Ben rose from his place at the counsel table, reached across to take the jury board from Lester Crewe. He stared at it as if to familiarize himself with the names. Actually, he was performing an exercise in basic legal accounting.

Six whites. Five blacks. One Hispanic. In New York

these days, he was lucky to have six whites on the jury.
Since Riordan's victim was black, blacks on the jury posed
a significant problem for Ben. Let them swear an oath of
impartiality and disclaim all prejudice, still it was there.
Just as it would be if Riordan were black and Johnson had
been white. There was no such phenomenon as an unprej-
udiced juror.

Ben would have preferred even more whites, if possible. But if he now dared to excuse any of these five blacks
by a peremptory challenge, he faced two great problems.

Uncle Harry used to point out that by the end of any
court day, most of those jurors who had been excused and
returned to Central Jury were black, since prosecutors
usually tried to get a predominantly white jury. "Therefore," Harry had cautioned, "unless your defendant is
black, don't ask for any new jurors near the end of the
day."

There was also a second risk for Ben in excusing any
black juror. Those blacks who remained would resent it
and unconsciously accuse him of racial bias. He felt hand-
cuffed by circumstance. Still, he had to make some pre-
tense at shrewd jury selection.

"When I read off your name, please raise your hand.
Elihu Prouty?"

The lean, aging black man in Seat 1 raised his hand.

"Violet Tolliver?"

At the mention of her name, two new jurors in the
second row leaned forward to make sure she was indeed
the woman they had seen on television. Ben studied her,
curious as to why she was here.

He called the name of the man in Seat 3. "Walter
Grove?"

Grove raised his hand.

"Mr. Grove, it says on your slip you're an author."

"Yes, sir."

Violet could not resist glancing in Grove's direction, for now his name was somewhat familiar.

"Tell me, Mr. Grove," Ben continued, "have you ever written crime stories? Courtroom drama? Legal stories of any kind?"

"No, sir. Intimate fiction. Personal revelations. No crime."

Ben Gordon paused, pretending to ponder challenging Grove. Secretly, he was delighted to have him. An author with a fertile imagination, and most likely an idealistic need to defend the underdog, could prove an unexpected bonus. All it took to get a hung jury was one such quixotic, stubborn maverick.

Finally, after what he figured was an impressive and grave silence, Ben passed on to Juror Four, Harold Markowitz, and to the others on the jury board he held: Aurora Devins, a black woman. Armando Aguilar, a Puerto Rican. Deborah Rosenstone, white, Jewish. Luther Banks, a black commercial artist. Anthony Mascarella, white, Italian. Mildred Ennis, black. Eudora Barnes, black. Veronica Connell, white and, Ben hoped, like Dennis Riordan, Catholic as well as Irish.

It was as balanced a group as Ben Gordon could expect. He turned to Judge Klein. "I accept the jury."

Klein nodded to the court clerk, who faced the jurors. "Please rise and raise your right hands!"

Twelve jurors and two alternates complied.

The clerk read from the card he held. "Do you solemnly swear that you will well and truly try the action of the People of the State of New York and Dennis Riordan, the Defendant at the Bar, in a just and impartial manner to the best of your judgment and to render a verdict according to the law and the evidence, so help you God?"

The jurors having signified their assent, Judge Klein admonished, "From this moment on you are not to discuss anything that happens during this trial with anyone, especially with each other. I also impose on you the legal obligation not to watch any television newscast, listen to any radio broadcast, or read any newspaper which carries any report of this trial.

"Your verdict must be based solely on the evidence presented in this courtroom. You will report here tomorrow morning promptly at nine-thirty! Dismissed!"

As the jurors started to file out of the box, Walter Grove whispered to Violet Tolliver, "No need to be puzzled. We've met twice before, very casually at publishers' cocktail parties. I won't blame you for forgetting if you don't blame me for remembering."

Resenting his attempt to turn this situation to his social advantage, she said, "The judge said jurors were to have no conversation with each other."

"About the case," Grove corrected her.

"I don't think he intended to encourage familiarity between jurors," Violet Tolliver replied.

"And between judge and juror?" Grove asked.

She did not reply, but left the jury box at once. She felt no need to admit to Grove or anyone the events leading to her attendance at the jury call this morning.

10

BEN GORDON SAT at the bay window that looked out on New York Harbor. He ignored the panorama to make a cold assessment of the jurors he had accepted.

Six women. Six men.

Two Jews. One Italian. Good family people. They should sympathize with Dennis Riordan. Normally, so would all the blacks on the jury, except that in this case Riordan's victim was black. That was a strong negative.

Three Catholics. The Irish woman. The Puerto Rican. And the Italian, Mascarella. They were a distinct plus.

Women, Ben decided, were his greatest asset. They could be counted on to react very emotionally in any case involving rape. To capitalize on that, he must introduce as much explicit testimony as Judge Klein would allow concerning the rape of Agnes Riordan.

Yet once, while still in the D.A.'s office, Ben had suffered a shocking surprise. He ended up with a hung jury in a rape case in which the defendant was clearly guilty. On questioning the jurors afterward, Ben discovered that the sole holdout for acquittal was a bitter spinster who believed that rape never occurred unless the victim invited it.

The jury, Ben pondered, as he studied their names. How much better he might be able to sharpen his strategy for the defense of Dennis Riordan if he knew more about this jury than merely names, addresses and occupations.

That old black man in Seat 1, a tailor according to his slip, would, if custom prevailed, be appointed foreman of the jury. What had he lived through in his sixty-odd years that might predispose him to favoring or resenting a white man like Dennis Riordan?

Violet Tolliver? Why, Ben questioned, had a woman with one of the most publicized faces in America not sought to be excused from jury duty? It was most unusual for a person of her prominence to serve.

That author, Graves. Or was it Grove? Ben consulted the jury list. Yes, Grove. Originally, Ben was delighted to find an author on the jury, hoping he would prove to be a maverick idealist, fighting for underdog Dennis Riordan. On second thought, suppose, instead of being the maverick he hoped for, Grove intended only to capitalize on the case, as several had done on the trial of that school-mistress who shot the diet doctor? Unfortunately, Grove would remain an enigma to Ben Gordon, right to the end. As, in truth, so would they all.

For what did he really know of them? Of the lives they had lived, the experiences they brought with them that would predispose them to hear his client's case and judge him?

The jury, the jury, the jury. . . .

In his own living room, in his apartment on the upper East Side of Manhattan, Lester Crewe was studying the same list of jurors in preparation for opening the prosecution's case in the morning.

He made his own analysis. Six whites. Five blacks. One Puerto Rican. Even split between the sexes. Those six women troubled him. The mention of rape, which was unavoidable in Riordan's confession, was bound to affect them. So it was vital that he focus the jurors' attention solely on the fact of the crime under consideration. Murder. Deliberate, planned, intended murder. Women, and probably most men on the jury, would tend to sympathize with Dennis Riordan. Crewe himself did.

But there was a principle at stake here which he must make the jury confront. No man, regardless of the degree of provocation, had the right to take justice into his own hands. All other elements, sympathy, race prejudice, emotional reactions to rape, all must yield to the undeniable facts in this case.

Lester Crewe's responsibility was to ensure that all those other elements, most especially emotion, be kept out of this trial. Particularly, he must block every attempt by Ben Gordon to enlarge on the rape and death of Agnes Riordan. To that end Les had armed himself with detailed memoranda of law, supported by many court citations, in which such testimony had been ruled out under similar circumstances.

Secure in his preparation, his witnesses and the physical evidence, Lester Crewe went to bed repeating to himself over and over, *Make Ben Gordon stick to the facts and emotion could not affect the outcome.*

But more than an hour later, he was still awake and restless, trying to lie as still as possible so as not to wake Hortense. She had to rise early, prepare the children's breakfast and still make an uptown bus in time to greet her class in Harlem by eight-thirty.

Out of consideration for her, Les eased out of bed, went back into the living room to study the jury list and ponder, *among those six whites, was there one who might be so prejudiced that, despite the sworn oath, he or she would hold out for Riordan's acquittal in face of overwhelming evidence?*

He knew he would never have a case as solid as this

one. All he had to do was present it in a methodical, straightforward manner, alert always to combat all diversions Ben Gordon might seek to introduce.

Still the jury; always that nagging doubt about what a jury, any jury, might do.

To a prosecutor that thought was as unsettling as an unresolved biopsy to a physician.

The jury, the jury, the jury. . . .

Juror One:

Elihu Prouty. Sixty-eight years old. A tailor with his own small shop on Columbus Avenue in the Eighties, where he took in clothes for cleaning and pressing and himself diligently did all the repairs and alterations. A black man, a widower, he lived a frugal life. Between his shop, his television set and his church, his life was full, if not particularly eventful.

Juror Two:

"Jury duty?" Violet Tolliver had exclaimed in a fury when the notice was handed to her by her secretary. "You know I don't have time for jury duty! Send that notice down to Gene Cordes. He takes care of such things. Then get me those contact prints and page proofs. These ads have to be approved by tomorrow morning!"

This one time her secretary did not obey.

"Anne, don't just stand there! Get hold of Gene!" Violet ordered, her green eyes blazing. Many people, most of them men, thought Violet Tolliver was at her most fascinating when she was angry. Tall, willowy, with hair a striking shade between blond and red, she had been one of the most highly paid models in America until she decided to capitalize on her fame and produce a line of beauty products which were now known worldwide, thanks to her own persistent promotional efforts.

She appeared in many of her own television commercials and personally supervised every phase of her operation, which was vast and vastly profitable. One thing everyone knew who knew Violet Tolliver, she was a woman with little time to spare. Two ex-husbands could testify to that.

"Anne, get hold of Gene!" When Anne stood there almost trembling, Violet knew there must be something terribly wrong. "All right, Annie, what is it?"

"This jury notice came from Mr. Cordes."

"Impossible! These things come in every year or two. And he always gets me excused. Always!"

"But this time . . ." Anne started to say.

"Get him up here!" Violet ordered angrily.

Within minutes, Gene Cordes, attorney and house counsel to Beauty-by-Tolliver, Ltd., was at Violet's door. As she flipped back the Pliofilm sheet that protected one of the sketches for a new ad, she saw him enter. She dropped the ad and brandished the jury notice.

"Gene, what's the meaning of this?"

"Computers," he replied calmly.

"What the hell does our having computers have to do with my jury duty?" she demanded.

"Not *our* computers. The *court's* computers," Gene corrected her.

"I don't give a damn about their computers. You got me off every time before!"

"Exactly," he pointed out, "but now down at the County Clerk's office in the Supreme Court, they have a computer system on which they accumulate the lifetime record of every candidate for jury duty. All those years I've been getting you off are listed there. So when I sent my law clerk down to get you excused, the lady punched up your record and said, 'Sonny, according to our records Miss Tolliver has been called for jury duty twelve times in the past seventeen years. But has never served once. Sorry.' "

"What are you saying, Gene?"

"Vi, this time you have to go down there yourself. Appear before the judge who's sitting in Jury Part. Work your wiles on him. After all, you're a beautiful woman."

In chambers that day Judge Aaron Klein did not wear his black magisterial robe. As he studied a legal order he had been asked to sign, Violet Tolliver noted that he wore a dark blue suit with a distinct pencil stripe and that he had committed the egregious sartorial error of also wearing a striped shirt and a striped tie. He had no style sense at all and worse, he was overweight with not the faintest concern for his physical fitness.

Klein finished reading, signed the order, then looked up at Violet Tolliver. She could see from the light in his eyes that he was startled.

"Well, well, the little lady from the television commercials. Not so little. How tall are you, five six, five seven?"

"Five eight and a half," Violet informed him.

"And such a beauty," Judge Klein said as he took a cigar from the battered old humidor with the brass nameplate which his wife had bought when he was appointed years ago. Once he had bitten off the end of the cigar, he asked, "So what can I do for you?"

"Judge Klein, I am here to clear up some widely held misconceptions about me. People who see me on television or read about me in the columns think that my life is all glamour, parties, gala nights and discos. What they see is only the publicity part of my work. Actually, my life consists of long hours, hard work, sometimes seven days a week of day-to-day office work, meetings, battles, competition and decisions, all of which I have to make alone. That takes time, a great deal of time. So I'm sure you can understand that I can't possibly sacrifice two weeks to serve on a jury."

Then, as she had been instructed by Gene Cordes, she concluded, "After all, my business gives employment to more than three hundred people. I'm sure you wouldn't want to jeopardize their jobs."

Klein nodded and picked up a computer printout.

"Miss Tolliver, according to our records you have never served on a jury. Not even when you didn't own your own large business. Now, I'm sure you're opposed to crime in the streets and I'm sure you'd like to see justice fairly administered. Well, in our system *you* are a vital player in that game. As judge I am only the umpire. I interpret the rules. But jurors decide guilt or innocence. Just as you can't play baseball no matter how many umpires you have on the field, so without players there is no game here. You are one of the players. Let us say, like in a war, a war against crime, you have been drafted!"

"Suppose I'm called on a case where I feel I can't be impartial?"

"It's your right to say so when the issue comes up," Klein pointed out, relighting his cigar.

"Why do I have to waste two weeks of my valuable time to find that out?" Violet Tolliver demanded in the imperious tone with which she dominated her employees.

Calmly, Judge Klein replied, "Because, lady, nobody should be so famous that she is exempt from being a conscientious citizen. And also if you don't do it, I'll sentence you to two weeks in jail for contempt!"

She stared into Judge Klein's brown eyes. He stared back and she knew he would make good his threat.

She had been about to respond, but the judge shook his head in fatherly fashion. She was wise enough not to try. Then he smiled. "You know something, Miss Tolliver? If you had a small business, employed three people or less,

I could have let you off. But a big business, three hundred people? The law says you've got to serve!"

By the time her limousine had returned Violet Tolliver to her office on Fifth Avenue, her practical side, the side that made her a successful executive, had adjusted to the dismal prospect of two long, dreary weeks of jury duty.

She had planned her routine. Her limousine would deliver her to the courtroom every morning. She would bring along work to do during the wasteful waiting hours. Then the car would return to the office to pick up Anne, who would bring down Vi's lunch along with all urgent mail, proofs and advertising schedules. She could have lunch in her limousine and transact her business at the same time, one of the advantages of having a phone in her car. Promptly at four the car would return to whisk her back up to the office for the rest of the afternoon and evening.

On that hectic, if inconvenient, basis it would be possible for her to survive this ordeal. Most important, if Gene gave her a list of acceptable excuses, she would be able to avoid completely being selected to serve on a case.

Her careful plan had miscalculated in only one regard. That she would decide to serve in the case of *The People* v. *Dennis Riordan*.

Juror Three:

Walter Grove had been struggling over the last page of Chapter 19 of his novel when he heard the mail being dropped at his front door by the elevator man.

Grove now lived and worked alone, and was quite accustomed to all morning sounds, the thud of *The New York Times* when the elevator man threw it against his door at seven o'clock and the sound of his mail being dropped, usually at around nine-thirty.

On days when he was writing well, he ignored all sounds, including his doorbell. Today he had opened the door for the *Times*, which he knew he would not read until much later. Now he found himself going to the door at the sound of the mail. Anything to escape his typewriter, which had taunted him all morning.

He had flipped through the mail and found the jury notice. His instinctive reaction was, *I'll never make my deadline if I have to serve.* He ripped open the envelope, glanced at the date and the little notice which informed him that if he wanted to be excused he would have to appear and make his reason known during the week previous to the date of service. He had always asked, and had always been excused, mainly because lawyers never wanted authors to sit on their juries, considering them too eccentric and unpredictable.

This time, however, he looked favorably on the idea of serving. But his professional conscience, which drove him to write seven days a week, starting punctually at six o'clock each morning, demanded a more acceptable excuse. He satisfied it by arguing, if he did get to serve on a jury and it proved to be an interesting case, it might provide him the basis for an episode in some future novel.

In truth, he was aching to get away from his typewriter, most unusual for him. Martha could testify to that. The day she had asked for the divorce she said, "You're not married to me, only to that damned typewriter. When you're not working at it, you're thinking about it. I can't go on talking to myself forever."

Since then, he had been alone, a hermit in a crowded city. He had his work. He had his editor. He read the newspapers, listened to the television news and thought about tomorrow's writing. He missed Martha. But he did not miss women as a group. He was sublimating his sexual drive in his work.

This latest novel, which he knew could be very good, was for that reason his most demanding. Exhausting was a more apt word. As a juror he would be able to sit back for two weeks and let lawyers spin the plots and introduce the characters. As for his deadline, they couldn't hang him if he was a few weeks late.

Juror Four:
Harold Markowitz, in charge of a plumbing supply warehouse, led a frustrating life, between suppliers who were always late with deliveries and contractors who needed everything at once. To him, jury duty was a welcome relief from his usual harried days in which he dreaded every ring of his telephone and instinctively reached for an antacid tablet each time it did.

Juror Five:
Aurora Devins, a young black woman, worked as a secretary in a small real estate office in Harlem and looked upon jury duty as an inconvenience but a necessary obligation. In this city these days, with most defendants being black, she wanted to make sure they received fair consideration.

Juror Six:
Armando Aguilar, fifty-two, was superintendent of a large apartment house on the upper West Side. If he resented the long subway trip down to court every morning, he consoled himself that it meant two weeks of freedom from constant nagging by tenants about lack of heat, breakdowns in elevator service and noise created by other tenants.

Juror Seven:
Deborah Rosenstone, thirty-nine, wife of a successful real estate operator, she looked forward to serving, not only out of a sense of duty but because it might afford her

a chance to give some judge a piece of her mind on the loose way the courts dealt with criminals in this decaying city! She was a woman who spoke only in sentences that ended in exclamation marks.

Juror Eight:
Luther Banks, twenty-seven, black, assistant art director for a national drug manufacturer. He had no interest in serving on a jury; it interfered with his work, to which he was devoted. But when he brought the jury notice to his office, the personnel director told him that the company's effort to have employees excused covered only the top echelon of executives. All others were encouraged to serve at full pay to prove that the company was public-spirited.

Juror Nine:
Anthony Mascarella, manager of the produce department of a large, expensive market on the upper East Side, resented serving on a jury because it interfered with the proper purchase and display of his wares, of which he was very proud. But like most citizens, grumbling and unwilling, he had yielded to his jury notice and reported for duty.

Juror Ten:
Mildred Ennis, a young black woman of twenty-six, was a trained, highly experienced X-ray technician in the office of a busy roentgenologist on Park Avenue in the Sixties. To her, serving on a jury would be a relief from patients who trooped in day after day, trying to appear calm and even casual but betraying fear in their eyes. All of them dreaded the same fatal diagnosis, and when it occurred Mildred Ennis felt that somehow they blamed her.

Juror Eleven:

Eudora Barnes, twenty-three, teller in a large bank on Fifth Avenue in the Fifties, attended night school in pursuit of a degree in business administration that would allow her to rise to the executive level at the bank. Once she had determined that it would not interfere with her precious night classes, she had no resistance to serving on a jury.

Juror Twelve:

Veronica Connell, a lay teacher at St. Ignatius School, was a woman of strong convictions. Because she deemed conditions unjust, she had led the recent teachers' strike in the diocese. She approached life with the same stringent standards that she applied to her young students in the classroom. She had rigid ideas about right and wrong, and principle was more dear to her than human beings.

Into the hands of those twelve citizens, some reluctant, some merely seeking to escape the burdens of their everyday lives, Ben Gordon had entrusted the fate of Dennis Riordan.

He fell asleep reassuring himself, women must be compassionate toward a husband and father who suffered as Dennis Riordan had. But how to exploit that without putting Riordan on the stand? Because if he did, he was practically conceding the vital element of intent to kill. On the other hand, in the course of any trial unforeseen developments arose which could force an attorney to alter radically his original strategy. Uncle Harry used to say, "A defense attorney must be firm and fluid at the same time."

Finally, Ben fell asleep. But within the hour he woke in a cold sweat. Barefoot, he moved silently across the bedroom floor out to the living room to stand in the bay window and look out at the harbor. Aside from the lights on the Verrazano Bridge and the bridges into Manhattan, the city seemed blacked out.

"Ben?" Arlene called to him softly from the bedroom. He did not answer, hoping she would fall asleep again and relieve him of the need to confide in her. But soon he heard her bare feet pad across the living room carpet. She embraced him.

"My God, you're in a cold sweat!"

"I . . . I had this dream. Les had presented his last witness. He turned him over to me and I had no questions. Then Les said, 'The People rest.' Judge Klein stared at me. 'Mr. Gordon, call your first witness.' I looked at the bench. I looked at the jury. But I couldn't speak. I began to tremble so that I had to hold onto the counsel table to support myself. I woke in a sweat and trembling. No attorney should go into a trial feeling that way."

"Your uncle Harry always said when he went into court, unless his hands were icy cold and he felt extremely tense, he knew he wasn't going to be at his best. You did tell me that, didn't you?"

"Yes," Ben conceded.

"Well, that's all you're going through now. Nerves. Stage fright. And that's good. It means you care, you're deeply concerned about Riordan's fate."

"You don't understand . . ." He tried to argue.

Because she felt he needed it, she persisted. "Those days and nights in the law library, those cases you read, surely you're prepared. You said you had your trial strategy all worked out."

"You don't understand!" he exploded. He began to pace and speak in intense, rapid-fire sentences. "My entire strategy is based on the fact that legally and factually we have no valid defense. All those cases I read? They only confirmed that. Well, what does a lawyer do when he has no defense?"

"Pick away at every witness. Keep looking for those loopholes that create a reasonable doubt," Arlene said.

"In any other case that would be the thing to do, because the prosecution usually has to rely on witnesses with criminal records or unsavory reputations, on policemen who exaggerate in an effort to get a conviction, on confessions that can be attacked because they were illegally obtained. But in this case Les's witnesses have no reason to lie or exaggerate. They are solid witnesses whose character and veracity I can't attack."

"Then what can you do?"

"Pick away," Ben said.

"But you just said that wasn't good enough."

"In this case picking away is not a strategy but a tactic, a diversion to cover up my real strategy."

"Diversion?" Arlene asked, puzzled.

"Les expects me to pick away. He's undoubtedly prepared his witnesses for it. So I'll persuade him to go on thinking that, by actually picking away. But all the time I have to be like a magician who keeps you looking at his innocent hand while he does the trick with his other hand. While picking away I have to be searching for other opportunities."

"Opportunities for what?"

"Uncle Harry used to quote an old lawyer's maxim, 'When the law is against you, argue the facts . . .'"

"'And when the facts are against you, argue the law,'" Arlene recalled.

"Right!"

"But when both are against you?" she asked.

"That's where Uncle Harry's own maxim came in. When they're both against you, take the jury's mind off what your defendant did by putting his victim on trial. All during Les's presentation of his case, while I divert him by picking away at his witnesses, I will actually be looking for openings to drag Cletus Johnson into this case and put him on trial for the rape and murder of Agnes Riordan. I want that jury to experience every harrowing, painful, bloody detail of how it occurred. I want every woman on that jury to feel that it might have been her and if it had been, the horrors she would have lived through before she died."

"That sounds like a powerful strategy to me," Arlene said. "Why are you so worried?"

"Because, my darling, those cases I've been studying, those textbooks on evidence I've been reading, all add up to one thing. It will be very, very tough to introduce Johnson's crimes into this trial. It may even turn out to be impossible. And if it is . . ."

Ben broke off and was silent for a long moment before admitting, ". . . if it is . . . well, that's what woke me. If I haven't made my case by the time Les says, 'The People rest,' I have no case."

"Can I come to court?" Arlene asked.

"I'd rather you didn't."

"Okay," she agreed, unable to completely conceal her hurt at being shut out of this most important part of his life.

In the morning before he left for court, Arlene checked him out. Dark suit, light blue shirt and a neat tie with a subdued stripe, all met with her approval. She studied his hair, still damp from his shower, and approved, though she knew before the morning was half over it would be dry and unruly again.

She kissed him, whispered, "Good luck, darling," at the same time discreetly reaching for his hand. It was icy cold. If Uncle Harry was right, then her lover was ready for battle.

THE TELEVISION CAMERAS were waiting for Ben Gordon when he arrived at the courthouse. He tried to brush by them, but he was imprisoned by microphones thrust into his face like weapons, hand-held cameras that attacked him from all angles. Reporters, women as well as men, hounded him with questions.

"We hear you're going to plead insanity. Can you confirm that?"

"Is it true your client tried to hang himself in his cell?"

"Do they have him isolated from the other prisoners on Riker's so that the blacks there won't kill him?"

"Will you make him available for interviews during the trial?"

"We hear his neighbors out in Astoria are getting up a defense fund. Any truth to that?"

One female reporter, who traded on her beauty to ferret out interviews which others failed to get, smiled and said, "Mr. Gordon, our producer took a minute-by-minute survey. Do you know that next to unemployment and President Reagan, this case is the item with the highest rating on our six o'clock news? You owe it to a very interested public."

"And do you know, young woman," Ben responded, "that courts were established to achieve justice, not sup-

ply items for the television news so we can boost your
ratings? I am going in there to defend a man against the
charge of murder. My mind is on that, not on answering
questions for your viewers. Excuse me."

He pushed his way through the crowd and heard the
frustrated reporter threaten, "I'll take care of that sonofabitch at six o'clock!"

When he arrived in the holding pen where he could
confer with his client, he discovered that Dennis Riordan
had been confronted by the same assault from newspeople when he stepped out of the bus that brought him from
Riker's Island. His guards were able to protect him only
by using physical force to keep the reporters away.

Ben asked to be alone with his client.

"Mr. Riordan, now it starts. Once we go into that
courtroom, time begins to run, like the ticking of a clock.
Every day, every hour counts. We have only so much time
to make our defense. Up to now, you haven't been much
help. If you change your mind and during the trial anything occurs to you that might help, tug at my sleeve. I'll
ask for a recess so we can discuss it.

"Anything at all, even if it seems inconsequential to
you, let me know. I need every point on which I can pick
apart every prosecution witness. It's vital to my strategy.
For instance, if they describe what you wore that day and
your tie was a different color, let me know. If they say you
said something one way and you said it another, tell me.
If you put the gun down with your right hand and the
sergeant testifies it was your left, let me know. I've got to
keep the prosecutor off balance with details. And I'm
depending on you to help me."

Riordan did not respond except to ask, "Are you going
to put me on the stand? I want to testify!"

Rather than alienate his client at the moment his trial

was to commence and deny his request, Ben said only, "We'll see how it goes."

"That was the main reason, I want to tell the people, warn them," Riordan insisted.

"We'll see," Ben reiterated, though, barring some unforeseeable circumstance, he had determined never to put Riordan on the stand.

The jury was already seated in the box. The prosecution's first witness was waiting in the front row of spectators' benches. Because of the notoriety the case had created, the rest of the seats were taken by reporters, newspaper and television sketch artists, and curious private citizens, white and black, who after being frisked were admitted to fill the few remaining seats.

The clerk called out, "All rise!"

Jurors, attorneys, newspeople and spectators stood respectfully as Judge Klein, garbed in judicial black, entered, trailed by his plump, dark-haired female law clerk. He whispered some last-minute instructions to her, then ascended the bench.

He looked out over the courtroom, feeling considerable irritation, thinking, *This whole trial is unnecessary. I know the outcome. Yet, in a way, it's my fault. If I had chosen an older lawyer to defend Riordan, he would have talked him into copping that plea. But young Gordon couldn't bring it off. Or else he didn't want to bring it off. Maybe he welcomes the challenge, or the television publicity, or the experience.*

In that intolerant mood, Judge Klein said, "Okay, okay. Everybody be seated!" He gestured to the clerk, who droned the usual opening pronouncing the court in session. Judge Klein looked in the direction of Lester Crewe. "The People ready?"

Crewe nodded, rose, and with a sweeping look in the

direction of the press, finally fixed his gaze on the jury. He adjusted his heavy-framed glasses, realized that his hand trembled a bit, took a deep breath and cautioned himself, *Take your time. Do it exactly as you rehearsed it last night.* Hortense said the slower the better, since it gave greater weight to everything he said and dispelled any hint of nervousness. And being a speech teacher, she should know.

He wet his lips, cleared his throat and began, "Ladies and gentlemen of the jury, according to the rules of procedure in criminal cases . . ."

Judge Klein interrupted. "Counselor, don't give us a course in trial law. Just make your opening statement."

"With all deference, Your Honor, I think that due to the circumstances in this particular case it is necessary for me to offer a prelude to the usual opening statement."

"The presence of all these reporters wouldn't have anything to do with that, I suppose?" Judge Klein shot back.

Crewe was tempted to reply, but decided to adhere strictly to his planned opening. He took no small degree of satisfaction from the fact that a white judge badgering a black prosecutor would win him sympathy from at least five members of the jury.

"Ladies and gentlemen, according to the rules of procedure in criminal cases, the prosecutor makes the first opening in order to outline for you the facts he will attempt to prove, because your verdict must be based not on emotions but only on the facts. Not on what Dennis Riordan may have felt, but what he actually did.

"The People will prove that on the twenty-first day of January, 1981, Dennis Riordan bought a pistol in another state, drove back to New York with the express intention of killing one Cletus Johnson. That on the twenty-fourth day of January he did indeed track down Johnson, fire five shots at him, hitting him four times, killing him instantly. We will prove all that by witnesses to those events and, most important, by a complete and uncontested confession of guilt by Mr. Riordan. Thank you."

As Lester Crewe returned to his seat, Judge Klein routinely asked, "Mr. Gordon?"

Ben rose to his feet, paused, then, because he did not wish to reveal his strategy even by inadvertence, he stated simply, "Your Honor, the defense chooses not to make any opening statement."

The excitement that erupted behind him told Ben that his announcement had created considerable surprise and speculation among the press.

"Counselor, is that your considered decision?" Judge Klein asked.

"Yes, Your Honor."

Privately, Klein did not approve, but he had no choice except to order, "Your first witness, Mr. Crewel"

"The People call William Simmons!"

A pale, nervous young man in the first row came through the barrier. Neatly dressed, wearing a proper tie, shirt and suit, all of which made him appear even more uncomfortable than he felt, William Simmons ascended the single step to his place on the witness stand. He carried a black-bound ledger. Judge Klein gestured the court clerk to administer the oath.

"PutyourlefthandontheBibleandraiseyourrighthand-anddoyousolemnlysweartotellthetruththewholetruthand-nothingbutthetruthsohelpyouGod?"

"I do."

"Beseatednameplease!"

The witness replied, "William Simmons."

Lester Crewe approached the witness box and proceeded to elicit from Simmons that he was the clerk who sold the 38-caliber pistol to Dennis Riordan. He asked

Simmons to rise and identify Riordan. Then, relying on the black ledger in which he had noted the information, Simmons testified to every detail of what had occurred on that day in the gun shop. He especially pointed out that Riordan had given him a false address, failed to offer his driver's license when asked for identification, mentioned that the gun was for the protection of his wife, who, it later turned out, was dead at the time. Once Simmons had identified the murder weapon by checking the numbers on it with the numbers in the ledger, Lester Crewe offered the gun in evidence and turned to Ben Gordon. "Your witness."

Ben rose to his feet, yellow pad in hand, and moved to the witness box thinking, *Now it begins, the diversionary tactic, the picking away. Watch closely, Les, else it won't work.*

"Mr. Simmons, you testified that Mr. Riordan did not show you his driver's license when you asked for identification. Did you specifically ask for his driver's license?"

"We like a driver's license best because it usually has a photo on it. So I said, like I always do, 'Driver's license, owner's registration, anything official?' "

"So it wasn't that you said to Mr. Riordan, 'Show me your driver's license' and he refused?"

"No, sir. But he didn't show it to me," Simmons volunteered.

"Suppose Mr. Riordan had shown you his New York driver's license? After all, New York licenses do not have identifying photos on them like some states."

"I know that, sir," Simmons said.

Sensing an opportunity he had not expected, Ben asked, "How do you know that?"

"We sell lots of guns to people from out of state. Provided they got good identification."

"So that if Mr. Riordan *had* shown you his New York

driver's license, even without a photograph on it, you would have sold him the gun anyhow," Ben pinpointed.

"Yes, sir."

"Tell me, Mr. Simmons, if Mr. Riordan had never mentioned his wife, never said the weapon was intended for her protection, would you have sold him the gun?"

"Well, I . . ."

"Let me put it another way," Ben interrupted. "Did *you* ask him if this gun was intended for his wife's protection?"

"No, sir."

"Then it didn't matter to you if she was alive or not? Right?"

Crewe rose to intervene. "Your Honor, he's badgering the witness."

"Your Honor, the prosecution made a big deal out of the fact that my client said he was buying the gun to protect his wife. The fact is, that was a matter of absolutely no consequence. Therefore, that entire line of questioning by the prosecutor was misleading and I want to demonstrate that."

"The witness may answer," Judge Klein ruled. "Would it have affected the sale of that gun whether Mrs. Riordan was alive or not?"

"No, sir," Simmons finally admitted.

Ben resumed. "Mr. Simmons, in that ledger, what name do you have written down for the purchaser?"

"Dennis Riordan."

"So he made no effort to disguise his identity, did he?"

"No, sir."

"Is that the action of a guilty man?"

"Well . . . no, sir."

"Mr. Simmons, do you know the neighborhood in which Mr. Riordan resides?"

"No, sir."

"Do you know it is considered a high-crime area?"

"I wouldn't know."

"Do you know that while Mr. Riordan has been in confinement his home has been broken into and looted?"

The reaction of surprise among the press was almost as loud as the objection which Lester Crewe rose to shout:

"Your Honor, I object! Counsel has laid no foundation for the question, nor has any evidence been introduced that the defendant's home was looted! I insist the question be struck!"

But Ben responded softly, "Your Honor, if the prosecutor would like, I will take the stand myself and testify in detail as to what I found in the defendant's home."

Judge Klein pondered for a moment, then ruled, "I will allow the witness to answer."

"No, I didn't know his home was looted," Simmons acknowledged.

"So, Mr. Simmons, in view of that fact, isn't it entirely possible that when Mr. Riordan said he was buying a gun for the protection of his home he was telling the truth?"

"I . . . I suppose . . ." Simmons admitted, looking to Lester Crewe to extricate him from this situation which neither of them had anticipated. But the prosecutor was impotent to help him.

"Only one more question, Mr. Simmons. Think carefully before you answer. Did anything Mr. Riordan said, or anything he did, lead you to believe that it was his intent to kill anyone?"

Simmons hesitated, his face reddened, and he finally answered, "No, sir."

"That's all, Mr. Simmons."

When Ben returned to his chair, Riordan tugged at his sleeve and whispered, "You know, kid, you're crazy.

When I get on that stand I am going to tell them exactly why I bought that gun."

But Ben Gordon was not disturbed. For the moment, to gauge by the distressed look on Lester Crewe's face, he had diverted him sufficiently to force him to repair the damage.

"Tell me, Mr. Simmons," Lester Crewe began on redirect examination, "did you have any reason to suspect that the defendant was not telling you the truth when you sold him that gun?"

"No, sir."

"If Mr. Riordan had told you that it was his intention to kill someone . . ."

"Object!" Ben called out.

"Your Honor, since the defense opened this line of questioning I have a right to pursue it," Lester Crewe insisted.

Judge Klein reflected a moment, then ruled, "You may ask the question."

"Mr. Simmons, if Mr. Riordan had told you that it was his intention to kill someone, would you have sold him this gun?"

"No, sir, I would not," Simmons responded righteously.

As Crewe turned away, Ben rose in place to ask, "Mr. Simmons, in all the time you've worked at that store, has anyone ever come in and said he wanted to buy a gun to kill someone?"

"Of course not."

"So that you don't know what you would have done if he had said he wanted to kill someone, isn't that true?" Ben asked. He did not wait for an answer, but sat down and pretended to make notes on his yellow pad.

Actually, he was doodling, *Diversions, diversions, diversions . . . it's working . . . working*

12

"WILBERT WARD!" Lester Crewe called out.

The guard at the courtroom door permitted a short black man to enter. Stocky, clean-shaven, neatly dressed for his court appearance, he threaded his way to the barrier. He took the stand, was sworn in, gave his name and address.

Crewe approached him to ask his first question. "Mr. Ward, did you know a man named Cletus Johnson?"

"Yes, sir."

"How long had you known him?"

"Most of my life," Ward said.

"Were you with Cletus Johnson the twenty-fourth day of January, 1981?"

"Yes, sir."

"Where were you with him?"

"The Avon Restaurant on Lenox Avenue."

Then Lester Crewe led Ward through routine questions which established that on that day he and Cletus Johnson had left the Avon Restaurant after lunch, were laughing over some joke Johnson had just told, when a strange white man called out, "Cletus Johnson!" Johnson turned. The man fired. Johnson fell to the sidewalk. The assailant then went to his car, got in and drove off.

Lester Crewe then asked, "Mr. Ward, is the man who fired those shots at Cletus Johnson in this courtroom?"

"Yes, sir!"

"For the sake of the jury, would you identify him?"

As Les had instructed him to do, Ward rose from the witness chair and pointed in the direction of Dennis Riordan.

"That's him!"

"You're sure?" Crewe asked.

"Yes, sir. Never forget his face."

"Will the record show that the witness identified the defendant, Dennis Riordan?" Crewe requested, then concluded, "thank you, Mr. Ward." He turned to Ben Gordon inviting him to cross-examine.

Slowly, glaring at him to instill a sense of insecurity in him, Ben approached the witness.

"Mr. Ward, did you say you were a longtime friend of Cletus Johnson?"

"Yes, sir, since we started in high school together," Ward answered promptly.

"Did you also finish together?" Ben asked.

"No, sir. Clete, he dropped out in the first year. I went on for another year."

"But you remained good friends?" Ben asked.

"Yes, sir!"

"And you were good and close friends right up until the time of his death?" Ben asked, laying a foundation for later use when his tactics would open the door to his strategy. Then he switched subjects suddenly to throw the witness off guard. "Mr. Ward, you testified that you and Cletus Johnson were having lunch that day at the Avon Restaurant?"

"Yes, sir!" Ward answered briskly, for the longer he was on the stand the more secure and confident he felt.

"Mr. Johnson was shot around four o'clock in the afternoon. Lunch, Mr. Ward?" Ben asked, looking at the jury.

Ward was forced to concede, "It was a kind of late lunch."

"I guess so." Ben seemed to agree, then asked, "What did you have for lunch?"

"Uh . . . we had . . . chops, pork chops. And greens, collard greens."

"Seems like a balanced diet," Ben observed before continuing. "Did you also by chance have a drink?"

"I . . . yes, I guess so, we had a drink."

"Or two?" Ben asked.

"I don't remember. No, sir. Not two," Ward insisted.

"You're sure now?" Ben asked in such an insinuating manner as to put Ward under the impression that he had proof to the contrary.

"Well, maybe just two," Ward finally admitted.

"Mr. Ward, isn't it a fact that the Avon Restaurant is not really a restaurant but a bar?"

"No, sir!"

"Mr. Ward, I have been up to the Avon Restaurant and I did not see any food served there. How do you account for that?"

"Well, could have been off hours," Ward tried to explain.

"It was four o'clock in the afternoon, *lunchtime*, Mr. Ward!" Ben pointed out.

Lester Crewe sang out with an air of impatience, "Object as to both form and relevancy!"

"Sustained as to form," Judge Klein ruled. "Make your point in a proper way, Counselor!"

Ben resumed. "Mr. Ward, do you still maintain that at four o'clock in the afternoon you and Cletus Johnson were having lunch and not drinking?"

"I already said we had a few drinks." Ward began to fight back to preserve his credibility with the jury.

Ben had drawn some blood, not enough to score any vital points but enough to becloud the issue. So he again changed subjects abruptly.

"Mr. Ward, what did you do when you claim that Mr. Riordan started shooting at Cletus Johnson?"

"When I hear gunfire I duck. Learned that in the Army."

"So you ducked." Ben bore down. "When?"

"Soon as the firing started."

"Where did you duck?" Ben pursued.

Ward glanced at Crewe, then at the bench as if harassed by such unexpected questions. Finding no help, he answered, "When the firing started, I ducked behind this stoop. Like any man in his right mind would do."

"At the sound of the first shot?"

"Yes, sir. Wouldn't you?"

"Indeed I would, Mr. Ward," Ben agreed. "So if I understand correctly, you and Clete Johnson were having . . . uh . . . lunch . . . and a few drinks, finished, came out of the bar laughing at some joke that Clete had just made. A man called out, 'Cletus Johnson.' And Clete turned around. How soon after that was the first shot fired?"

"Soon as Clete turned."

"Instantly?"

"Yes, sir."

"And you ducked behind the stoop at the first shot?" Ben asked.

"Yes, sir, like I said."

"You mean, Mr. Ward, you crouched there and just watched a man pump four bullets into your dear, close friend Clete?"

"I didn't just watch him. I was trying to stay out of the line of fire," Ward protested.

"So what really happened was, after having a number of drinks, you came out, heard Clete's name, heard a shot fired and ducked behind a stoop. Am I right, Mr. Ward?"

"Just about."

"Then the only time you could have had a look at Clete's assailant was in a fraction of a second between turning and ducking?"

"Well, I . . . I did get a look at him!" Ward insisted.

"For a fraction of a second, perhaps one one-hundredth of a second!" Ben declared. "A man with three or four drinks in him gets a flash look at a strange white man, then comes into court and testifies very smugly that was the man who shot his old friend Cletus Johnson. Really, Mr. Ward . . ." Ben said, then turned and started back to the counsel table with an air of great disdain which he invited the jury to share.

As he expected, Lester Crewe rose to his feet and from his place at the table asked, "Mr. Ward, did you ever see this defendant at any time *after* the shooting?"

"Yes, sir."

"Will you tell the jury how that happened?"

"I was asked by the police to come down to headquarters to make an identification," Ward said.

"And did you, on that occasion, when the defendant was in a lineup, pick him out?"

"Yes, sir!"

"Do you now have any doubt whatsoever that he is the man you saw shoot Cletus Johnson?"

"No doubt at all!" Ward insisted with finality.

Crewe turned the witness back to Ben with a curt "Thank you, Mr. Ward."

Ben Gordon approached the witness. "Mr. Ward, when Cletus Johnson fell mortally wounded and the shooting had stopped, what did you do?"

"I went to his side. To see what I could do for him."

"But you testified that you saw the defendant go to his car, get in and drive off. Now which did you actually do? Tend to your dear, close friend? Or watch his assailant?"

"I . . . I guess I did both." Ward defended his previous testimony.

"Since you saw the defendant clearly enough, long enough, so that you could identify him in a lineup, and then again in this courtroom, isn't it possible that while your dear friend was bleeding to death, instead of trying to save his life, you just stood there watching his assailant make his getaway, thus permitting your friend to die?" Ben asked. "And he was your dear, close, longtime friend. Ah, Mr. Ward . . . Mr. Ward. . . ."

As Ben had anticipated, Ward felt the need to insist on his close friendship with Cletus Johnson. The small black man almost rose up from the witness chair as he proclaimed, "He *was* my friend! And I did everything I could for him, everything! It just . . . just wasn't enough!"

"Just how close a friend of Cletus Johnson were you?" Ben asked.

"How close . . . ?" Ward repeated, puzzled. "Close. Very close. I don't know how you say how close . . ." And he looked at Lester Crewe for some assistance.

"Well, for example, what did you two talk about?" Ben asked, almost casually.

"We talked about lots of things. Sports. Sometimes politics, like Reagan is not very good for black people. Things like that."

"Women?" Ben asked, smiling.

Ward permitted himself a slight smile. "Yeah, we talked about them, too."

"Ever exchange names, phone numbers, descriptions of what went on, like men sometimes do?" Ben asked, still smiling.

Ward hesitated, then conceded, "Yeah. Sometimes."

Ben paused, looked down at his pad as if he had run out of questions. The witness, assuming the cross-examination was over, had started to rise when Ben said, "One more question, Mr. Ward."

The witness sank back into his chair.

"Tell me, Mr. Ward, did your dear, close friend Cletus Johnson ever describe to you the manner in which he raped and strangled Agnes Riordan?"

Before Ben could even enunciate her full name, Lester Crewe was up and shouting, "Object! Irrelevant and immaterial!"

"Counselor?" Judge Klein invited Ben's rebuttal.

"Your Honor, since the prosecution made it clear in his opening statement and during the questioning of his first witness that the defendant's intent is crucial to this case, I wish to probe the question of intent in all its aspects, mostly as to its inception," Ben argued.

Judge Klein considered that for a long moment, then ruled, "I will sustain the objection." Before Ben could remonstrate, Klein added, "And I will preserve your exception for the record."

Ben caught a glimpse of Lester Crewe's face as he suppressed a relieved smile and pretended to make notes. *Well might Les smile,* Ben thought grimly. For not only had he just frustrated the best possible defensive strategy Ben could mount, but he had laid the groundwork for shutting it off in the future. Ben's chance of making Cletus Johnson the focus of this trial had just suffered a severe blow.

13

THE NEXT MORNING Lester Crewe introduced as his first witness Sergeant Kalbfus, to whom Dennis Riordan had surrendered and turned in his pistol. Ben picked away at his testimony, lightly, sparring for an opening which he never really expected to find. Then Crewe introduced Detective Marchi, who had kept Riordan in the interrogation room and prevented him from confessing so that his rights under the Miranda rule would be protected.

It was early afternoon when the young prosecutor called to the stand Medical Examiner Dr. Allan Frost. Once the doctor had been sworn, Lester carefully led him through his educational background in general medicine and his specialized training in forensic medicine. Frost answered all questions with the ease and confidence that came from years of serving as a State's witness in murder trials. When Lester Crewe had established Frost's credentials as an expert, he was ready for the crucial questions.

"Now, Doctor, I ask you, did you, on January twenty-fifth, 1981, perform an autopsy on the body of one Cletus Johnson?"

"Yes, sir, I did."

"Will you tell the jury your findings, sir?"

"The victim suffered four bullet wounds. To the chest, stomach, side and groin."

"During that autopsy, Doctor, were you able to determine the cause of Cletus Johnson's death?"

"I was."

"Will you tell the jury your findings?"

"All four bullets contributed to his death. But the one to the chest was the immediate cause of death, since it severed the aorta and found its way into Johnson's heart."

"Based on your findings, was death instantaneous?"

"Object!" Ben called out. "He is leading the witness!"

"Let me rephrase that, Doctor. In your expert opinion, when did death occur?"

"Considering the location and damage caused by that bullet, I would say that death was instantaneous," Frost declared.

"In your opinion, Doctor, could there have been any other cause of death?" Lester Crewe asked.

"Based on my examination of all the vital organs of the victim, the only cause of Mr. Johnson's death was the bullet wounds he suffered," Frost declared with finality.

"Thank you, Doctor."

Lester Crewe turned away and started back to his place, not expecting that Ben Gordon would attempt to cross-examine Frost, whose credentials and testimony were unassailable. When Ben rose, pad in hand, Crewe slipped into his seat very gingerly, wondering what his opponent had in mind. Frost was too experienced a witness to be rattled. And surely Ben had no expert forensic knowledge with which to shake him. More out of curiosity than concern, Lester Crewe watched Ben very closely.

On the bench, as puzzled as the prosecutor, Judge Klein leaned a bit in the direction of the witness, thinking, *Gordon must be doing this out of desperation. What can he possibly elicit from this witness that might help his case?*

Still, Ben approached the witness box, pad in hand,

pretending that he had a number of pertinent, probing questions to ask. He paused to ensure the total involvement of the jury, because what might emerge from this cross-examination could prove vital to his defense.

"Doctor," Ben began, "I believe you testified that you have done a great number of autopsies, several thousand, I think you said?"

"Yes, sir," Frost replied crisply.

"Spreading over a number of years?" Ben asked.

"Since 1966. That would make it sixteen years!"

"Sixteen years," Ben repeated slowly, giving the words inordinate significance to mislead Lester Crewe as to his intentions. "Tell me, Doctor, during those sixteen years, did you ever take any breaks from your duties? I mean, long leaves of absence?"

"Aside from my annual summer vacations, no, sir," Frost responded, glancing at Lester Crewe to see if he could clue him as to the direction of Ben's questions. But Crewe seemed as puzzled as he did.

Ben persisted. "Never took time off to get away on those nice, leisurely conventions that doctors always seem to attend?" He had asked the question as if he had some special and embarrassing information.

"Well," Frost began, obviously defensive, "there are times when forensic experts from various parts of the country convene to exchange experiences and discuss new techniques."

"And, by coincidence, always in nice, warm, pleasant places like Florida, Palm Springs, the Virgin Islands?" Ben asked, smiling.

Still puzzled but by now wary of Ben's tactic, Lester Crewe rose to intervene. "Your Honor, are such aspersions necessary?"

"Mr. Gordon," Judge Klein admonished.

"Sorry, Your Honor." But Ben kept his eyes fixed on the doctor. "Sir, did you ever attend such meetings?"

"Not on any regular basis."

"How many times a year? Five, ten, twenty?" Ben pursued.

"Not nearly that many," Frost protested. "I would say three, possibly four times a year. And then only for three or four days at a time."

"I see," Ben said, trying to give the appearance of being extremely thoughtful and calculating. "Would you say that this limit of three to four times held true for the year 1981?"

"In 1981?" Frost countered, still trying to discern the purpose of Ben's question. "It was certainly no more than four times. And most likely three. But I can call my secretary and find out exactly."

"That won't be necessary, Doctor. I accept your word. In 1981 no more than three or four absences for no more than three or four days at a time. Making a total of, say, twelve to sixteen days of absence during the entire year?"

"That would be about right," Frost said, looking in Crewe's direction for some clue.

"Then may I assume you were at work in the Medical Examiner's office during the month of February, 1981? With the possible exception of a few days?" Ben asked.

"Yes, you can assume that," Frost said.

Impatient with a seemingly irrelevant line of questioning, Judge Klein called out, "Counselor!" Ben turned to face him. The judge ordered, "Get to the point, if you have a point!"

"Yes, Your Honor," Ben said, slowly turning back to the witness. In a loud, clear voice he asked, "Then may I also assume that during February, 1981, you performed the autopsy on the body of Agnes Riordan?"

"Yes, I did . . ." Frost began to answer.

But Lester Crewe was on his feet, shouting to obscure Frost's answer. "Your Honor, I object! The question is irrelevant and immaterial to this case!"

Behind Ben the press section erupted in an outburst, the first of the trial. For this was the most important piece of news the trial had revealed, and with the public so involved, this was a bonanza for the press and the television reporters. But Judge Klein banged his gavel, furious. "Another such demonstration and I will throw the lot of you out. I respect the First Amendment, but we are trying a case here, not running a television show!"

Once order had been restored, he turned to Crewe and Ben Gordon. "Gentlemen, I think we had better remove the jury while we argue this." He signaled to the clerk to direct the jurors out.

But before they were out of hearing, Ben deliberately and loudly protested, "If the jury is going to be prevented from hearing all the evidence . . ."

Judge Klein banged his gavel so hard that a sudden and total hush settled over the courtroom. He glared down at Ben. Ben had taken an impulsive gamble, now he realized it might prove a costly one as well. He had antagonized Klein, and he suspected that from this moment on, for the rest of this trial, he could expect no favor from this judge who had been sympathetic. Yet in the interest of his overall strategy, it was a risk Ben had felt compelled to take.

Klein waited for his anger to subside before saying, "Counselor, one more little trick like that and I will hold you in contempt! Now, if you have a legal argument of substance to make as to admissibility of this testimony, make it!"

His hunch having proved out, Ben was determined to win the right to exploit it to the full. He must keep Frost on the stand and drag out of him every bloody detail of the manner in which Agnes Riordan had been seized, raped, then strangled by the strong hands of Cletus Johnson. Only the man who had done the autopsy on her could provide that. If he could win this argument, could present that to the jury, his strategy would have succeeded.

Confident, feeling for the first time he had full control of this case, Ben addressed the bench.

"Your Honor, by the People's own indictment, by the questions the prosecutor has asked, one of the crucial elements in this case is defendant's intent. Since the defendant's state of mind, without which there can be no intent, was based on his reaction to the brutal death of his daughter, it is of the utmost relevance for the jury to know the details of that death. If they could not stand alongside this man when he had to identify his daughter's body, they should at least know what it was he saw from the lips of the one witness, the only witness, who can tell them, first-hand, what happened to this poor girl. I would like them to hear from Dr. Frost what was the cause of death in *Agnes Riordan's* case! And was her death 'instantaneous' or was it a slow, agonizing death, preceded by terror and rape and worse? Without that, Your Honor, this jury cannot fairly consider the question of intent!"

Judge Klein seemed to nod his head almost imperceptibly before he turned to Lester Crewe.

"Your Honor," the young black prosecutor began, adjusting his glasses as he spoke, "this is exactly the kind of emotionalism which I had anticipated during the course of this trial. And while it may succeed in winning this defendant points with the press, I am afraid that inside this courtroom we must be guided by only two things. The facts. And the law. I wish to point out, and it will become even clearer when we introduce the defendant's confession, that almost a year and many incidents transpired between Agnes Riordan's death and the murder with

which this defendant is charged. If immediately after
viewing his daughter's body this defendant had taken action against Cletus Johnson, there might be some causal
connection between the two events. But not under the
facts as we know them."

Lester Crewe paused, then made his final point. "Riordan's action was not in response to his daughter's death,
but in response to his frustration with the orderly processes of the law. Hence, any testimony about Agnes Riordan's death is totally irrelevant to this trial. Therefore, I
insist this entire line of questioning be ruled out!"

Judge Klein pondered both arguments, then finally
said, "There being no immediate causal connection between Miss Riordan's death and the defendant's action, I
will rule it out." To Ben he added, "Defense counsel may,
if he wishes, submit a memorandum of law supporting his
argument. In which event, I may reconsider."

Ben did not respond, for he was sure no memorandum
would alter Klein's mind. He had failed after having come
so close. He took only one consolation from the encounter, at least he had created in the minds of the jurors the
unsettling thought that because of the intervention of the
prosecutor they were being denied access to testimony,
which, if not relevant, was certainly tantalizing. For the
first time during the trial, he had been able to jockey
Lester Crewe into disfavor with the jury.

But in his primary strategy to turn this into the trial of
Cletus Johnson, Ben Gordon had lost one more decisive
round.

In the waiting room several members of the jury,
thankful for the break, lit up cigarettes. Others merely
felt excluded from the case and curious. Walter Grove was
the only one who spoke.

"I did some research for a novel once. I found out that
they always send the jury out when questions of law are

being argued." Then he added, "I never did write that novel...." Suddenly mindful of Judge Klein's admonition, he asked, "I wouldn't consider this discussing the case, would you?"

He addressed the question to several of the jurors, but especially to Violet Tolliver.

"A general statement like that can't be considered discussing this particular case. At least I wouldn't think so," she agreed.

"Strange, isn't it?" Grove continued directly to her. "Out there are newspaper people, television people and people who just wandered into the courtroom out of sheer curiosity. Yet those unconcerned strangers are entitled to hear what we, the jury who has to make the ultimate decision, are forbidden to hear. It seems very perverse and arbitrary, doesn't it?"

"Yes, yes, it does," she replied, but now an aloofness appeared in her response that made her seem cool and distant. For she felt that by entering the conversation she had encouraged the very familiarity with Grove which she had sought to avoid.

He noticed the change and it was reflected in his perceptive gray eyes. *She's raised that barrier again,* he thought. *Can't she ever relax and forget she is so damned beautiful and famous and that possibly, just possibly, not every man in this world has a burning desire for her? If she could only relax.*

She read the reaction in his eyes and turned away. If her avoidance had been too obvious, she felt it was necessary. She had arrived at that stage where she had her life very well arranged. She had lived through two marriages, and two divorces, and several affairs which ended the way affairs always end. None of those relationships had been able to survive her fame and the pressures of her thriving career. She enjoyed the power that went with the success of her business. She enjoyed the publicity and the parties and the galas, though at times she had to admit they did become boring. But more, she enjoyed her solitude. She preferred to be aloof from the sport of sexual pursuit, deception and conquest. She was finished with being sought as a prize, as if a man achieved status by going to bed with her. She was tired, too, of the men in her set, the same tycoons, network executives, financial manipulators, motion picture producers and politicians she seemed to meet at every party and function she attended. Always the same men, always the same conversation, always the same sexual hints and ploys which she had grown tired of avoiding.

This tall, craggy-faced author, with the vaguely familiar name, did not move in those circles. Perhaps he was different from the men she knew. He didn't dress the same. His conversation did not abound with the very latest neologisms which in a single week became New York and Washington clichés. He seemed a plain, unpretentious, serious man. *That would be a change for the better*, Violet Tolliver thought.

But in the same instant she arrived at that conclusion, she suddenly resented him all the more, as if her thoughts about him were an act of aggression perpetrated by him. She was relieved when the jury was summoned back to the courtroom.

As they filed into the jury box and noticed the empty witness chair, involuntarily she found herself exchanging glances with Walter Grove to comment on the fact that obviously the District Attorney must have won his point. Each of them wondered what the doctor had been prevented from testifying to. But they had little time to wonder, for Lester Crewe was addressing the bench.

"Your Honor, at this point, for reasons that will

become obvious, I ask to take the stand and be questioned by an associate."

Judge Klein granted his permission with an abrupt nod.

Sitting at the counsel table, his client alongside, Ben appeared unmoved despite the fact that he was thinking, *Now it comes, the heavy artillery. If I can't keep this confession out, then by whatever means it takes I must do something to minimize its impact.*

Lester Crewe's associate read from the list of questions he himself had prepared, and Lester answered, informing the jury of the events of January 24, 1982, the call from the Twenty-sixth Precinct, the hasty trip uptown, meeting Detective Marchi, finally meeting the suspect, Dennis Riordan.

"Can you tell the jury what transpired then?" Crewe's young assistant asked.

"Just as Marchi said, the man was willing, almost eager, to confess to a murder he said he had committed only an hour before," Lester Crewe replied.

"Mr. Crewe, do you have a record of that confession?"

"I have a closed-circuit television tape of the confession made by the defendant, after he had been apprised of all his legal rights," Crewe said, glancing in Ben's direction.

To distract Crewe, Ben was furiously making notes on his yellow pad. It would do no harm to give the jury the impression that he considered Crewe's testimony faulty.

At that point Crewe's assistant turned to Ben. "Your witness."

"No questions at this time," Ben said. "But I reserve my right to question the witness later."

Crewe stepped down from the stand to resume his case. "Irving Rosenthal! Please take the stand!"

A man who had been waiting outside entered the

courtroom, passed the barrier, headed for the witness chair. Once sworn, Rosenthal settled into the chair. He was cadaverously thin, with a scraggly black mustache. His shirt collar seemed two sizes too big, and his pale face betrayed that he spent his days and, most times, his nights, working in smoky editing rooms.

"Mr. Rosenthal, what is your profession?"

"Television engineer."

"Exactly what does that entail, Mr. Rosenthal, please explain to the jury?"

"I tape television events, speeches, meetings, commercials, interviews."

"Confessions?"

"Yes, sir. I am a consultant to the New York City Police Department."

"And did you on the twenty-fourth of January tape a confession made by the defendant in this case?"

"Yes, sir."

"Did you or anyone ever tamper with that tape since the day it was made?"

"No, sir!"

"So it is in all respects the exact tape you recorded on that day?"

"Yes, sir!"

"Your witness," Crewe said, with magnanimous confidence.

Still smarting from his defeat over Dr. Frost's testimony, Ben rose, thinking to himself, *I'll give those TV newshawks something to lead off with on the six o'clock news and throw a little scare into Les at the same time.* He approached the witness box.

"Mr. Rosenthal . . ." Ben began, then stopped, studied the man, pretending to recognize him. He felt sure that would make the witness tense, and it did. He resumed. "Mr. Rosenthal, did I hear you say, and bear in mind you are under oath, did I hear you say that neither you nor anyone ever tampered with the tape you made?"

"Yes, sir."

"Are you sure of that?" Ben pursued, aware that the jury was leaning forward now. He could also sense behind him the stir of hungry anticipation from the press.

"Yes, I'm sure of that," Rosenthal responded.

"Absolutely sure?" Ben pressed.

"Yes, sir!"

Ben stared at Rosenthal until the man nervously cleared his throat.

"Mr. Rosenthal, on the tenth of February, 1982, I was shown a tape which purports to be the tape you intend to show this jury. . . ."

At the word "purports," Lester Crewe was on his feet. "Your Honor, if counsel is challenging the authenticity of the tape, or the fact that it is unedited, then I would like him to introduce expert testimony to that effect!"

"Mr. Gordon?" Judge Klein challenged.

"Your Honor, I would like permission to continue, subject to connection later."

"If connection is not established, I will throw out this entire line of questioning, is that understood, Counselor?" Klein reproved sharply. He had not forgotten the Frost encounter either, or Ben's attempt to influence the jury.

Ben turned back to the witness. "As I was saying, Mr. Rosenthal, on February tenth I was shown the tape of a confession purportedly made by Mr. Riordan. And then again it was shown to me on February eighteenth."

"Yes, sir?" Rosenthal responded, curious as to Ben's question.

"The tape was run for me in the District Attorney's office. Both times you were not present. A man, I forget his name, ran it for me. In fact, he was very obliging and ran it several times on that second occasion."

"Yes, sir?" Rosenthal asked, more curious now.

"Then that tape has not always been in your possession, has it?"

"That's right, sir. Once I make a tape I turn it over to the D.A."

"So that the tape you intend to show this jury might have been handled by another technician between the time you turned it over and when you show it to us in this courtroom?"

"Possibly," Rosenthal granted.

"And if it could be handled by another technician, might it not also have been handled by three other technicians, or four, or five, or fifty?"

"I wouldn't know that," Rosenthal admitted.

"So when you testified under oath that this tape had not been tampered with, you really had no way of knowing that, did you?" Ben asked.

"I can tell when a tape has been edited or tampered with!" Rosenthal protested.

But Ben had turned away and was starting back to the table. Crewe rose in his place.

"Mr. Rosenthal, how long have you been a television engineer and technician?"

"Twenty-two years."

"In that time have you become expert in detecting whether television tapes have been edited?"

"Yes, sir."

"Mr. Rosenthal, when was the last time you examined the tape in question?"

"Yesterday, to get ready for today's showing."

"In your expert opinion, has the tape we are about to see ever been tampered with?"

"No, sir, it has not!"

"Thank you." Lester Crewe turned to Ben, challenging him to question the witness further.

Ben rose in his place, determined to make one last effort to diminish the effect on the jury of his client's confession by creating some doubt as to the reliability of that tape.

"Mr. Rosenthal, before you leave the stand, one question. During your long career as a television expert, have you ever edited tape, rearranged tape, taken a segment out of sequence and put it in another place? Have you ever done anything like that?"

"Of course. Every television editor has done that."

Ben Gordon nodded, then, as if Rosenthal's answer had stimulated another question, he asked, "Would you say it was a sign of an expert, highly experienced television editor like yourself, if the cuts and rearrangements you made were done in such a skillful manner that they could not be detected by the viewer?"

"Yes," Rosenthal conceded.

"Therefore, is it possible if changes were made in this tape, a layperson like myself, or a member of this jury, would not be able to detect it?"

"Yes," Rosenthal was forced to admit.

Ben turned to the bench. "Your Honor, as long as the jury understands that, we have no objection to the tape being shown." On his way back to the counsel table, Ben cast a glance in the direction of the jury. He felt he had succeeded, if only in some small measure.

Lester Crewe addressed the bench. "Your Honor, the People would like to have the technicians come in now and set up the television monitors so the jury, the bench and the media can view the confession."

Klein nodded his agreement, thinking, *I'd love to take a break and have a cigar, anyhow.* "How long will it be?"

"No more than fifteen minutes, Your Honor."

Good, Klein thought, *enough time for a panatela I've been saving.* Addressing the courtroom at large, he warned, "Everybody at ease while they set up. If you want to talk, go out to the corridor."

More than half the media men and women rushed for the doors. They had their evening headline: Defense Counsel Attacks Riordan Confession Even Before Shown!

14

THE TECHNICIANS HAD wheeled in not one but three television monitors. One was positioned to face the jury. One faced the bench. One was angled in the direction of the press and the spectators.

When court reconvened, Ben asked, "Your Honor? May we?", indicating he and his client would like to ascend the platform where the judge sat in order to view the tape. For the first time, Dennis Riordan exhibited an interest in the proceedings, for he had never seen his own confession.

The clerk, stationed at the wall panel, flicked off all the lights. Then he proceeded to raise the shades of the high windows, blocking out all daylight.

"Now!" Lester Crewe ordered.

Rosenthal pushed the button of the tape player. The three screens were activated and after some leader had flicked by, the confession of Dennis Riordan appeared.

It started with Lester Crewe's meticulous questions which safeguarded Riordan's rights to remain silent, to have an attorney, not to make a statement, and the clear warning that anything he said might be held against him.

All fourteen jurors leaned forward, the light from the television set playing on their intent faces as they watched and heard a stolid, calm Dennis Riordan begin:

My name is Dennis Riordan. I live at Seventeen-oh-nine, Twenty-fourth Street, Astoria, Queens. I live alone, my wife having died two months ago. And my daughter having been murdered ten months before that.

Ben was less concerned with the screen than with studying the effect on the jurors as they watched his client's confession. They kept glancing from the screen up at the live and present Dennis Riordan as he watched himself. They were probably wondering what went through his mind as he witnessed his retelling of the rape and murder of his daughter, the freeing of her murderer, the grieving death of his wife, and his own resolve to carry out justice.

Riordan himself kept his eyes fixed on that screen, thinking, *Now they know, all the people know how and why I did it. And they have to do something about it, to keep other Agnes Riordans from being defiled and murdered. It was worth it, all of it, this trial and even what happens to me after this trial, it was worth it!*

In the press section, reporters scribbled frantic notes in the semidarkness, while artists sketched the scene at the bench: the judge, flanked by Attorney Ben Gordon and Defendant Dennis Riordan. Those sketches would appear on the six o'clock news, be repeated at eleven, and would be in the evening and morning papers.

The confession came to its conclusion:

And today, just about an hour ago, I found Cletus Johnson, the man who killed my Aggie. And I shot him. Fired five times. If there's anything else you care to know, just ask.

At that point Riordan had stared directly into the camera and said:

Now, I want to be tried!

Lester Crewe then asked:

Anything else you'd like to say, Mr. Riordan?
Yes. I'd like to talk to my priest.
If I may suggest, Mr. Riordan, before a priest you
need an attorney.
I want to see my priest!

So ended the confession of Dennis Riordan. Despite the dimly lit room, all eyes were on Riordan as he moved from the bench back to his place at the counsel table. All eyes but two. Ben Gordon's were fixed on the jury. Fourteen grim jurors actually seemed frightened by the calm way in which a man had confessed to murdering another man. The tape had had a far greater impact on them than Ben anticipated. He must improvise some tactic to diminish its effect. Before he could organize his next move, Lester Crewe was on his feet.

"Your Honor, before the lights are turned on, may I request that the tape be shown again."

"I think once is enough, Counselor." Judge Klein was inclined to dispose.

But Crewe insisted. "Your Honor, this time I ask the members of the jury to focus their attention on the wall clock under which the defendant is sitting. If there is any doubt in anyone's mind that this tape has not been tampered with, that clock will dispel all such questions."

Oh, Les, you shrewd bastard, Ben thought, but for him to object now would only bring greater attention to the authenticity and unassailability of the confession. He remained silent as Judge Klein ordered, "Run it again!"

All eyes were fixed on the clock, which proved that the tape was indeed continuous and had not been edited by even a single frame.

After such a defeat Ben was relieved when Judge Klein announced, "We will take a fifteen-minute recess."

The media people raced to report on the confession, the hottest piece of news they had been handed since the trial began. The jury, when asked by the clerk to file out, was slow in responding. For the confession, seen a second time, with the clock as silent witness to its veracity, had virtually decided for them what their verdict must be. More than any testimony, the confession had brought them face to face with the awesomeness of their duty.

Elihu Prouty, the elderly black man in Seat 1, glanced furtively at his colleagues, thinking, *We might as well vote now, what more can be said?*

But Anthony Mascarella, himself a father of two young girls, thought only, *Thank God it's never happened to one of mine. I don't know what I'd do. It'll be hell to vote this man guilty, but what choice do we have?*

Veronica Connell thought, *What good did he think a priest would have done him then? Or now? That District Attorney was right. He needed a lawyer, before he confessed.*

Because he could read their grim faces, Ben Gordon took his chair at the counsel table feeling more depressed than at any time since this trial had begun. He must do something to overcome the effects of this damning confession, to divert the jury's minds and emotions from it to some other aspect of this case. But Riordan was tugging at his sleeve.

"Listen, kid . . ."

Frustration and concern made Ben direct his anger at his client as he said in a hard whisper, "I told you, don't call me that in the courtroom. I'm your attorney!"

"Sorry," Riordan apologized sincerely. "I didn't mean any disrespect. I only want to say, it's more important than ever that you put me on the stand now."

Stunned, Ben asked, "Why?"

"There's a few things I wanted to say in that confession and never got to say."

"You said more than enough," Ben replied. "You spelled out intent. That's all that was missing from their *prima facie* case. And you just gave them that."

"I don't give a damn about that!" Riordan said. "I want to tell my whole story. Give me your word you'll put me on!"

"Sorry, Mr. Riordan, I can't promise that," Ben said, turning away and starting for the door. For the first time, he noticed that in the last row of spectator seats a blond girl was rising to her feet.

Arlene!

He pushed through the crowd, ignoring the reporters, who tried to elicit his reaction to the confession and any move he had planned to counter it.

"Honey, what are you doing here?" he asked.

"Came to watch Clarence Darrow in action," Arlene said, trying to joke because she knew how badly the last half hour had shaken him.

"Not even Darrow could have kept that confession out," Ben said. "I tried to discredit it. Didn't work. Shouldn't you be back at your office?"

"If the Market was down twelve points my phone wouldn't stop ringing. But today it's up twelve, so I'm safe," Arlene said. Then she added, "Oh, your mother called me again this morning."

"Just your luck, my beautiful darling, to have mother-in-law trouble without even being married. What does she want this time?"

"She's afraid to ask you. She would like to come and see you try this case."

"That's all I need," Ben replied.

"It's the least you can do. It'll give her something to brag about." Arlene pleaded his mother's cause.

"I'll . . . I'll think about it," was as much as Ben would concede.

But as he said that, he noticed that Arlene's eyes had fixed suddenly and she was studying someone. He turned to discover a stranger staring at him in a way that indicated he wanted to talk to Ben. Ben eyed the man, a short man, portly, with rimless glasses and, staring at him from behind those glasses, two penetrating and purposeful eyes.

"I noticed him when he first came in," Arlene said. "Though the attendant wasn't admitting any more spectators, he managed to get in. What do you suppose he wants?"

Ben said, "Maybe he knows something important to the trial. It happens that way, sometimes a witness appears out of the blue. Of course, sometimes it's just a kook who thinks he knows exactly what will get your client off. In either case, I'd better talk to him." He started in the man's direction.

"Mr. Gordon?"

"Yes?" Ben said cautiously.

"Victor Coles," the man announced, expecting to be recognized instantly. When Ben failed to respond with the proper degree of awe, the man continued, "The literary and motion picture agent. You've read about me."

"Oh, yeah. In the columns. Right," Ben admitted, though puzzled.

"Mr. Gordon, or can I call you Ben?"

"Suit yourself," Ben said, now suspicious and growing impatient.

"Ben, I read the papers last night, I watched the TV news, and decided to come here myself this morning and make sure. After that confession, I am positive!"

"Positive? Of what?" Ben asked, still shaken by the effect of that confession on the jury.

"Ben Gordon, you are sitting on a gold mine!" Victor Coles announced.

"Am I?" Ben asked. "Mr. Coles, right now I am sitting on a disaster that will make the *Titanic* look like a cruise ship in the Caribbean."

"The rights!" Coles declared. "Get your client to sign over to you the book and picture rights to his story."

"Are you serious?" Ben asked.

"Ben, you are talking to a man who nets in seven figures a year. I can smell a valuable property a mile away. I wouldn't be here now if I wasn't absolutely sure! This is big, very big. Trust me, Ben! Do as I say!"

"Big, eh? How big?"

"If I had to venture a ball-park figure, I'd say four hundred thousand dollars," Coles declared.

Ben stared at the man, whose eyes peered back from behind those elegant rimless glasses but did not blink. Coles knew that look of skepticism, he had seen it often.

"Take my advice. And it's easily done. You won't even have to write the book. I have a client who'd write it for you. He'd get a percentage, small of course. You would only have to go over the manuscript to make sure there are no legal errors and to point up some of the subtle legal maneuvers you're making."

"You noticed my subtle legal maneuvers, did you?" Ben asked, thinking to himself, *I may have fooled some spectators, but not that jury.* "Tell me, Mr. Coles, what happens to your grandiose plans if I lose this case? We're out of the ball park, right?"

Far from being discouraged, Coles only smiled. "Ben, some of the biggest deals I've made have been for lost cases. I have only one test, public interest. People are talking about this case, about Riordan. He's become a *cause célèbre* with the average citizen. Why? Because he's done what the average man says to himself a hundred times a day he'd like to do to protect his own family. You have a whole city out there, a whole country, of nice, average, middle-class Dennis Riordans. They're talking about this man and they'll talk a hell of a lot more as this case goes along. So don't worry about losing the case. In fact," Coles added, as though imparting a secret of great significance, "confidentially, it's much better for us if you lose."

"How?" Ben demanded, enraged because he had a feeling this man was trying to tamper with his ethical commitment to Riordan.

"Let's say the jury finds him guilty, what's your next step?"

"Appeal. In a murder case that's virtually automatic."

"Exactly!" Coles agreed, smiling. "And how long does an appeal take?"

"Months," Ben said. "Maybe as much as a year by the time it's decided."

"Right," Coles said enthusiastically. "And during that time where is Riordan? Out on bail? After being convicted of murder? Not likely."

Ben could not dispute that.

"So what do we have? In jail, an average simple man, a man people understand and sympathize with, and outside a fearless, daring young lawyer battling for his freedom. Don't you see, Ben, if he's found guilty it gives the property legs. During the time it will take to write and publish the book, we are keeping public interest fresh by what you're doing. Also, maybe we arrange some interviews with Riordan and shots of him in prison. Then, if your appeal succeeds and we get a new trial, that's perfect!"

Coles's intense eyes became even more more so as he

said, "Come to think of it, we'll insist on a percentage of the film, too, a percentage of gross. That could mean another hundred thousand, maybe more!"

"Five hundred thousand dollars," Ben said, even more skeptical now.

"The way publishing is these days it's either blockbusters or just plain busts. And this is a blockbuster. I know. I represent three different men who were with the Carter administration, and two Watergate defendants, plus a renegade cop who took bribes and then talked. And Ben, I have to say it, I think this one could be bigger than all of them. So you just get your client to assign to you all literary, motion picture and television rights as part of your legal fee."

"What about Riordan?" Ben asked, curious as to how Coles would dispose of him.

"If we're forced to, we cut him in for a small piece," Coles conceded.

Making no effort to conceal his anger, Ben said sarcastically, "That's mighty nice of you!"

"Ben, Ben, Ben," Coles tried to placate him, "there's nothing wrong in what I'm suggesting. Attorneys have done this before. Both defendants' attorneys and prosecutors. Look, let me put it another way. How much do you stand to make out of this case?"

"Several thousand dollars," Ben admitted reluctantly.

"This is the chance of your lifetime. You may never get a case this hot again. Consider the personal publicity that goes with a book and a TV mini-series. Imagine what that can do for your career!"

To bring the conversation to an end, Ben said, "I'll think about it. Now I have to get back to work."

"One thing," Coles said, seizing Ben's arm. "Give me your word that if you decide to do it, you won't sign with any other agent. Gentlemen's agreement?" He extended his hand.

"Oh, sure. Gentlemen's agreement," Ben said, but he did not shake Coles's hand.

Coles turned and left the courtroom. Arlene drew close.

"What did he want?"

Before Ben could answer, the clerk was announcing, "All rise!"

The judge was back in the courtroom. Everyone rushed to resume his place. Judge Klein peered over his reading glasses at Lester Crewe. "Mr. Crewe?"

"The People have nothing to add to the confession."

"Mr. Gordon?"

"I would now like Mr. Crewe to resume the stand!"

He deliberately made his announcement in a sudden and dramatic way. Not that he had any illusions about being able to attack the confession, but he felt a need to offset the emotional impact of it on the jury, who had resumed their places looking as disturbed as before. He must not allow them to leave this courtroom for the day in that same frame of mind. He desperately needed a tactical diversion. Lester Crewe was his only chance. Ben glanced up at the clock. It was already twenty minutes to four, not much time to accomplish his purpose.

Crewe resumed the stand puzzled, curious and yet sympathetic to Ben Gordon's predicament, for the confession had had even more impact than Crewe originally hoped. Having been sworn once before, he was still under oath, so Ben was free to begin his cross-examination.

"Mr. Crewe, you have just exhibited to this jury the tape of a confession purportedly made by Dennis Riordan, the defendant in this case."

With a faint smile, Crewe asked, "Mr. Gordon, is that

a statement or a question to which I'm supposed to respond?"

Ben ignored that to continue, "Mr. Crewe, was that the first confession you have ever taken?"

"No."

"The second, fourth, eighth, tenth?" Ben pursued.

"I've taken a great many."

"How many? Can you give us an estimate?"

"I'd say upward of a hundred."

"Upward of a hundred . . ." Ben repeated slowly. "Tell us, if you will, during all those confessions have you ever encountered a man who was as insistent on confessing as this defendant?"

Puzzled by Ben's purpose, Lester Crewe responded cautiously, "I have never seen a man so lucid, so completely in possession of himself, and so insistent on making a confession."

Ben could hardly disguise a smile at the precise phrasing of Lester Crewe's answer.

"Now, then, Mr. Crewe, wouldn't the fact that he was so unusually calm be highly significant?"

"Different, perhaps. Significant? No," Crewe responded.

"After all, here was this man who had never before in his sixty-six years committed the most minor of crimes. He doesn't even have a traffic ticket on his record. Yet he calmly insists on confessing to the most heinous of crimes, murder! And you don't think that's significant?" Ben demanded.

"That's right," Crewe responded, limiting his reply to as few words as possible, not to offer Ben any gratuitous opportunities.

"It didn't disturb you at the time, Mr. Crewe?"

"Mr. Gordon, once I had apprised him of his rights,

which you and the jury saw on that tape, I felt justified in taking his confession," Crewe stated.

Ben deliberately paused for a moment before asking, "Mr. Crewe, in conversations with me concerning this confession, do you recall ever using the word 'compulsion'?"

Taken aback, Lester Crewe repeated, "Compulsion? I'm afraid I don't."

"Then let me refresh your recollection. Did you or did you not say about this defendant, quote 'He seemed to have a compulsion to confess' unquote?"

"It's possible I may have said that," Lester Crewe admitted, curious about what use Ben intended to make of that remark.

Seeking to involve the jury in his question, Ben half-turned to them as he asked, "Mr. Crewe, as an understanding human being, you never thought for a single instant, this man doesn't know what he's doing? He has a 'compulsion to confess,' the compulsion of a religious zealot? He should be protected from his own dangerous impulses? From his own ignorance of the consequences of what he is doing?"

"Mr. Gordon, once I made him aware of his rights . . ." Lester Crewe began.

Ben interrupted. "We know all about that, Mr. Crewe! You read him his rights! Big deal! My question is, didn't you feel it incumbent on you to protect that man from his 'compulsion,' from himself?"

With ill-concealed impatience, Lester Crewe pointed out, "Mr. Gordon, in the Miranda case the Supreme Court of the United States laid down precisely what my duty was. And I performed it. Precisely!"

"Did the Supreme Court ever hand down a ruling exempting a prosecutor from having a little common decency? A little humanity?"

"Now, just one moment, Mr. Gordon . . ." Crewe turned to invoke the intercession of the judge.

But before Klein could rule, Ben thundered on, "A little compassion for a man who had suffered such grievous wrong at the hands of the man he confessed to killing?"

Klein brought down his gavel with a loud, resounding crash. "Mr. Gordon! No flights of fancy, please. No summations. If you have proper, relevant questions, ask them. If not, do not badger the witness."

"Sorry, sir," Ben said, pretending regret, but from the corner of his eye he noted that he had at last intrigued the jury by this line of questioning. He decided to continue and, glancing at the clock, asked, "Mr. Crewe, at the time of the defendant's confession were you aware of his religion?"

"Only at the end, when he asked for a priest," Lester Crewe said.

"The name Dennis Riordan never indicated to you that in all likelihood he was of Irish extraction and thus almost surely Catholic?"

"I don't recall having such thoughts," Crewe said, while trying to discern the direction in which Ben was now attempting to lead him.

"It never occurred to you that a man who was a staunch and faithfully observant Catholic might look upon confession in a quite different light than other people?" Ben asked, hoping to exploit the sympathy of the Catholics on the jury sufficiently to take the edge off that damaging confession in some degree.

"I don't understand the question," Crewe said.

"Mr. Crewe, you are aware that confession is a basic practice in the Catholic Church?"

"Of course."

"That a Catholic is brought up from earliest childhood

to believe that if you sin, you confess. And if you confess, you are granted absolution. Not put on trial for murder! I ask you, Mr. Crewe, didn't you take advantage of a simple God-fearing man by letting him confess without trying to protect him? Didn't you take advantage of his religious convictions?"

Before Crewe could respond, the judge rapped his gavel sharply, ruling, "The witness need not answer! For obvious reasons! Counselor, I warned you. No flights of fancy, no argumentative questions! Is your cross-examination of this witness quite finished?"

Ben Gordon hesitated, glanced up at the wall clock, which now read three minutes to four. In one last desperate effort to overcome the damaging effect of the confession, Ben looked at Lester Crewe and asked, "Mr. Crewe, would you have felt the same way, acted in the same way, if Mr. Riordan's victim had not been a black man?"

The instant he uttered those words, Ben Gordon rebuked himself, *Christ! What a thing to say!* To Lester Crewe of all people! Even a desperate man had no right to level such an accusation against Les.

But it was too late. Ben could tell from the agitated stir behind him that the press had seized on his question. Suddenly race had taken undue and unfair prominence in this case. He saw the astonished, hurt look in Lester Crewe's eyes, and he turned away.

Crewe paused before responding, thinking, *In the end it always comes down to this. You're a colleague, a co-worker, even a friend, until the heat is on, then you're just a black man after all.*

Slowly, softly, Lester Crewe responded, "Mr. Gordon, I would have acted in the same manner whether the defendant's victim had been black or white, Catholic, Protestant or Jew. And you know that."

Inwardly, Ben kept apologizing, *I'm sorry, Les, sorry,*

sorry, sorry. But all he could say was, "No more questions." He stared up at the clock. Four o'clock. Strategically, he had accomplished two purposes. He had beclouded the effect of the confession and brought the day to a close without having to open his own case.

In the process he had also accomplished one purpose he had not intended. He had smeared, besmirched and tarred with the brush of bigotry an innocent man.

Lester Crewe stepped down from the stand, turned to the bench and announced, "Your Honor, the People rest."

Ben knew what was expected of him now. A pointless formality in this case.

"Your Honor, the defense moves to dismiss the indictment on the ground that the People have failed to prove a *prima facie* case."

"Denied!" Klein ruled perfunctorily.

"Exception!"

"The record will so indicate," the judge said. "Mr. Gordon, will you be ready to present your first witness tomorrow? Or will you have other motions to make?"

"I will present my first witness," Ben said.

As he left the courtroom, he searched for Arlene. He pushed his way through the crowd, ignoring the reporters, who pursued him with questions.

As he descended the courthouse steps, he spied Arlene waiting at the curb. He started toward her, but cameras, microphones and shouting faces converged on him until he was surrounded and imprisoned.

"Mr. Gordon, do you want to enlarge on what you said in the courtroom? Have you had any previous experiences with the District Attorney that led you to believe he's a racist?"

"No comment," was all Ben would say, for he could

not now defend Lester Crewe without exposing his court-room tactic for what it was, a desperate trick.

"Mr. Gordon, didn't you and Mr. Crewe work together in the D.A.'s office at one time?"

"No comment."

"Mr. Gordon, do you think that such an exchange as happened between you and Mr. Crewe damages the already fragile relations between blacks and Jews in this city?"

"No comment," Ben kept repeating, inwardly at the ragged edge of his patience and tormented by guilt.

Finally, the men and women of the press realized Ben could not be tempted or provoked into making any newsworthy statement that might give an added lift to the six o'clock news. They departed, since it was already close to four-thirty and they had film and tape that had to be edited to make the air by six.

Arlene was waiting at the curb. He would have to face her. Before he reached her, Victor Coles intercepted him.

"Clever, Ben! Diverting the jury from Riordan's confession to the problem of racial tension. It adds another element of controversy. The kind of thing that makes people discuss the case." Then Coles asked, "What did Riordan say?"

"Riordan?" Ben responded, confused.

"You talked to him, didn't you? About the book and film rights?"

"No. I . . . I didn't get a chance."

Coles reached into his pocket and drew out a folded paper.

"Here is the usual release I get defendants to sign. It's been upheld in one court in California and another in Texas. Remember that sexy blonde who was accused of killing her millionaire husband? I made the book and picture deal for her lawyer. This agreement was upheld in her case. Have Riordan sign it."

He seized Ben's hand and pressed the paper into it. A long blue limousine rolled up. "Can I drop you anywhere, Ben?"

"No, no thanks," Ben said, desperately wanting to be alone with Arlene.

When he reached her, she said nothing. He tried to kiss her; she permitted only her cheek.

"Well, go on!" he demanded. "Say it! It was a lousy thing to do!"

"Since you are already aware of that, just tell me one thing. Why?"

"I swear to God, I don't know. It just came out," Ben confessed. "I kept thinking, don't let that jury go home with Riordan's confession the last thing they remember. Do anything, just shake that damned confession out of their minds. I was like a quarterback who, before he hits the ground, throws a desperation pass."

"Desperate is one thing. That was despicable!"

"I know, I know, I know," Ben kept saying, watching the jurors leave the courthouse. They noticed him and stared.

Elihu Prouty, the thin, elderly, light-skinned black man, stopped, seemed about to say something to Ben, but decided it would not be proper for a juryman. So he proceeded toward the subway thinking, *He seemed such a nice young man. I actually felt sorry for him, considering the strong case young Crewe put in, and then he does something like this. Is there never going to be an end to the prejudice?* He paused at the newspaper stand at the subway entrance, but remembered Judge Klein's instruction not to read about the case. He started down the steps, fingering his senior citizen's reduced-fare card.

15

A CAN OF COLD BEER in hand, Ben sat before the television set and watched as the young black woman reported on the trial of Dennis Riordan. Light-skinned, pretty, very neat, with non-Negroid features, her hair beautifully coiffed, she looked like a movie star, not a reporter.

In the Supreme Court today, the trial of Dennis Riordan for the murder of Cletus Johnson took on the aspects of a racial confrontation as white Defense Attorney Ben Gordon accused black District Attorney Lester Crewe of prejudice in accepting the confession of the defendant. What had seemed a murder trial up to this point suddenly erupted into a race war and, alongside it, even Riordan's confession faded into relative insignificance. The prosecution rested its case, so tomorrow the defense will have its turn. And perhaps have the chance to further enlighten the jury and us on the prosecutor's prejudice.

Ben flicked from Channel 4 to Channel 7. The reporter was concluding, ". . . tomorrow when the defense gets in its licks in The People versus Dennis Riordan."

He flipped over to Channel 2. They were onto news

156

about another impending rise in subway and bus fares, obviously having already covered the trial. He turned off the set.

Arlene was sitting in the big wing chair with her end-of-day vodka martini in hand, the glass frosty and still full. She said nothing. He wished that she would.

"Well, at least . . ." he began, ". . . at least I made them play down the confession."

Arlene finally took a sip of her martini.

Her silent accusation made him explode, "It isn't me! It's our system of criminal justice. Guilty or not, it guarantees every accused a defense. As Riordan's attorney I am charged with giving him one. And it is my duty to use every tactic I can to see that he gets it. That's the adversary system. Set up smoke screens. Seduce the jury. If you know your man's guilty, play on any prejudice at hand in hope of getting a hung jury. That is not only permissible, it is my job as a defense lawyer. I sometimes wonder whether lawyers corrupt the system. Or is it the system which corrupts lawyers?"

Finally, Arlene was provoked to speak.

"That, my dear friend and bed partner, is one lousy cop-out! Lester Crewe is a man with whom you worked for two years, a man we have socialized with, a man you respect as a lawyer and a human being. You have come home from the office many times and told me what a terrific prosecutor he is, what a courtroom presence, what a quick mind. But never, until today, did I hear you accuse him of being a bigot!"

Ben shot up from his chair, hurling his beer can against the far wall, where it splashed and left a stain that ran down the pale gold wall in rivulets of foam.

"Accuse me of whatever you choose, you won't come within a mile of what I've been calling myself."

He started toward the kitchen for a towel to wipe away the damage he had done to the wall.

Quietly, she said, "I'll do it." It was the first sign of forgiveness from her.

She had almost obliterated the stains when he admitted softly, "You're right. I was blaming the system for what I did. With all its faults, it's the best and fairest system there is. Tomorrow morning, first thing, I will stand up in court and apologize to Les."

Arlene kissed him, then said, "I'll make your dinner."

She was broiling lamb chops on the grill in the kitchen when she called out, "What did the man want?"

"What man?" Ben asked, looking up from the notes he was making for his examination of tomorrow's character witnesses.

"Coles," she reminded him.

"Oh," Ben said and went for his jacket to find the agreement the agent had pressed into his hand.

It stated that in consideration for Ben's defending him, Dennis Riordan assigned to him the exclusive rights, title and interest in all material, recollections and documents concerning the events leading up to, occurring in the course of the trial and in any subsequent legal proceedings that might eventuate therefrom. It went even further, granting Ben Gordon the right to impersonate Dennis Riordan in any medium, including, but not limited to, the stage, motion pictures, television, radio and media yet to be invented.

Coles was right. It was an ironclad agreement, right down to the place at the bottom where Riordan was to sign and a notary was to witness his signature.

Arlene served their dinner. Before they began to eat, he passed the document to her. She skimmed it, looked across at him.

"Are you going to ask Riordan to sign this?"

"Coles says it's worth half a million dollars."

"Are you going to ask Riordan to sign this?" she reiterated, this time more forcefully.

Instead of answering, Ben asked, "Remember the first day I ever asked you to marry me?"

Puzzled by this non sequitur, she recalled, "Yes, it was on that pier on the East River."

"Right. I was talking to you but looking at a big garbage scow that was being towed out to sea. There were gulls hovering around it, every so often one would dart down to pick up a bit of garbage. When I read this very carefully drawn document, I was reminded of that. I wonder, is that what publishing has become, and television and movies, scavengers on the garbage, the misery of unfortunate people? And do I want to be one of the scavengers? No, thank you. What right do I have to sell another man's life, another man's misery?"

"Thanks, Ben."

"What for?"

"For complicating my life. Every time I find a good reason to leave, you do something that makes me say, he's not such a bastard after all." Then she became firm and maternal with him. "Eat your lamb chops!"

He stared at her and then declared, "You can't leave me!"

"Why not?" she challenged.

"Because this is your apartment, silly. But I could leave you."

"Ben, my darling, don't threaten me. You're not very good at it. You're like a little kid who keeps threatening to run away from home. But never does."

"Is that my trouble?" he asked.

"What?"

"Am I too soft to be the lawyer I want to be? No killer

instinct. No need to win at all costs. Do you think that's what's wrong with me?"

"Honest? Straight? No holds barred?" she asked.

"No holds barred," he said, staring into her bright blue eyes.

"I think the man who refused to prosecute that cop for murder because he didn't think he was guilty, the man who feels bad about what he did to Les today, that man is as tough as I would ever want my man to be. Better than tough is being principled. I like that. In fact, I love it."

He had tried to sleep but could not. He eased out of bed and quietly made his way to the living room. He snapped on the chairside lamp, took up the yellow pad he had abandoned earlier in the evening and reviewed his notes for tomorrow.

Thomas Boyce. Father Nelson. Mrs. Delahanty. . . . Then a long list of dots. For after he had presented only three character witnesses, he had no more defense.

The order of witnesses? Boyce first, Mrs. Delahanty, the Riordans' neighbor, second; save Father Nelson, his most impressive witness, for last. Ben had considered and researched the legal question presented by having a priest testify. Would that open the door and permit Lester Crewe to cross-examine Father Nelson on the subject matter of Riordan's confession? If it did, that would reinforce, from the mouth of a defense witness, the fact that Riordan was unrepentant, adding more proof to the question of his intent to kill. The cases Ben had researched were not precisely clear on the point. That could prove to be an advantage, for if Judge Klein allowed such cross-examination of the old priest, it could provide Ben an additional ground for appeal.

When Ben's thought fixed on that, he suddenly realized, ever since the judge had ruled out the Medical Examiner's testimony on the rape and death of Agnes Riordan, he had unconsciously come to think more and more about appeal and less and less about defense.

He now determined that he must find some way to reach that jury, if not by factual testimony then by emotional testimony. There must be some way to touch them and make them overcome any scruples they might have against the only act of violence Dennis Riordan had ever committed.

If only there were some way. . . .

Outside, rain was beginning to beat against the window. He turned off the light and padded back to the bedroom. He eased himself into bed so as not to wake Arlene. Once he was settled, his cold back up against Arlene's soft warm back, he patted her gently on the behind. She stirred and made a sound.

"Shhhh. Go back to sleep," he whispered. He patted her again. "Are you gaining weight?"

That made her wake and half-turn. "What?"

"Are you gaining weight?"

"I don't think so."

"Then are you . . . you're not getting pregnant, are you?"

"Idiot! You don't 'get' pregnant in stages. You either are or you aren't."

"Well, are you?"

"I don't think so. Why?"

"It just felt . . . I don't know. My hand used to fit exactly and now it doesn't."

"Is that what you woke me up to tell me?"

"Sorry. Go back to sleep."

"I can't. So now you'll have to make love to me."

Warm, fragrant, she turned to him and enveloped him.

* * *

It was almost dawn. Arlene had made coffee and brought two cups to bed. She sat up, her back against the headboard. She lit up a cigarette and took two deep puffs.

"If you're pregnant, you shouldn't be smoking."

"If I'm pregnant, I shouldn't even be talking to you."

"It's not my fault. You're the one who is supposed to take the pill."

"I was joking," she said. "I'm not pregnant. I was just trying to get you to relax. What's this morning?"

"I told you at the outset, I had to make my case while Les was presenting his. I had to turn this into the trial of Cletus Johnson. Well, I failed. Klein ruled me out every time. So now the entire case for the defense comes down to three character witnesses."

"You could put Riordan on the stand. Will you?" Arlene asked.

"It's got pluses and minuses. He is a nice, honest, sincere man. That's got to impress the jury. But he will also tell them that he intended to commit the crime they have to decide about. So how much better off are we?"

"Shall I come?"

"If you like dull character testimony, be my guest."

"I'd like to be there when you apologize to Les."

"Are you sure you can take time off? You were there all day yesterday," Ben reminded her, hoping she would decide not to come.

"When the father of the child I am not having does something decent like that, I would like to be there."

"Counselor, are you ready with your first witness?" Judge Klein asked while handing his female law clerk an order which he had just signed.

Ben rose in his place. "Your Honor, before the defense puts in its case, I would like to make a statement for the record."

"Oh? What?" Klein asked, suspicious.

"A statement in relation to something that occurred in this courtroom yesterday."

"Provided it has relevance to the course of this trial," Klein said.

"I think you will find that it does," Ben said. He turned to the jury.

"Ladies and gentlemen, yesterday in the heat of cross-examination, I accused the prosecutor of having a racial bias in this case. I wish to withdraw that unfortunate remark. I have known Mr. Crewe for several years and I have never found his actions to be racially motivated. I'm sorry."

He turned to the counsel table. "I'm sorry, Les."

There was a stir behind him in the press section. From the rustling sound and the rush of footsteps which followed, he knew that several of the reporters had slipped out with the news.

"And now, Your Honor, the defense calls Thomas Boyce!"

Thomas Boyce rose from the first spectator's row and looked at Ben, who gestured him through the barrier and toward the stand. A man in his middle sixties, with a physique that testified to his having been a strong and efficient freight handler in his early years, Boyce was now displaying a bit of executive bloat. He was dressed in the same plain suit he wore to church. A pale blue shirt and a solid maroon tie testified to his life-style, plain, simple, honest.

Once Boyce had been sworn, Ben led him through his forty-year association with Dennis Riordan, both as friend and as his boss at the warehouse.

Then Ben asked, "Mr. Boyce, are you acquainted with Dennis Riordan's reputation in the community?"

"Yes, sir!" Boyce replied eagerly. "Dennis Riordan has

always enjoyed an excellent reputation among all his neighbors. He is regarded as a man of the highest character. At work, he's never shirked, never asked for special privilege or days off."

Then, as Ben had coached him to do, Boyce added, "Except, of course, when his daughter Agnes was . . ."

Before Boyce could enunciate the word "murdered," Lester Crewe was on his feet, drowning out Boyce's voice with a loud "Object!"

"Sustained," Judge Klein ruled.

Defeated on that maneuver, Ben continued, "Did Dennis Riordan ever ask for days off at any other time?"

"Yes, sir, when he went down to testify at a hearing for the man who murdered . . ."

Again Crewe was on his feet. "Object! The witness is drawing a conclusion!"

"Sustained!" Klein ruled once more.

Ben asked his last question. "Mr. Boyce, was there another time when Dennis Riordan asked for time off?"

"Yes, sir. When poor Nedda died of grieving," Boyce said softly.

Feeling that Boyce had accomplished as much as possible in recalling for the jury events which would have an emotional effect when they considered Riordan's fate, Ben said, "Thank you, Mr. Boyce."

Lester Crewe rose in his place at the counsel table. "Mr. Boyce, wasn't there another time when Mr. Riordan asked for time off?"

"Another time?" Boyce seemed puzzled.

"During January of this year," Crewe reminded him.

"Oh, you mean when he went to buy the gun?"

"Yes, Mr. Boyce," Crewe repeated slowly and with emphasis, "when he went to buy the gun."

"He . . . he did ask for two days off then," Boyce was forced to admit.

"And after that, did he ask to be transferred from the day shift to the night shift?"

"Yes, sir," Boyce conceded, cursing himself for his blunder.

"And it was when he was on the night shift that during the day he tracked, found and shot . . ."

"Object!" Ben interrupted.

"Sustained!" Judge Klein ruled.

Boyce stood up in the witness box and shouted, "Dennis is a good man. The best! Always was. Still is. What he did was out of love for his family. And if the same thing happened to my daughter . . ."

Klein, who had tried to silence the witness with his gavel, interrupted in a loud and angry voice. "The witness will be silent! And the stenographer will strike everything after 'Always was, still is.' "

"No more questions," Les said, quite satisfied with the results of his cross-examination.

"No more questions," Ben replied, thinking it too dangerous to take Boyce through a redirect examination which might only lead to a recross that could be even more devastating.

"The witness is excused," Judge Klein said.

Thomas Boyce stepped down from the stand, approached Dennis Riordan, who rose to greet him. The men shook hands, then embraced. Boyce passed through the railing and toward the door of the courtroom. There he turned suddenly and cried out, "Still is! And always will be. Dennis Riordan is the best!" He was gone before the judge could invoke any admonition or punishment. Klein contented himself with a remark to the jury.

"Ladies and gentlemen, you will ignore that. Sometimes witnesses become emotional. Next witness, Mr. Gordon!"

"Mrs. Theresa Delahanty!" Ben called out. He looked to the glass insert in the courtroom door and beckoned.

A woman in her early sixties entered shyly, staring about the crowded courtroom. Ben went to meet her and escort her to the witness stand. He smiled, partly to reassure her, partly, too, because when he had first interviewed her she was wearing a plain cotton housedress and her gray hair was tied in a bun. Today she wore her finest dark maroon silk dress, and her hair had obviously been coiffed at a beauty parlor yesterday and was no longer gray but brown.

Ben indicated she climb up to the witness stand. When the oath had been administered, Ben asked, "Your name, please?"

"Theresa Delahanty," she said. Leaning in the direction of the court stenographer, she instructed her, "That's with an *a*. Many Delahantys spell it d-e-l-e. We was always with an *a*. When my husband come over, as a small boy, there was a mistake at the Immigration."

To put her at ease, Ben asked, "Mrs. Delahanty, is this the first time in your life that you have ever been on a witness stand?"

"First time I ever been in a courtroom. 'Course I've seen them on television, but this is the first time for real."

"Mrs. Delahanty, how long have you known Dennis Riordan?"

"Oh, let's see now. Was about the time my Catherine was three, we moved next door to the Riordans. And his Dennis Junior, the one who became the priest, he was about six . . . I'd say onto twenty-nine years."

"During those twenty-nine years," Ben continued, "did you have occasion to see Dennis Riordan often?"

"Every day. Well, almost every day."

"And do you know his reputation in the neighborhood?"

"Oh, yes, sir!" she responded promptly.

"And what is that reputation?" Ben asked in the legally prescribed fashion.

"The very highest!" she declared, then looked at Ben in a way that asked, *Did I say that like you told me to?*

Her ingenuous manner was such that Judge Klein smiled. While in the jury box Walter Grove shook his head, Violet Tolliver could not resist glancing at Grove, and for an instant their eyes met in shared amusement.

Ben continued, "Mrs. Delahanty, in all the years you have known Dennis Riordan, did you ever know him to be a dangerous man?"

"No, sir! He was always a fine, gentle man. Considerate, too. Why, since my Sylvester died, if there's a snowstorm overnight, Dennis Riordan never goes off to work without shoveling out my walkway, too. He's always doing nice things for people. When that dreadful thing happened to his Aggie . . ."

Crewe called out, "Your Honor . . ."

Klein leaned in the witness's direction and said gently, "Mrs. Delahanty, please do not make any reference to that."

"But it happened," she started to protest.

"According to the rules you are not permitted to mention it," Klein explained.

"I'm sorry, Judge. I didn't know what the rules was." She began to cry from tension and embarrassment.

"No further questions," Ben said.

Lester Crewe rose slowly, contemplated cross-examining the woman, but decided to confine himself to a single question.

"Mrs. Delahanty, if a man bought a pistol for the purpose of shooting another man, and then did shoot him, would you call that a 'fine, nice, considerate' thing to do?"

The woman's lower lip trembled, her tears came faster, she could not respond.

"You don't have to answer, Mrs. Delahanty," Crewe said softly.

Ben escorted Theresa Delahanty from the witness stand through the courtroom to the door. All the way she continued to weep. "I hope I didn't say nothing wrong, didn't hurt Dennis in any way."

"No, you were fine, Mrs. Delahanty, fine." At the door Ben kissed her on the cheek and said, "You were terrific. A great help!"

As he opened the door for her, she noticed Father Nelson waiting in the corridor. She burst into tears once more. The priest comforted her, patting her on the shoulder. When he felt free to do so, he followed Ben into the courtroom.

Father Nelson had taken the stand. The clerk held out the Bible for him to place his left hand on. Father Nelson opened the cover, turned to the title page, then said, "I would rather it was the Douay Version, but this will suffice for the purpose." He raised his right hand and was sworn.

"Your name?" Ben began.

The frail, bald man, who seemed too small for his black clerical suit, replied, "Peter Nelson."

"And from your garb may we assume that you are a priest, sir?"

"Yes, yes, of course."

"Father, do you know the defendant, Dennis Riordan?"

"I do. He is one of my parishioners. Has been for almost forty years."

"Has he been a faithful parishioner? In his attendance at church? Communion? Confession?"

"Oh, yes! He takes communion regularly. And makes his periodic appearance in the confessional. He is also very active in church matters. Any time I call for volunteers I can always depend on Dennis." The priest sighed. "Except, of course, in the last year, which has been a very sad time. Very sad. Not only for Dennis but for all of us who have watched the little family torn apart."

Ben waited, hoping the priest might volunteer some specific reference to Agnes and her death. But the old man did not, for he was shrewd enough to notice that the prosecutor was ready to pounce if he tried.

"Father, knowing Dennis Riordan's reputation, would you say that people regarded him as an angry man? A man with criminal tendencies?"

"No, sir, absolutely not!"

"How would you say the community characterizes him?"

"As a good, decent, hard-working human being, a devoted husband, and a loving father who raised his children to be as fine as he is."

Ben could not have written a better answer himself. He was quite satisfied when he said, "Thank you, Father." He started back to the table to take his place alongside Dennis Riordan.

Lester Crewe decided to ask his questions from his place at the counsel table.

"Father, you said that Dennis Riordan made confession regularly?"

"Yes, sir, that he did."

"Did he also make confession on the twenty-fourth of January, 1982?"

The little priest drew himself up in the witness chair. "Sir, I do not think that confidentiality allows me to answer that question."

"Surely it is no breach of the sanctity of the confessional merely to tell us whether or not he made confession."

Judge Klein intervened. "Mr. Crewe, don't press it."

"Your Honor, may I recall to you and the jury, the last words on the tape of the defendant's confession were, 'I want to see my priest.'?"

"Then let that be sufficient answer," Judge Klein advised.

Once Father Nelson left the witness stand, Judge Klein asked, "Mr. Gordon, your next witness?"

"Your Honor, I would like a recess at this time until after lunch."

"But it's only eleven-fifteen," the judge pointed out.

"Please, Your Honor, it is quite important to my case."

Klein motioned both attorneys to the bench for a sidebar conference. Out of hearing of the jury, the judge spoke in a confidential whisper.

"Gordon, what's the problem? Are you trying to decide whether to put your client on the stand?"

"That's one consideration," Ben conceded.

"If the prosecution doesn't object, I'll give you a little advice. Don't!" Judge Klein cautioned.

"That jury has got to know what happened to that man before he killed Johnson!" Ben argued.

"Why?"

"Because if I can prove extreme emotional disturbance, I am going to ask you to instruct the jury in your charge that they can consider a verdict of Manslaughter in the First."

"With that man's calm attitude when he made his confession an hour after the murder, you are going to claim extreme emotional disturbance?" Klein scoffed. "Gordon, I would never give a jury such a charge under these conditions."

"Still, the jury has a right to know . . ." Ben protested.

Klein had to gesture to Ben to keep his voice down. In a tense but emotional whisper, the young lawyer continued, "I am sitting in this courtroom with my hands tied and my mouth gagged, and I am supposed to give my client an honest defense. This jury has a right to know and I have an obligation to tell them!"

Crewe urged, "Ben, be reasonable. Look at the facts. Your client was not emotionally disturbed, so you can forget Manslaughter One. He was not in any position of danger, was not protecting himself, so that wipes out Justifiable Homicide. This is, under the law and you know it, Murder Two. Face it!"

"I still want a chance to tell his story. I owe him that much," Ben insisted.

"Okay, then put him on the stand!" Crewe challenged. "I tell you right now, if you do, I will take him through every step of that crime from the moment he decided to kill Johnson until he fired those shots. I will make his confession look like a church picnic by comparison. During his confession I did not question him, I just let him talk. Well, not on cross-examination! I will pull it out of him. Bit by bit."

Ben evaluated the risk: the beneficial impact on the jury of Dennis Riordan, father, husband, decent human being, as against Dennis Riordan, defendant, in effect confessing all over again, and this time with Lester Crewe eager to underline every incriminating nuance with his probing questions. It was the most crucial decision he would have to make in this case.

"Counselor?" Judge Klein prodded impatiently.

"I would like a recess until tomorrow morning," Ben said.

Considerate of Ben's plight, and feeling guilty at having involved him in this difficult case, Klein looked at Lester Crewe. Lester nodded. As the attorneys were about to depart from the bench, Klein said, "Gordon, I liked what you did this morning. That apology. This city has enough hatred without creating any more."

"Thank you, Your Honor," Ben said. "Now, if you don't mind, I'd like to see that confession tape again. It might help me make up my mind."

"I'll set it up for you, Ben," Crewe volunteered.

As the attorneys resumed their places at the table, Judge Klein turned to the jury.

"Ladies and gentlemen, you are excused for the rest of the day. But report here tomorrow morning when Mr. Gordon will continue with his case. In the meantime, I caution you once more, do not discuss this case among yourselves. Do not read or listen to any news reports."

He banged his gavel. The jurors began to file out. The press contingent rushed to the barrier to try to extract from Ben Gordon or Lester Crewe some explanation for this sudden recess. Neither attorney would make a statement.

As the reporters abandoned the courtroom, Lester Crewe said, "I can't wait to hear the speculations that will fill the air at six o'clock tonight." He laughed. "Hortense and I sit home and watch the news and learn more about this case than I know."

When Ben did not share in his laughter, Crewe realized why. "Oh, yeah, you want to see that confession again."

The courtroom had been locked to bar any curious intruders. The tape machine and the monitor screen, which remained from the session in which Riordan's confession had been played for the jury, were moved into place. The clerk pulled up the blinds on the high windows and extinguished the lights. The stenographer, into whose possession the tape had been entrusted as an exhibit in the People's case, inserted the cartridge into the machine and flicked the switch. She slipped out by the judge's door, leaving Ben Gordon alone to witness once more the confession of his client. He watched intently, pad in one hand, pencil in the other, hungry to seize on any detail that might offer a clue to his next move.

16

THE JURY HAD BEEN dismissed before the usual lunch hour. Thus, when Violet Tolliver reached the foot of the courthouse steps, her long black Mercedes limousine had not yet returned. The television reporters, camera crews and sound engineers capitalized on the opportunity to surround her, photograph her and try to elicit her reactions to the case.

Mindful of the legal restrictions imposed by the judge, she refused to answer any questions, including those relating to her impressions of Riordan and her personal reaction to the two young attorneys. But the television reporters permitted her no escape. Walter Grove, coming down the steps, realized her predicament, pushed his way forcefully through the clutter of microphones, hand-held cameras and cables to say, "Miss Tolliver has an appointment with me. I hope you won't mind!"

He took a firm grip on her arm and steered her through the protesting reporters toward the corner and around it, along narrow streets devoted to small restaurants that catered to courthouse and government personnel. He led her past the Italian *ristorantes* and several blocks beyond to an area of small Chinese dining places.

"Lunching in your elegant limousine every day, you miss a lot of the local color," Grove said. "Some of the best

Chinese restaurants in the city are down here, small, simple places, but excellent."

He guided her to an unpretentious restaurant with a simple, neat sign over the door announcing itself in white Chinese letters on a red background. Violet stared through the window at four small bare tables surrounded by plain wooden benches. Beyond was an open kitchen presided over by a single chef. Instinctively, she turned toward Grove to protest, but he anticipated her comment. "Take my word for it. The finest Chinese food in New York. I eat here every lunch break."

She relented and was somewhat reassured when the lone waiter greeted Grove with a broad, warm smile and in Chinese, which she did not understand. They were directed to a table with a mere wave of the hand.

Once they were seated, Grove asked, "Have you ever been introduced to the surprising world of Chinese dumplings? Terrific, fluffy white pastries with the most pungent and exotic fillings. And the fried dumplings. Incredible! We'll start with some."

He ordered in Chinese, then continued. "The great Chinese food is found in simple places like this, where they take basic ingredients and do wonderful things with them. Not like those elegant, chi-chi, overly expensive places uptown, where they concentrate more on writing enticing descriptions for their menus than on the food. If you could eat the adjectives it would be fine. Well, down here, no adjectives, just terrific food, surprisingly delicious, earthy, yet, as one of those uptown menus would say, 'fit for kings and gods.' And goddesses, of course."

Their dumplings arrived. Violet tried one and found it every bit as delicious as Grove had promised. She started on another, found it quite different in tang and texture but equally tantalizing and delightful.

"Excellent," she exclaimed enthusiastically between

mouthfuls. "You're right. Far better than we get up-town."

He was not only delighted with her approval but surprised at the zest with which she ate.

"With a figure like yours, I got the impression you never eat."

"Actually, I have a very hearty appetite," she confessed.

"And all these days I've been feeling so sorry for you, cooped up in that big limousine, lunching on low-fat cottage cheese. Or is it yogurt, plain, because it has fewer calories and is probably more fit for hanging wallpaper than eating?"

Violet laughed and admitted, "It drives women crazy. They always want to know my secret, how I can eat everything and still keep my figure."

"You've kept it, I can see that."

She found herself blushing, something she had not done in a long time. He noticed and said, "Sorry, I didn't mean this lunch to become personal. I was only trying to rescue you from a difficult situation."

"Which you did very effectively. Thanks."

"It's my personal war against the media. Against people who have the outrageous insensitivity to shove a camera into the face of a poor woman who has just lost her children in a fire and ask her how she feels. That's part of the reason I interfered. However, I must confess I do find it very pleasant being here with you. With a woman, I mean."

She looked up from her food to glean his meaning.

"When I'm working, I'm a recluse, surrounded only by my characters to the exclusion of everyone else. As my former wife would tell you."

"Oh?" she replied. "A recent member of the club?"

"A year ago. And I started on my new book at the same

time. Maybe as an antidote. So I've been quite alone, but never realized how alone until I began sitting on this jury. That's why being here talking to you is a distinct pleasure."

"I know the feeling."

"You? Lonely?" he asked, incredulous.

"I've been divorced, too, twice. And for the same reason. No fierce battles. No messy infidelities. Just too involved with my work."

"It's like an amputation, isn't it?"

"Without anesthetic," she added. "I did the same thing as you, tried to recover by plunging more deeply into my work."

The waiter interrupted by bringing two more dishes to the table, chicken in a spicy, pungent brown sauce, embellished with large, flowery black mushrooms, and a platter of pink shrimp in a sauce whipped to a frothy white. Grove waited for her to sample both dishes.

"Do they cater limousine lunches?" she asked, laughing.

"I think it could be arranged."

They ate, laughed and talked, about food, about weather, about pudgy Judge Klein, about the two young attorneys. About everything but themselves. As if they had briefly opened parts of their private lives, into which each was permitted only a glance, not a penetrating look.

"Mrs. Delahanty with an *a*," Grove said. "I loved her. I'll use her in a book one day."

Violet confessed, "When she was testifying about Riordan I felt she was more than just a character witness. She not only respected him but, in her way, cared for him a great deal. And, being a romantic at heart . . ."

Grove interrupted. "Mrs. Delahanty or you?"

"Me, I'm afraid. I don't often admit that. People assume I'm the essence of unemotional sophistication. Actually, I'm hopelessly romantic, still fantasizing that one day I am going to meet the man who'll be all the things I want."

She became self-conscious suddenly. "How did I get onto that?"

"Mrs. Delahanty and her feelings about Riordan," Walter Grove reminded her.

"As I watched her on the stand, the proper, nice old Catholic lady from Queens, a widow. And living next door to her Riordan, a widower. I thought, wouldn't it have been nice if they got married and were companions for each other in their old age, got to know each other's children, and grandchildren."

Grove pointed out, "Riordan doesn't have any grandchildren, won't ever have any. Only one son left, a priest."

"True. His other son was killed in Viet Nam. And then his daughter . . ." Violet stopped abruptly. "Are we discussing the case when we shouldn't be?"

"I don't know if romantic fantasies come under the heading of discussing the case."

They continued eating until he asked, "Your two husbands, what did they do?"

"The first was my agent. When I started my line of beauty products, he reacted as if I were deserting him. The more my business grew, the more he resented it. After a while, he just up and left."

"And the second?" Grove asked.

"Very solid. Vice-president of the bank that financed me at the start. He had been married before, with two delightful children. We got along famously until he wanted more of my time than I could give. I also think he grew resentful of being known as Violet Tolliver's husband."

"That must be something to contend with," Grove agreed.

She changed the subject at once. "About the trial, do

you think it's got much longer to go? Are we allowed to discuss that?"

"As long as we don't discuss guilt or innocence, or whether we believe or disbelieve certain witnesses. You see, I've never served on a jury before either."

"Well," she asked, "how much longer, do you think?"

"Not a hell of a lot. Unless Gordon puts Riordan on the stand."

"And if he does?"

Walter Grove shook his head discouragingly but only said, "I guess we're at the point where we'd better not discuss it any further."

"I guess," Violet agreed reluctantly.

They stared down at the two platters to discover that they had devoured what had seemed impossibly large portions only a short while ago.

"I told you I have a ravenous appetite," she reminded him.

"I like a woman who can come to the table with enthusiasm and not feel she's walking through a minefield when she studies the menu."

They were strolling back to the courthouse.

"I want to thank you," she said.

"My pleasure. Frankly, I get tired of eating alone, working alone, living alone."

"I meant for rescuing me from that mob of TV people."

"Any time, lady, any time."

She turned to look up into his craggy face. His comment was more than a polite rejoinder or a casual invitation.

"There's your car," he said suddenly.

The long black Mercedes with the dark windows was waiting obediently at the foot of the courthouse steps. Her secretary, Anne, was standing outside, anxiously searching in all directions, grasping in her hand a thick file of papers which called for immediate decisions. When she spied Violet, she was relieved, smiled and waved with her free hand.

To Violet, it was a summons back to duty. She asked, "Can I drop you uptown somewhere?"

"I prefer walking. I need the exercise."

"Well, thanks again."

"You're welcome again," he said, turned and started away.

She watched him go, tall, lanky, angular, with a frame that fit with his craggy face. A nice man, she decided, not at all the pushy type she had suspected at the outset. And so lonely. But Anne was waiting. Violet started for the car. Anne held the door open for her. She slipped inside, settled into the deep, luxurious velour seat.

"Bloody Mary?" Anne asked, referring to the bar in front of them.

"Today, no drink," Violet said, reaching for the file. The first item was a letter from the Arizona attorneys she had retained to defend her in a lawsuit by a woman who claimed to have suffered a severe allergic reaction to one of Beauty-by-Tolliver's costly creams. The woman's attorney indicated she was willing to settle.

And why not? Violet thought. All that was in that very expensive cream was about eleven cents' worth of vegetable oil. Nothing to provoke an allergic reaction.

Anne started to unwrap the sandwich she had brought, but Violet said, "No lunch today, Annie. In fact, for the rest of the trial, no lunch. I'll eat out."

Ben Gordon was walking across the Brooklyn Bridge, the most direct route from the courthouse to the apartment on Brooklyn Heights. Ordinarily he would have taken a cab or the subway, but not today. He had time.

Not enough time to muster an effective defense for Dennis Riordan and too much time to ponder that fact.

He had just viewed the tape of Riordan's confession again and had come away without making a single note. He had found no hint of a new defense.

He blamed himself, recalling how many times he had seen his uncle Harry manufacture defenses for men who were flagrantly guilty of crimes against innocent people. Yet this man, Dennis Riordan, who had rid society of an acknowledged rapist and murderer, stood naked and defenseless in the eyes of the law.

The one element he had hoped to rely on, jury sympathy, had been denied him. He had been ruled against each time by Judge Klein.

As he walked, he argued the case legally. Strictly, according to the rules of evidence, Klein was right. What had happened to Agnes Riordan was immaterial to this case, unless Riordan's motive was relevant. But under the definition of Murder Two as defined in the New York statutes, motive was not a factor. Intent was, and only intent. And that was limited solely to one question: Did Dennis Riordan intend to kill Cletus Johnson when he shot him? Why he had formed that intent had no legal relevance.

Still, the jury should know that, Ben argued. This man Dennis Riordan, now called the defendant, did not deserve the rap that fate had handed him. A son killed in Viet Nam, a daughter raped and murdered, and a wife who died of a broken heart. And now, the final irony.

The same system of justice that had set free confirmed criminal Cletus Johnson was going to send Dennis Riordan to jail for at least fifteen years. Which, for a man his age, even with parole, meant for life!

And I, Benjamin Franklin Gordon, can't do a thing about it!

Suddenly he found himself as angry with Riordan as with his own helplessness. Damn it! If the man would only show some concern, some fear, some anger. But Riordan would only say, "Don't worry, kid, it's all right." *I'm his lawyer, he's in jeopardy and he's comforting me!*

Looking at it from Riordan's point of view, he had felt outraged at the way the law had dealt with his daughter's death. So, in the same methodical way he had lived his life, he went out and did what he had to do to rectify that very legal, but morally offensive, miscarriage of justice. Having done that, he feels justified. As far as Riordan is concerned, what happens now *is* all right.

Well, it is not all right as far as I am concerned, Ben protested in his silent fury.

But by the time he was climbing the front steps of the old brownstone on Brooklyn Heights, he was no closer to a viable defense. At the door he fumbled for his key. Arlene opened it before he could. She had been waiting impatiently for him.

He gave her a hasty kiss on the cheek, dropped his briefcase on the chair in the foyer, crossed the dark living room, slipped onto the cushioned seat of the bay window and stared at the harbor. Arlene brought him a drink, pressed it into his hand. It was icy cold, condensation running down its sides. He took a sip but said nothing.

"You're so late. Subway tie-up?"

"No."

"How did you get home?"

"I needed lots of time to think, so I walked."

"How?"

"Across the bridge, of course," he answered impatiently.

"That's funny."

"What does that mean?"

"Based on everything you told me, I just assumed Uncle Harry would have walked across on the water."

Ben turned to glare at her.

"What the hell does *that* mean?" he demanded, furious.

"While you were walking, because you needed time to think, I baked us some veal chops. I ate mine while I watched yours grow dry and tasteless. Which gave *me* plenty of time to think about a lot of things. Us. You. The trial."

"And?" he demanded, impatient but curious.

Arlene studied Ben a long moment before asking, "Tell me, when Uncle Harry was alive and practicing law . . . whom did *he* quote?"

"What?" Ben asked, irritated by what he deemed a foolish question.

"Didn't your uncle Harry have an uncle he quoted?"

"Of course not!"

"That's a surprise," Arlene said, her blue eyes glistening so that he was able to read her anger even in the dark.

"Meaning?"

"Meaning you break your heart trying to imitate your uncle, whom you idolized. But that's not what you really do. Uncle Harry never relied on anyone else. He never went around quoting his uncle, or his father, or his nephew. What made Uncle Harry a successful lawyer was Uncle Harry! What *he* thought. What *he* did. What *he* innovated. The one thing he did *not* do was go around quoting anyone else!"

Though furious, Ben did not reply. For the first time someone had held a mirror up to him, let him look at what he had become. It was a shock. If she had done it out of any other motive but great love, he would have lashed back at her. But the combined look of compassion and defiance in her blue eyes made him turn away.

More softly, she continued, "Darling? Don't you see? You've been using Uncle Harry like money in a nonexistent bank account. You have to live your life on the basis that there is no Uncle Harry. There is only Benjamin Franklin Gordon and Dennis Riordan, his client, who is being tried for murder. The question now is, if you can't try the victim, as you planned, what is *Ben Gordon* going to do? Not Uncle Harry. Not Louis Nizer. Not F. Lee Bailey. But Ben Gordon. Now, you start thinking and I'll make some coffee."

She sat on the sofa, her long, shapely legs curled up under her. She watched Ben as he stared out at the darkness, vaguely reaching for his coffee cup, which eluded him. *Just as well*, she thought, *he's already had four cups.*

"You ought to go to bed, it's cold out here," he said.

"Does my being here bother you?"

"Should it?"

"After what I said . . ."

"It had to be said," he admitted.

"Only if it helps," she offered.

"It helped me decide what Ben Gordon should do. Made me put all the pieces of this case together in every way I can."

He rose and started to pace briskly.

"And what are the pieces?" he began. "Cletus Johnson. Rape. Murder. And the system that set him free. Riordan. His outrage against the system. His act of killing. And now, what is it prevents me from bringing all the facts into that courtroom? The same system. Well, if the system won't let me put the victim on trial, I will put the system, the law itself, on trial!"

"Will they let you?"

"Klein? Les Crewe? I'd like to see them stop me!"

"What are you going to do?"

"Not just me. You, too!" he said.

"Me? What can I do?"

"In the morning, before court, I am going to the office and draw up a very important document."

"And then?"

"Then you will do exactly what I tell you to do!" he said. "Now, go to bed. You may have a very long, tough day tomorrow."

She started for the bedroom, but he reached to catch her hand and draw her close. He looked into her bright blue eyes and said, "Years from now when I am a famous lawyer they will invite me to lecture at law schools. And I am going to tell those kids, what every young lawyer needs, more than a swivel chair, a desk, a telephone, a law library or a Xerox machine is an Arlene Robbins. You see, by that time they'll be able to clone beautiful, bright girls like you."

He kissed and released her.

Alone, he began to pace excitedly, for her challenge had led him to devise a whole new approach to the defense of Dennis Riordan. Through his mind raced all the cases he had spent days researching: *Mapp* v. *Ohio, People* v. *Wright, People* v. *Rogers* and dozens of others, all the cases he had been prevented from using thus far in this trial. Well, tomorrow morning he would use them.

"Tomorrow morning, Judge Aaron Klein," he defied him silently, "you are going to be faced with a situation unprecedented in your years on the bench! Let's see how you rule then!"

By the first light of day, Ben was still making notes at a furious pace. It had never even occurred to him to get any sleep. He was ready!

17

THE NEXT MORNING shortly before ten o'clock, Ben Gordon entered Part 4, Criminal Division of the Supreme Court, New York County. This time he was not alone. Arlene accompanied him. He seated her in the place usually reserved for the first witness to be called.

Before this morning was over he might have need of her testimony. As he turned to pass through the barrier, she seized his hand and whispered, "Good luck, darling!"

He approached the counsel table, laid out his pads, his pencils, his legal memoranda and notes. He bade a pleasant good morning to the woman who served as court stenographer. He greeted Lester Crewe when the young black District Attorney arrived. Ben tried to perform all these amenities with an appearance of complete calm, but his eyes kept glancing nervously toward the door to Judge Klein's robing room. Just before ten o'clock, the defendant, Dennis Riordan, in handcuffs, was escorted into the courtroom by two uniformed guards.

"Good morning, Mr. Riordan."

"Good morning, Ben," Riordan said simply, without emotion. Prepared to face another day in which he was unconcerned about his fate, he seemed far more at ease than his young counsel.

"How much longer is this going to go on?" Riordan asked.

"Depends," Ben said.

"If you're not going to put me on the stand, don't the time come soon when you have to sum up? I thought that's the way it worked."

"Only after all the evidence is in."

"You mean it isn't?" Riordan asked.

"No," Ben said, his eyes fixed on the judge's door.

"Look, would you do something for me?" Riordan asked suddenly.

"Of course. What?"

"Mrs. Delahanty."

"What about her?"

"She thought I didn't look well yesterday. So she brought me some food this morning. And she made a big fuss when the guard refused it."

"I'll talk to the guard," Ben promised.

"No. Talk to her. Tell her to stop."

"Okay."

"And do whatever you can to get this trial over with. Fast!" Riordan said.

Mister, Ben thought, *that is precisely what I am not going to do!*

The jury filed in promptly at five minutes to ten. Elihu Prouty, Violet Tolliver, Walter Grove and eleven other citizens of New York County.

When all was in readiness, the court clerk disappeared into the robing room to alert the judge. The clerk was gone for a very long time. It was almost ten-thirty when the door was flung open. Not the clerk but Judge Klein himself entered, his face florid with anger. When everyone started to rise, he growled, "Forget that!"

He climbed to the bench, glared down at Ben Gordon,

who pretended to be engrossed in one of his legal memoranda.

"*Mr.* Gordon!" Judge Klein bellowed, "approach the bench!"

At that angry command, everyone in the courtroom instantly came alert. The jurors sat up tensely in their chairs. The men and women of the media leaned forward. The artists started sketching furiously, for they sensed that something of enormous moment was about to take place in this trial.

With forced deliberateness, Ben Gordon slowly put aside the memo he was pretending to read, got to his feet and came forward. Curious, and in the interest of protecting his case, Lester Crewe started to rise. But Judge Klein ordered him back down with a sharp gesture. "Later, Mr. Crewe!"

Ben had reached the bench. He leaned forward so that Klein could address him in a whisper.

"Gordon!" Klein began, as furious as a man could be who was operating under the strictures imposed on him by the presence of the jury. "Do I understand that this morning you had a subpoena served on Judge Michael Lengel?"

"Yes, sir." As if oblivious of the unusual nature of his action, Ben asked with pretended ingenuousness, "Was the subpoena defectively drawn?"

"The document was properly drawn," Klein admitted. From inside his black robe he produced the folded subpoena and held it out to Ben.

"Your Honor, I don't understand," Ben said.

"Take this back, Gordon! And we will proceed on the basis that it was never served!"

"I don't really see how I can do that, Your Honor." Ben directed Klein's attention to the first row of spectators. "You see that blond girl sitting in the first seat? She is the one who served the subpoena on Judge Lengel. And I have here her affidavit of service. She is also available to testify in person that she made valid service on the judge. And also what the good judge said when she served him. I can put her on the stand to testify if you'd like. Or will you be content to accept her affidavit?"

Ben slid the paper across the wide desk. Klein glared at the affidavit but avoided touching it, as if it were the carrier of a deadly disease. He glared at Ben. He glared in the direction of Arlene. He glared at Ben again. Ben stared back, as innocent as he could pretend to be under the circumstances.

Klein could not resist asking, "What did Lengel say?" Lengel was a martinet in the exacting standards of conduct he demanded from attorneys and witnesses who appeared in his courtroom. He also would resort to very earthy language when personally provoked.

"I'd rather you heard it from her, Your Honor," Ben said. "She's ready to testify."

"Never mind!" Klein was contemplative for a moment, then blurted out, "Gordon, what the hell do you expect to accomplish . . . ?" Aware that he was raising his voice in the presence of the jury, he lowered it once more to an angry whisper, "Come up to my chambers!"

"Your Honor, if there's to be any question as to whether Judge Lengel will honor my subpoena, I prefer to have it argued out here, in the presence of the court stenographer, for the record. You may have to remove the jury. But I think the press has a right to know. Else I will go out on the courthouse steps and make a statement. Something I have refrained from doing thus far. I will tell them how I have been muzzled during the course of this trial."

Klein did not respond at once. His lips twitched in nervous frustration as he wished he had the comfort of a cigar. "Gordon, I can hold you in contempt for any derogatory statements you make about the fairness with which this trial is being conducted. Even if made outside this courtroom!"

"I know that," Ben agreed, clearly indicating it was a penalty he was willing to risk.

As if it were an ultimatum, Klein said, "Judge Lengel does not wish to comply with this subpoena!"

"Then I will take the steps an attorney is forced to take with a recalcitrant witness," Ben countered.

"You won't withdraw this subpoena?" Klein asked for the last time.

"I had it served in full expectation that Judge Lengel, being a law-abiding citizen and an officer of this court, would honor a legally drawn, lawfully served subpoena. I will be greatly surprised to find out otherwise."

"I don't know what you expect to achieve," Klein sputtered, "but if you insist, I will have to give the prosecution the opportunity to be heard before I decide."

"I expected that you would, sir."

Klein was thoughtful for a moment, then beckoned to the clerk. "Remove the jury!"

Fourteen puzzled citizens filed out of the jury box. Once outside, and though each was extremely curious, none of them dared venture a guess.

Only Anthony Mascarella, the produce manager, grumbled, "Every time it gets interesting, we're kicked out. The jury's the only ones in the world not allowed to know what's going on."

An admonishing look from the clerk silenced him.

Freed from the restraining presence of the jury, the ground cleared for battle, Judge Klein invited Lester Crewe to the bench with a single, angry gesture of his forefinger.

"Do you know what this bastard has done?" Klein began in a whisper that was both hostile and conspiratorial. "He has had the goddam nerve to subpoena Judge Lengel to appear as a witness in this case!"

Aware suddenly that the stenographer had drawn close to record the sidebar conference, Klein, with great annoyance and embarrassment, instructed her, "Strike that! And make it read, 'Mr. Crewe, I'm afraid I must inform you that your opponent in this case has taken a most regrettable step. He has had a subpoena served on Judge Lengel to appear as a witness in this case.'"

Lester Crewe looked at Ben, not in dismay but with concern, almost with pity. Had his friend and onetime colleague lost his mind? Aside from the serious question of the admissibility of Judge Lengel as a witness in this case, what did he hope to prove?

"Your Honor, the People oppose such a move on several grounds." He spoke in full voice so everyone in the courtroom could hear. The men and women of the press grew silent and poised, eager for their first hint of the subject of the long, secret, tantalizing conference at the bench.

Crewe continued, "In the first place, Judge Lengel has no firsthand knowledge of the crime in this case. So he would not be competent to testify even if he were a private citizen. As to the propriety of subpoenaing a judge to testify, I am sure I could, given the opportunity, produce a number of cases that would substantiate my objection.

"I'm afraid I must state for the record that I am shocked that an attorney whom I have long considered an ethical and honorable member of the bar should resort to such tactics. I urge Your Honor to vacate the subpoena under the powers which you have."

Klein looked at Ben to hear his rebuttal.

"Your Honor, in the first place, as to the liability of a judge to a subpoena, I have looked up some law on the question. I find no case that holds that *any* citizen is immune to service of a subpoena. Just as when a man takes the oath as an attorney, he becomes an officer of the court, so the judge's oath does not diminish his responsibility but enlarges it. I invite my colleague to search the law, but I do not think he will find a case exactly in point to substantiate his contention.

"Now, as to the second part of his argument, the admissibility of Judge Lengel's testimony on the ground of relevance, I must admit that if the subject of Judge Lengel had not been introduced by the prosecutor, there might indeed be some question. But since the prosecutor himself introduced the subject during the presentation of his case, I feel I must be allowed to present evidence, the best evidence, firsthand evidence to counter that."

"The People never mentioned Judge Lengel in their case!" Crewe challenged. "Search the record! Find me one single State's witness who referred to him!"

"We don't have to search the entire record, Mr. Crewe. I can tell you exactly where it is," Ben said.

Judge Klein and Lester Crewe exchanged glances that remarked on their doubts not only as to Ben's memory but his sanity as well.

Ben turned to the stenographer. "Mrs. Harrison, do you have your notes of Wednesday with you?"

"Yes, Mr. Gordon."

"Will you find for me that place where, after considerable dispute, the confession of Dennis Riordan was placed in evidence?"

Mrs. Harrison flipped through the long, narrow pages of stenotype notes, did not find it in the first batch, went on to the next and found it finally in a fifth batch.

"Will you read that confession to the court?" Ben asked.

She looked at the judge. "The whole thing?"

Before Klein could answer, Ben said, "The whole thing, Mrs. Harrison!"

Somewhat dubious and ill at ease, she began to read:

"I am Dennis Riordan. I live at seventeen-oh-nine, Twenty-fourth Street, Astoria, Queens."

With Judge Klein listening impatiently, Lester Crewe listening with great skepticism, and the spectators silent and puzzled, Mrs. Harrison continued reading.

Finally, she reached that portion of the confession which read:

> Then they got to yelling at each other, both lawyers. Until this Judge Lengel, he bangs his gavel and says . . .

Ben Gordon raised his right hand and extended his forefinger. Mrs. Harrison read on until she came to:

> And the District Attorney, his face red, stands up and says something like 'Judge Lengel, confronted by Your Honor's rulings, the People find it impossible to make a *prima facie* case.

Ben Gordon raised a second finger. And so he did each time Lengel's name was read by Mrs. Harrison, until when she was finished, Ben had all five fingers on his right hand raised.

"Five times, Your Honor, five times Judge Lengel is mentioned in that confession. It is our contention that when the prosecution introduced that confession into evidence it introduced the subject of Judge Lengel as well. It also introduced the subject of the exclusionary rule upon which Judge Lengel ruled out the confession of Cletus Johnson and barred Mr. Riordan from identifying his daughter's jewelry which was found on Johnson. In order for the jury to approach their deliberations with a complete understanding of my defendant's confession, they are entitled to know what the exclusionary rule is, and how it works."

"I can cover that in my charge." Judge Klein tried to dispose.

"I'm sorry, Your Honor, but I'm afraid I will have to insist that since Judge Lengel is the person who invoked the exclusionary rule, he is the only witness who can explain his thought process in making those decisions. I must insist that this subpoena be sustained, not vacated. And that Judge Lengel be ordered to honor it or be held in contempt of this court."

With a sense of impatience, and in an attempt to trivialize Ben's argument, Lester Crewe interjected, "Your Honor, to ask a judge of this court to delay or interrupt a trial he is presiding over is a burden on a judicial system that is already overburdened."

"Your Honor, as far as I am concerned," Ben rebutted, "there is only one case of importance before this court. The People versus Dennis Riordan. In my mind, my client's rights supersede any judge's convenience, desires or obligations. I want Judge Lengel on that witness stand. And I am willing to wait hours, days or weeks until he clears his calendar and can comply with my subpoena!"

"Mr. Gordon!" Klein thundered. "We can't be asking every judge to appear and testify about every case he's presided over. It would make the life of a judge intolerable!"

"Your Honor," Ben suggested in a low but strong voice, "I am not asking every judge to appear. Only one judge. And I am not asking him to testify about every case he's ever presided over. Only one case. A case involving a situation for which I do not think you will find any precedent. Your Honor, I urge that exceptional cases demand exceptional rulings."

Klein stared down at Ben. "Counselor, are you aware that the Supreme Court of these United States has ruled, more than once, that a judge is immune from all lawsuits deriving from his official actions and decisions?"

"Yes, Your Honor. As I understand it, the judiciary is the one profession exempt from the astringent effects of malpractice suits," Ben replied.

With greater emphasis and increasing wrath, Klein responded, "The reason is that a judge cannot effectively and fairly carry out his duties if he is under constant fear of reprisals, legal or otherwise!" He stared at Ben in such a way that he hoped to end all argument with that statement.

But Ben refused to be cowed. "Your Honor, may I point out that we are not attempting to sue Judge Lengel, or even to affect his judgment. His judgment was made long ago. We are only asking that he explain to the jury what happened so they can understand the conditions leading to my client's confession."

"It is the feeling of this bench that forcing a judge to do so violates the spirit of those Supreme Court decisions. The judiciary must be protected from harassment!" As if he had made his final ruling, Klein was about to bang his gavel.

But with the suggestion of an implied threat, Ben urged, "Your Honor, the defense will not allow this question to rest here. There will be an appeal."

With a resentful glance at Ben, Judge Klein turned his attention to Lester Crewe, who had been impatient to respond.

"Your Honor, the People view this entire move as a dilatory tactic on the part of counsel to prolong this trial and to conceal the fact that the defendant has no legitimate defense. The People insist this subpoena be vacated!"

"The People?" Ben said. "Which 'People,' Mr. Crewe? The bureaucracy you call the People? Or the people out there?"

Ben turned to the press. "The average citizens, who really *are* the People. If it's those people you're representing, why this legal conspiracy between you and Judge Klein to keep them from knowing what goes on in the minds of their judges? After all, who are judges, high priests whom we must obey blindly and dare not question? Who wrap themselves in the black robes of office and proclaim, 'We are holy, you must not touch us?' 'We are above the duties and obligations of ordinary citizens, therefore we are not required to obey subpoenas lawfully served on us'? Is that what has brought us to where we are now, when the 'people' you claim to represent live in constant fear of their safety and their lives?"

Pointing his finger at the reporters, who were leaning forward listening to and recording his every word, he said, "If it's the people you represent, Mr. Crewe, answer to *them!*"

Confronted with a situation unprecedented in his experience on the bench, Judge Klein said, "We will stand in recess for thirty minutes!"

He banged his gavel and started down from the bench, regretting that he had ever assigned Ben Gordon to this case. It was one thing to contend with legal arguments, but quite another to contend with the press. That young upstart had suddenly removed this case from the courts to the public arena. Well, there were ways of dealing with him later. For the moment, Klein had a more urgent problem.

The instant Judge Klein was out the door, the courtroom exploded in a flurry of activity. Reporters representing all branches of the media rushed to the barrier to interview Ben, but he refused to answer any questions.

"I will await Judge Klein's ruling."

He glanced beyond them to Arlene, who smiled and winked her encouragement and support.

In chambers, after he had snatched a cigar and lit up, Klein shouted, "Esther!"

His plump niece, who served as his law clerk, came in, pad in hand.

"Wait till I tell you the argument that sonofabitch Gordon just made about that subpoena!" Klein exploded.

When he had finished, Esther said thoughtfully, "He's got a point. True, the Supreme Court has held that a judge is immune from suit because of a decision he has rendered. And there might even be a case where some lower court has held a judge immune from a subpoena, though I can't think of any at the moment. However, I'm sure there is no case in which the facts are identical with this one. After all, by introducing the confession, the prosecution did introduce the subject of the exclusionary rule and Judge Lengel. And, in a case involving Murder Two, I think the Court of Appeals would grant the defense the broadest latitude in rebuttal. I think that 'sonofabitch' is a very smart young man. And not bad-looking, either."

Klein drummed his fingers on the desk, pondering his next move. He made a decision. "Get Lengel on the phone!"

"He must be on the bench," Esther pointed out.

"Then get him *off* the bench!" Klein said impatiently. "And start looking up precedents. Maybe there is a case in point somewhere, in some jurisdiction."

Below in the courtroom, having given up trying to coax a statement out of Ben Gordon, the newspeople had departed, some going to phone their papers and report this unexpected development, others outside the court-room being taped for the television news, in which they tried to assess the importance and possible outcome of the questions Ben had raised.

In the well of the courtroom, Lester Crewe, more concerned than he was willing to admit, warned, "Ben, you must be out of your mind! Even if you get Lengel on the stand, which I doubt, what do you hope to prove?"

Ben avoided disclosing his strategy by saying, "Maybe it's just a fishing expedition. After all, I can't sum up with what I've got now."

Lester nodded, accepting that explanation. He started out to the men's room and was cornered at the door by reporters, cameras, microphones and lights. In the inter-est of protecting his case he, too, refused to make any statement.

Inside the courtroom Dennis Riordan beckoned Ben close.

"Look, kid . . . I mean, Counselor, don't get the judge mad at you because of me. It won't change anything. And if you get a reputation for being a troublemaker, all the other judges will always have it in for you. Judges are only human, you know."

"I intend to make damned sure of that," Ben said, giving Riordan no further clue to his plans. Arlene sig-naled him from the railing.

"I hope you're not getting yourself into more trouble than you can handle," she said.

"The worst that can happen is we get turned down. But Mr. Riordan is going to get all the defense he's enti-tled to, whether he wants it or not!"

Up in his chambers, Judge Aaron Klein impatiently chewed on his already damp, mashed cigar as he waited for Lengel to respond to his call. Of all the judges in New York County, Klein fretted, this had to happen with Lengel, the stickler for judicial propriety. Old Simon Legree, lawyers called him, for he was known to correct them not only about their courtroom demeanor but their attire as well. He had even once reprimanded a revealingly clad female witness, "Lady, go home and put some clothes on before you appear in my courtroom!" Lengel conducted his courtroom and himself with the same degree of gravity as a justice of the Supreme Court of the United States. As strict as he was on courtroom conduct, so was he in adhering to legal precedents in his decisions. *Lengel, of all judges,* Klein kept repeating to himself.

Finally, the call came.

"Michael? Aaron!" Judge Klein announced, trying to sound as hearty as he could. "Well, I tried to get him to withdraw it. But that young bastard won't retreat an inch. And my law secretary says he may have a point."

"Mine, too," Lengel admitted grimly.

"So unless I want to run the risk of being reversed on appeal, in a case that is sure to get lots of press coverage, I'm afraid I'm going to have to ask you to honor that subpoena."

"Aaron, do you mean to say you are going to ask a fellow jurist to submit himself to the demeaning, degrading indignity of being questioned like any ordinary witness? It's unheard of!" Lengel protested. "It's not only me, Aaron, think what it will do to the image of all judges with the public!"

"Frankly, Mike, that's exactly what I'm thinking of. That shrewd young bastard now has got the press and the jury believing that you, I and the prosecutor are in one huge conspiracy to prevent the public from discovering what went on in the Johnson case. While he was making his argument, I noticed the reporters were making notes like crazy. Michael, it is precisely because of our public image that I say it's important for you to appear. After all, the public is too critical of courts and judges as it is."

Hoping Lengel would consent, Klein paused, but when he did not, he resorted to the one argument that he knew might budge Lengel, who had pretensions of his own. "You know, Michael, I forget who said it, but it's still true, 'The Supreme Court of the United States follows the election returns.'" He knew Lengel would relish being compared with the highest judges in the land. "We're none of us immune to public pressure."

"What do you want me to do?" Lengel finally asked.

"In view of the fact that this is a unique case, I think from a public relations point of view, it would be in our best interest if you could make time to appear. At least long enough to give the impression we're not covering up anything."

Lengel was silent for a time, then asked, "How long do you think this would take?"

"I promise you one thing, if this kid is on a fishing expedition or just stalling, I'll put a stop to it very fast!" Klein said.

"You think we could dispose of it this afternoon?"

"Don't see why not." Judge Klein would have promised anything to get off the hot seat onto which Ben Gordon had placed him.

"Okay. I'll go down and recess my own trial until tomorrow morning. See you at two o'clock sharp!"

"Thanks, Michael. I'll return the favor sometime." He was about to hang up when he asked, "By the way, what did you say to that girl when she served you with the subpoena?"

"I don't remember. Why?"

"Oh, nothing," Klein said. "This afternoon. And if Gordon is just fishing, he'll rue the day!"

18

Ben Gordon stood up in his place at the counsel table and announced, "At this time, Your Honor, the defense calls Michael Lengel to the stand!"

Aware of the unprecedented moment and fearful of Judge Lengel's awesome reputation, the court clerk slowly approached the courtroom door to admit the tall jurist, who was distinguished by his shock of gray hair and his erect military bearing. Lengel paused in the doorway, surveyed the crowded room and, his disapproving look evidencing distaste for the situation, came into the room.

He strode down the center aisle between two banks of benches filled with curious, excited reporters and spectators. Michael Lengel had been known to say to a fumbling lawyer appearing before him, "Counselor, sit down. I'll question your witness." Then Lengel would proceed to ask sharp and penetrating questions and accomplish in minutes what the attorney had not been able to do in an hour. Now, Judge Michael Lengel himself was being forced to take the stand, and he would become the one who would be questioned. To make the situation even more irksome, he would be questioned by a young upstart lawyer. Lengel felt this reversal of roles demeaned not only himself but the entire judiciary.

He approached Ben, glared at him disapprovingly,

then proceeded to the witness box. His disdain carried
over to the clerk, who presented the Bible to administer
the oath. Tall, erect, his bearing evidencing his defiance,
Lengel placed his left hand on the Bible, raised his right
hand and listened impatiently as the clerk recited:

"Do you solemnly swear to tell the truth the whole truth
and nothing but the truth in the matter of the People versus
Dennis Riordan?"

"I do," Lengel replied, glaring in Ben Gordon's direction as the young attorney assembled his notes with cal-
culatedly provocative deliberateness.

In the jury box, Violet Tolliver looked at Walter Grove
on her left, who returned her glance with the same air of
anticipation and puzzlement. On her right, old Elihu
Prouty exchanged a hasty look with her. Sensing the com-
bative attitude of the witness, all the jurors leaned forward in expectation of a level of heated conflict surpassing
any which this trial had yet produced.

After a look in Arlene's direction, and with his notes
in hand, Ben Gordon approached the witness.

"Sir, would you give your name to the stenographer?"

"Lengel, Michael Lengel," he replied briskly and impatiently.

Purposely employing a form of address he knew would
provoke a reaction from the bench, Ben began, "Now, Mr.
Lengel . . ."

Judge Klein leaned across the desk and made no attempt to conceal his irritation. "Counselor, as you well
know, the gentleman in the witness chair is a judge of this
court. As such he is entitled to be addressed with respect
equal to his position. From now on you will address him
not as *Mr.* Lengel but *Judge* Lengel. And preferably, *Your
Honor.*"

"Yes, sir." Ben was delighted to agree. For Klein had
established a sharp line of distinction between judges and

ordinary citizens such as jurors. He turned his attention back to Lengel. "Now, *Your Honor,* since it is, to say the least, unusual for a judge to occupy the witness box, I wonder if you would tell the jury how you happen to be here?"

Barely controlling his anger, Lengel replied, "Early this morning, in my chambers, I was served with a subpoena requiring me to appear here as a witness in this trial."

"Was that subpoena served in accordance with the requirements of the law?" Ben asked, with a look toward Arlene.

Lengel hesitated, then conceded, "Yes, I suppose so."

"Come, come, Your Honor, you are known not to accept such an inexact answer from a witness in your courtroom. Was it or was it not served in accordance with the law?"

"Yes, it was," Lengel conceded brusquely.

"Having received that subpoena, which was served in a lawful manner, what did you do then?"

His lean face puckering in anger, Lengel turned in the direction of the bench to invite Judge Klein's intervention.

"Counselor, what is the purpose of this line of questioning? You subpoenaed Judge Lengel. He is in attendance. Why waste our time?"

"Because, Your Honor, it didn't happen quite that simply. True, I subpoenaed Judge Lengel. But between that time and his attendance here a number of things occurred which I think the jury should know."

"Mr. Gordon, in case you have forgotten what you learned in law school, I decide what the jury should or should not know!" Judge Klein admonished.

"There is also another reason for this line of questioning, Your Honor," Ben replied.

"Approach the bench!" Klein ordered angrily. When both Ben and Lester reached the side of the bench farthest from the jury, Klein spoke in his most furious whisper, "Gordon, you screw around with the judicial process and I am going to hold you in contempt! Understood?"

"Yes, Your Honor," Ben replied.

"Now, what is this 'other reason'?" Klein demanded.

"I am only trying to establish the ground rules for my examination of this witness. Since I called him to the stand he is considered my witness, and by the rules of evidence, I will be bound not to contradict or challenge any answer he gives. I will not be allowed to impeach him if he makes a misstatement, intentional or otherwise. Unless, of course, I can prove that he is a hostile witness."

"Don't lecture me on the law!" Klein said, casting a glance in the direction of the jury to make sure he had not been overheard. "You may continue. But watch it. I don't want to say any more!"

"Yes, Your Honor."

Ben returned to the witness box to confront Lengel. "Your Honor, having been served with the subpoena, which called for your attendance here at ten o'clock, did you in fact present yourself this morning?"

Another glance at the bench, a slight shrug from Klein, and Lengel finally admitted, "No, I did not."

"At the time you were served weren't you in this very building?"

"I was in my chambers!" Lengel snapped.

"Which is only several floors above us and no more than two minutes away from this courtroom, am I right?"

"Yes!"

"Yet you could not attend until four hours later?"

"Young man, I run a very busy courtroom! I have pressing matters which I cannot simply brush aside," Lengel replied.

"Is that the reason why, instead of honoring my sub-poena, you sent it down to Judge Klein and asked him to quash it?" Ben asked.

Lengel's lean, pale face slowly grew crimson. His lips tensed as he sought to control his fury before answering.

"There is a very substantial legal question as to your right to invade my chambers and serve me with a subpoe-na to appear in this case, with which I have no connection. I was merely asking Judge Klein to determine that ques-tion."

"Then, sir, I owe you my most profound apology," Ben said with a slight edge of sarcasm. "I had assumed you sent the subpoena down to Judge Klein in order to have him threaten me so that I would withdraw it." He deliberately avoided looking toward the bench, for he knew what Klein's reaction would be. "In any event, sir, is it fair to say that you did not receive my subpoena with great joy? And that you did try, albeit on legal grounds, to avoid coming here?"

Lester Crewe rose to his feet. "I object to the form of the question and the inference contained therein."

"Then let me rephrase it," Ben volunteered. "Sir, isn't it a fact that you tried to avoid coming here as a witness?"

Lengel hesitated, glared at Ben, then responded impa-tiently, "Yes, yes, it is true! I think your tactic is a disgrace-ful misuse of the judicial process and I resent it!"

"Thank you, sir, that's all I wanted to know." Ben turned to the bench. "Your Honor, I must now proceed on the basis that the witness is hostile and cannot be considered my witness in the ordinary sense of the term. Therefore, I will avail myself of the usual rules governing the examination of hostile witnesses."

To avoid being inhibited by Klein's manifestations of anger or disapproval, Ben took a position between the bench and the witness box, facing the jury. If his client were to have any chance at all, it would be reflected on those fourteen faces he could now study.

"Judge Lengel, you made the statement a short time ago that you had no connection with this case."

"Yes!" Lengel replied sharply.

"Yet in the defendant's confession, this jury has heard of certain rulings you made, which rulings are germane to the actions for which my client is now on trial."

"Counselor, is that a statement or a question?" Lengel snapped in his officious manner and with the same stern attitude he adopted in his own courtroom. "Either way, I am not answerable to you, only to the highest courts of this state."

"I understand that, Your Honor. I am only asking you to explain those rulings to this jury, who are all lay persons and do not understand the refinements and intricacies of the law."

"Counselor!" Judge Klein interrupted. "Confine yourself to questions, not lectures!"

Ben paused to reorganize his attack, but also to glance at the jury to determine if they were beginning to appreciate how openly hostile Klein had become. If he was expecting sympathy, he had not evoked any. He might even be in danger of antagonizing them by his bold attack on Lengel.

"Questions," Ben remarked, as if thinking aloud, "questions." When he had formulated his new approach, he resumed, "Judge Lengel, are there times when the opinion of one judge does not agree with that of another?"

"Of course. That's what Appeals Courts are for," Lengel replied crisply.

"So that on a given set of facts one judge might rule one way and another judge might rule in a quite opposite way?"

"Yes."

"Am I correct, then, in saying that the mental process of a judge is individual, personal to him alone, a highly introspective process, shall we say?"

"Each judge makes his decisions based on his own understanding of the facts and the law involved," Lengel explained with the impatient air of a professor lecturing a backward student.

"So that any time one wanted to discover *why* a decision was made in a particular way one would have to ask the judge who made it. For he would be the only one who would know his mental process at the time. Is that correct?" Ben asked.

"Counselor, as you well know, there are times when a judge hands down a written opinion in which he specifically states the reasoning behind his decision," Lengel said.

"Yes, sir, and you have a reputation for writing many excellent decisions," Ben concurred, but then he added, "In the case of People versus Cletus Johnson, did you hand down a written decision?"

"There was no reason to, since it was on the whole a rather simple case," Lengel replied.

"Therefore, the only record of the mental processes involved in your making that decision would be contained in your own memory, am I right?"

Instead of replying, Lengel reared up in the witness box, looked beyond Ben and addressed the bench. "Judge Klein! If it is counsel's intention to ask me to justify my decision in a past case, I will not submit to it! I absolutely will not!"

Ben Gordon could feel Klein's hostile glare as if it were a hot sun burning a hole in the back of his head, but he refused to face him.

"Counselor!" Klein called sharply.

Slowly, Ben turned. "Yes, Your Honor?"

"Is it your intention to ask Judge Lengel to justify his decisions in the Johnson case?"

"No, sir," Ben replied, most innocently. "Not justify. Merely explain. After all, this jury has witnessed a confession in which two of Judge Lengel's decisions played an important part in the action for which my client is now on trial. I only ask Judge Lengel to explain to the jury what happened and why. Because I am sure if you polled the jury . . . which I am willing to do right now . . . you would discover that they are as confused as Dennis Riordan was when all charges against Cletus Johnson were dropped without even a trial. Since judicial decisions are, as Judge Lengel himself has just admitted, completely subjective and highly individual, and since there was never any written opinion in that case, I am sure he is the only person able to explain to the jury precisely how those decisions were arrived at."

Sensitive to the reaction in the press section, where diligent and continuous note-taking had gone on ever since Judge Lengel had assumed the stand, Klein considered carefully before ruling. "Mr. Gordon, insofar as your questions are confined solely to eliciting information for the benefit of the jury I will allow them. But when they cross the line and become argumentative, or ask for responses that demand that Judge Lengel justify his decision, I will rule them out. Clear?"

"Very clear, Your Honor," Ben said. As he turned from the bench to the witness, he caught a glimpse of Arlene, who was leaning forward, her face more intense than pretty now. For his own sake, as well as Riordan's, she wanted him to succeed.

"Judge Lengel," Ben resumed, "since laymen are usually exposed to a courtroom only on television or in the movies, I trust you will be patient with me for several elementary questions to enlighten the jury. Is a judge's sole duty to preside over jury trials?"

"Of course not," Lengel replied. "There are trials without juries. There are motions argued before judges when trials are not necessary. And many cases are disposed of by judges without going to trial."

"Settled?" Ben asked. "Or plea bargained in criminal cases?"

"Exactly."

"Are there any other judicial proceedings which are not trials but are conducted in courtrooms?"

"Yes."

"Such as the kind of hearing Dennis Riordan referred to in his confession?"

"I am not aware of the contents of Mr. Riordan's confession," Lengel pointed out.

"He referred to a hearing in which evidence against Cletus Johnson was ruled out," Ben said.

"You mean a hearing to suppress evidence," Lengel volunteered.

"Exactly, sir. Would you explain to the jury precisely what such a hearing is?"

Lengel angled himself in the jury's direction and was startled to discover Violet Tolliver's familiar and striking face among them. "One of the most crucial decisions to be made in any criminal case is what evidence may legally be presented to the jury and what may not."

"Shouldn't all the evidence that's available be presented if the jury is to reach an informed and fair verdict?" Ben asked.

"That is a very simplistic approach to evidence," Lengel replied dogmatically.

"Your Honor, since the jury might not understand, could you give us some illustrations that would clarify that?"

Lengel studied Ben for a moment before giving expression to his impatience. "Counselor, I do not see why I have to instruct this jury as if they were a first-year class in law school." He looked at the bench.

"Your point, Counselor? The relevance?" Klein demanded.

"Your Honor, there are unexplained references in my client's confession. I cannot allow this case to go to the jury without their knowing fully what happened."

"Then get to the specific questions you want to ask!" Klein ordered, with a quick glance at the press section. More and more in recent years he had found himself considering the television reactions to his more newsworthy cases. He resented the intrusion, but he could not ignore it.

Ben resumed his questioning, his strategy not altered in the least.

"Judge Lengel, can you give the jury some examples of questions that are argued and decided in hearings to suppress evidence?"

With a sign of obvious annoyance, Lengel began. "Over the years, many cases have been decided by our Court of Appeals and by the United States Supreme Court that define what evidence is admissible in a criminal case. For example, under the Fifth Amendment to the Constitution, an accused cannot be forced to testify against himself. So, when a witness is questioned, he can refuse to answer on the ground that it might incriminate him. But there are other ways a person can incriminate himself. So the courts set certain limits as to how far you can compel a defendant's participation or cooperation."

"Such as?" Ben prodded.

"If, for purposes of identification, it is necessary to take the fingerprints of an accused, the judge will allow that. Or, let us say, it is obvious there was a struggle preceding a murder, and there are blood and strands of hair under the fingernails of the victim. It is considered proper to draw the accused's blood or use his hair for comparison purposes," Lengel explained.

"Now, sir, can you give the jury any instances of what an accused may *not* be asked to do, things that would be ruled out in a hearing to suppress evidence?" Ben asked.

"The basic rule is, nothing will be allowed that shocks the conscience of the court," Lengel declared, as if dictating an opinion.

"For the jury's sake, and since we already know that these things vary from case to case, could you give us some specific examples?"

"It is questionable in my mind that a judge is justified in asking the accused in a rape case to provide a sample of his semen. Or that a suspect at the time of his arrest be forced to regurgitate if he is suspected of having swallowed some drug," Lengel replied.

"And if he were made to do so, and that question were raised on a hearing to suppress, then the judge could rule that all evidence secured in that manner was not admissible at the trial?" Ben asked.

"Exactly!" Lengel agreed quickly, to close the issue.

But Ben continued, knowing what the judge's response would be but seeking to inform the jury of the latitude granted judges. "And these rules remain fixed and firm?"

"They are not fixed. They change with the times. For instance, we had a case in New York some years ago in which a suspect in the murder of a policeman had a bullet lodged in his leg. The State contended the bullet came from the policeman's gun before he was killed. If that could be established, the suspect would be identified as the man who had engaged in the gun duel with the policeman and was the killer."

"And how did the court hold in that case?" Ben asked.

"The judge ruled that the suspect could not be forced to undergo complicated and possibly life-threatening surgery to produce the bullet. That would constitute forcing him to testify against himself and would violate his Fifth Amendment right not to incriminate himself."

"And so it was ruled out?" Ben asked.

"Yes. But in a later case, where surgery was superficial, another judge did order an operation to produce a bullet," Lengel stated.

Now Ben changed both the substance and the tenor of his questions as he embarked on the most crucial phase of his strategy. "Your Honor, based on what we heard in the defendant's confession, are we correct in assuming you presided over such a hearing in the case of People versus Cletus Johnson?"

"I presided over that case. And, in the normal course of my duties, conducted a hearing. Yes!" Lengel replied crisply.

"Tell us, if you will, which of the questions you have just outlined arose in that case?" Ben asked.

"In that particular case, none of those questions arose."

"Then I'm confused," Ben said. "Why the need for a hearing?"

Though tempted to reply with the anger and impatience he ofttimes exhibited in his own courtroom, Lengel maintained an attitude of judicial calm. "Those are not the only questions that come before a judge during such a hearing."

"What other kind of questions are there, Your Honor?" Ben pretended innocent puzzlement.

"Questions as to the admissibility of evidence based on other grounds."

"Such as?" Ben prodded.

"Whether the police came into possession of evidence in a lawful manner. The conditions under which a suspect made his confession. Was he coerced? Did he know his rights? Was he offered an attorney? If he had one, was he present? Questions such as those."

"And in People versus Cletus Johnson, what specific questions arose? Or shall I refresh your recollection?"

"I have no need to have my recollection refreshed!" Lengel protested. "I am well aware of the case and its consequences."

"Then will you enlighten the jury?"

Since Klein could detect the signs of an incipient outburst of anger in Lengel's attitude, he intruded to say, "Counselor, this is obviously going to take longer than anyone anticipated, and since it is already close to four o'clock, I suggest we adjourn at this time!" To preclude any protest from Ben, he banged his gavel. Then he ordered, "Judge Lengel, Mr. Gordon and Mr. Crewe, we will adjourn to the robing room!"

As the men retired, Arlene listened alertly to catch fragments of conversation from the newspaper and television reporters around her.

The man directly behind her, whom she had seen many times on the nightly news, said, "This morning I thought Gordon was on to something really hot. But all this legal jazz, how do I cover it in a minute and fifteen seconds? Which is all my producer will give me on camera. I think Crewe's right. Gordon doesn't have much of a case and he's trying to cover it up with this stunt."

A woman reporter from the *Daily News* agreed. "Unless Gordon gets with it, I have a hunch Klein is going to throw him out of court. Either way, I don't think he's fooling the jury."

Inside the robing room, Klein lit up his usual fat and odorous cigar. While he was doing so, Lengel demanded,

"Aaron, how long are you going to allow this to go on? Where is judicial propriety? I'm being humiliated for no good reason." He turned to glare at Ben.

"Your Honor," Ben replied, "I don't see how explaining confusing matters to a jury can be termed humiliating. It's not much different from what you do when you charge a jury."

"There is a vast difference and you know it!" Lengel shot back. "When I charge a jury I am explaining the law to them, explaining their duties and limits to them. I am not called on to discuss my own actions." He turned to Klein. "This arrogant young bastard is doing exactly what you warned him not to do. I will not be put in the position of justifying my decisions!"

Ben replied, "Your Honor, I am merely going to ask Judge Lengel to explain what went on in the suppression hearing in People versus Johnson. Anything he cares to add is entirely of his own volition."

"Did you hear that?" Lengel demanded. "Do something, Aaron!"

"We will reconvene at ten o'clock tomorrow," Judge Klein decided, then turned to Ben Gordon. "And if this goes any longer than lunchtime, I will hold that the defense is merely stalling and I will rule out further testimony and excuse the witness."

19

"I'M AFRAID YOU DIDN'T make many friends in the press this afternoon with all those legal technicalities," Arlene commented gingerly as she served Ben his late dinner.

"From now on I'm not interested in the press!" Ben exploded. "They were useful in forcing Klein's hand. But starting tomorrow morning, I am only interested in twelve people in that jury box."

He pushed back his plate of broiled squab in Chinese seasoning salt, another exotic "Sixty-Minute Gourmet" specialty from *The New York Times*.

"Sorry, I can't eat. Not tonight."

He went into the living room to stare across at Manhattan, where, depending on what he did tomorrow, the fate of Dennis Riordan would eventually be decided.

It was the first time in his brief career that he felt responsible for the life of another human being. In his relatively few previous cases, his client's freedom had been at stake for a comparatively brief time. His obligation to Dennis Riordan was far more important, and far more personal.

He settled down in the chair that allowed him a view of the entire harbor. He took up his pad and started to frame his questions for tomorrow's session. They would have to be carefully drawn, in such manner as to evoke a

215

minimum of resistance from Lengel and the fewest adverse rulings from Judge Klein. And he must keep within the guidelines set down this afternoon, ask only those questions that would elicit information to enlighten the jury. As to the time limitation imposed by Judge Klein, it had been rash of Ben to let that pass without protest. But he would have agreed to anything to assure him his chance at Lengel.

Therefore, framing each question now demanded the same precision as microsurgery. He became aware of Arlene standing in the doorway. Without looking up, he asked impatiently, "Yes, darling?"

"Shall I keep your dinner warm?"

Sensitive to her concern, he laid aside his pad. "I didn't realize how hungry I was. I'll eat now."

He stopped in the doorway, kissed her, patted her on the bottom and promised, "This case won't last forever. Bear with me. Please?"

She kissed him on the lips, a long kiss. Then she released him.

He ate quickly, without genuine appreciation of the dish she had prepared to tempt him. She realized, *He isn't hungry, he's doing this to please me.*

"You don't have to," she said softly.

"I love it. It's great. If my mother cooked this well I never would have left home." He tried to joke but didn't succeed. He put down his fork. "You're right. I'm forcing it."

"You'd rather work."

"I'd rather you weren't so understanding. I'd rather you would just explode, blow off steam. Maybe even cry. At least accuse, 'For God's sake, talk to me! Pay attention to me! A week from now this case'll be gone but I'll still be here!'"

"I don't feel that way," she said.

"I wish you would. Because your long-suffering silences, your concern, your understanding are worse than any accusation you could make!"

She continued to remain silent.

"I'm an idiot!" he finally confessed. "Angry with myself, fearful of failing tomorrow. I have to lash out at someone. You're close, so I let you have it. The one person on earth who loves me, who doesn't ask anything of me."

"You knew it was a tough case when you took it on," she reminded him.

He reached for her hand and drew her close. "Remember when you warned me about becoming too emotionally involved in the case? Today he said to me, 'Look, kid'—that's what he calls me, except when he remembers and calls me 'Counselor.'—'Look, kid, why are you getting the judge mad at you because of me? If you get a reputation for being a troublemaker, all the other judges will take it out on you.'

"His life is on the line and he's worried about my reputation. When he said that, I realized that's exactly the kind of advice my father would have given me. That attitude which says, 'Son, let me bear the brunt of it to make it easier for you, safer for you.'

"He's like my dad in other ways, too. That same belief in the system. That same indignation and need to set it right when it fails. My dad was a married man during World War Two. He didn't have to serve. But he volunteered. Not because of what was happening to Jews in Germany. But because he believed in this country, in freedom. In his simple way, my dad had ideals. Just as Riordan has ideals. He's not a profound thinker. He can't even articulate his feelings. But he did what he did to let people know what's wrong, so it can be changed before it's too late. It was his way of saying, 'World, pay attention!

Your house is on fire!' I can't let him down. But I have this terrible feeling I might," Ben confessed.

The phone rang.

"If that's a reporter or a TV producer, I am not available for interviews!"

Arlene made a reassuring gesture. "I'll take care of it."

He went back to the living room to resume drafting his questions for Judge Lengel. Arlene was on the phone for a long time before she returned.

"I can't get her off the phone. She insists on talking to you."

"My mother?"

Arlene nodded.

"Tell her, given a choice, I would rather get married than go into that courtroom tomorrow."

"The trial is what she wants to talk to you about," Arlene said.

"What did she do, spend her afternoon in the law library?" Ben asked, irritated. He slammed his pad down on the couch and started for the phone in the bedroom.

"Hello, Ma, how are you?"

"Me?" she countered. *"I'm* fine!" thereby announcing her estimate of his condition.

"All right, Ma, what is it this time?"

His mother only replied, "Mr. Bienefeld."

"Who?"

"Mr. Bienefeld. I told you about him once. The man I met at the Golden Age Club. A widower."

Suddenly Ben became enthusiastic. *My God, she wants to remarry. Wonderful!* In his most anticipatory and pleasing manner, he asked, "Yes, Ma, what about Mr. Bienefeld?"

"He's a lawyer. That is, he used to be, until he retired."

"So?"

"He was watching the six o'clock news to-night . . ."

"And?" Ben asked, slowly beginning to become incensed.

"Well," his mother confessed, "since all the neighbors watch the TV news about your case, every night I serve a little coffee and cake and we discuss it."

"Really?" Ben asked angrily.

"Tonight, Mr. Bienefeld gave a long talk on what you're doing wrong and what he thinks you should do."

"Oh, did he?"

"He asked me to give you his phone number. In case you want to call and get his advice."

"Ma, tell me one thing. Before Mr. Bienefeld retired, what kind of law did he practice."

"He ran a collection agency," his mother said, then added defensively, "but he did very well. Well enough to retire and live nicely. He has a big car and he doesn't care how many miles he gets to the gallon."

"Well, you tell him to keep watching the six o'clock news and stay out of my case!" He slammed down the phone.

Arlene came into the doorway to ask, "Mr. Bienefeld?"

"Yeah!" Ben said. "Everybody who watches the six o'clock news is a legal expert!"

"Did I hear you shout at your mother?" Arlene asked. "You get right back on the phone and apologize!"

He reached for the phone, asking, "You get the feeling there may be something cooking between my mother and Mr. Bienefeld?"

"Could be."

"Maybe that's what she has in mind? A double wedding!" Ben laughed. "What do you say?"

"Nothing. Until this trial is over."

"You only go with winners. I know your type," he joked.

"I only go where I'm needed," she said, staring at him.

He did not attempt any more jokes but dialed his mother's number.

"Ma? Sorry I lost my temper. Tell Mr. Bienefeld I didn't have time to call him. But I look forward to meeting him soon. Okay?"

"Okay," his mother said. He could tell she had been weeping. He was glad now that Arlene had insisted he call back.

He hung up, kissed her on her pert nose and said, "You're a good kid, Arlene Robbins."

He kissed her again, then went back into the living room to resume planning his questions for tomorrow. Every question had to further his strategy, somehow to make twelve people in that jury box experience what Dennis Riordan had experienced, feel what he had felt, understand and empathize with what he had done. To Ben Gordon, Dennis Riordan was no longer simply one man, one client, one defendant. He was all people who felt frustrated and fearful in the face of a vast government which the greater it grew, was less and less able to guarantee its citizens that most basic right for which governments are created, the right to live in peace and safety.

If Dennis Riordan was willing to sacrifice the rest of his life to make that clear, Ben Gordon felt he could not do less than give himself completely to the cause. Nervous as he might be about tomorrow, about Judge Lengel's resistance and Judge Klein's punitive powers to silence him, Ben knew his strategy was right and his cause was important.

He took up his pad and pencil and began to write,

thoughtfully, meticulously choosing certain words, discarding others in order to frame each question so as to force Judge Michael Lengel to give him the answers he wanted.

20

LONG BEFORE JUDGE LENGEL arrived, the courtroom was crowded, some spectators insisting on the right to remain though they had no seats. The court attendant expelled them. The press corps had been reinforced by editorial writers as well as additional reporters. Newspaper and magazine editors along with television news producers had begun to appreciate the bold and innovative strategy Ben had embarked on once he succeeded in forcing Judge Lengel to take the stand.

When Ben arrived he discovered that Victor Coles had returned and had a seat on the first bench. The portly, pushy man had a way of maneuvering himself into preferred positions at all times. As Ben was setting out his questions for Judge Lengel, Coles strode past the barrier with such an air of belonging that the clerk made no attempt to stop him.

"Morning, Ben," Coles said, smiling.

"Not now, Mr. Coles, I'm busy," Ben said, trying to concentrate on his opening questions.

"Won't take but a moment. I wanted you to know that after the sensation you created by putting Judge Lengel on the stand, I sent up a few trial balloons. Called a few editors I know, at the bigger publishing houses."

"Look, I told you I wasn't interested. . . ."

"Ben, it doesn't do any harm to sample the market. I got two offers. Combined hard-cover–soft-cover deals."

Ben could not resist turning to look at Coles, who was beaming. "Now will you get Riordan to sign that paper?"

"I don't have it," Ben admitted.

"Where is it? Home?"

"I tore it up."

"You what?" Though he was angry, Coles continued to smile. "Look, I'll phone uptown, have my secretary draft a new one and have it down here by the lunch break!"

"Don't bother."

"Gordon, you can work your whole life as an attorney and not earn as much as I can get you for this deal!" Coles was no longer affable.

"Coles, this is not a piece of fiction or what you call a hot property. I'm dealing with a man's life. His freedom. His heart and soul. It is not for sale. Unless he chooses to sell it. It's his, not mine!"

"I like to deal with lawyers, not clients," said Coles. "Clients are too emotional. Lawyers are more practical. They can see the value of a story like this. The personal value."

Ben realized that he was asking him to put his own interests above those of his client, and he resented it.

"Don't you realize what this book can do for you, aside from the immediate money?" Coles persisted. "This is becoming one of the most promotable stories in years, thanks to your shrewd handling!"

"Coles, this is not the time . . ." Ben tried to terminate the conversation.

Coles studied him for a long, silent moment, then suddenly said. "I know! The William Morris Agency got to you! Right? I was first to approach you, but you didn't respect that. You have no sense of ethics."

"Nobody got to me! Now just let me get on with my case. If you persist, I'll have the clerk put you out!"

In a more conciliatory tone, Coles said, "I'll have another agreement drawn up. And I'll see you later."

The jury filed in. Ben knew that Judge Klein was ready. And Judge Lengel was ready. Ben turned to look out toward the spectators. Arlene was there, in what had become her customary seat, for the court attendant would let no one else occupy it.

She encouraged him with her smile, and he turned back to ready his questions as the clerk announced, "All rise!"

Klein entered and ascended the bench. He expressed his distaste for Ben's strategy with a look of total disapproval, intended to intimidate the young lawyer without leaving any trace in the trial record in the event of an appeal.

Judge Lengel resumed the stand, his attitude of disdain even more evident than it had been the day before.

Ben approached him respectfully. "Your Honor, when we recessed yesterday we were just getting to the questions involved in the case of People versus Cletus Johnson. Would you explain to the jury the specific questions in that case?"

"Counselor, as you well know, or should know, there are two kinds of evidence that a defense attorney can seek to suppress. There is physical evidence. The suppression of which is considered in a Mapp hearing . . ."

"A Mapp hearing, sir?" Ben asked. "Could you explain to the jury?"

Annoyed, Lengel turned to the jury to spell out "M-a-p-p. From the classic case of Mapp versus Ohio in which the Supreme Court of the United States declared that, like the federal courts, the state courts had to exclude all physical evidence that was illegally obtained." He turned back to Ben. "Young man, do you seriously intend to burden this jury with such legal detail?"

"Far from burdening them, I thought we were enlightening them," Ben replied.

"You are asking a jury of laymen to comprehend matters which law students have difficulty learning," Lengel protested.

"Your Honor, perhaps I have greater respect for the intelligence of laymen than you do. In any event, I'm afraid I must pursue this in my client's interest."

Judge Klein intervened. "Counselor, forget the noble speeches. Get on with the trial!"

"I'm doing my best, Your Honor," Ben said, turning back to his witness. "Judge Lengel, you were informing the jury about the case of Mapp versus Ohio and the exclusion of evidence in a criminal case in a state court."

Controlling his usual impatience, Lengel faced the jury. "You see, not every piece of evidence that comes into the hands of law-enforcement agencies can be admitted in a criminal case. Under the Fourth Amendment to the Constitution . . ." Lengel turned to Ben to ask, "Counselor, would you also like me to recite the Fourth Amendment for them?"

"Only if you happen to know it by heart," Ben responded, staring into the judge's eyes to let him know that he refused to be cowed or embarrassed into abandoning his line of attack.

Fully aware of Ben's resolve, Lengel turned back to the jury.

"There is no need to read you the Fourth Amendment. Let me say only that it protects a person from unreasonable search and seizure. If the police suspect you of having in your possession evidence that would involve you in a crime, they can't just break into your home and search. They need a warrant issued by a judge for reasonable cause. And if they don't have one, your rights have been violated and you could sue the police. But, more important, the Supreme Court long ago decided that when officers break the law, any evidence they find cannot be used against you during your trial. So when such a thing occurs, your attorney asks for a hearing to suppress all evidence which has been unlawfully obtained."

"Thank you, sir, for a very clear explanation," Ben said. "Now, will you relate that to what happened in the Johnson case when it came before you, sir?"

Lengel turned to the bench. "Your Honor, I thought we had an understanding as to justifying my decisions."

Before Klein could rule, Ben intruded. "Your Honor, I call the court's attention to the fact that I specifically asked the witness to enlighten the jury as to what *happened* in the Johnson case. I did not question the decision or ask that Judge Lengel justify it."

Unable to dispute Ben, Klein merely shrugged. Lengel had no choice but to reply.

"Johnson's attorney made a motion for a hearing to suppress both physical evidence and statements made by . . . Look, we are getting into an entirely different matter now. A Huntley hearing. This is becoming far too complicated. . . ."

"To make it as simple as possible for the jury to follow," Ben suggested, "may we confine ourselves to physical evidence for the moment?"

Secretly, Ben was delighted that Lengel had teased the jury's interest in questions yet to come. For he had his own fears about how to sustain their interest in the vital but more technical aspects of his strategy. To bring Lengel back to the subject, Ben reminded him, "Your Honor, you were saying that one part of the hearing in the Johnson case related to physical evidence."

"As I recall, it had to do with certain articles of jewelry

found on Johnson when he was searched after being taken into custody. A woman's watch. And a gold chain."

"With a cross attached?" Ben pinpointed.

"Yes."

"In other words, the same jewelry described by the defendant in his confession?"

"I am not familiar with the defendant's confession, so I can't answer that," Lengel declared.

"Of course. Sorry. I withdraw the question," Ben said, now that he had reminded the jury of Agnes Riordan's jewelry. "Sir, you said that Johnson's attorney moved to suppress that evidence. Yet, as far as we know, no one broke into Johnson's home without a search warrant. In fact, no one ever broke into his home at all."

"Counselor, you are deliberately trying to mislead the jury!" Lengel accused.

"I only asked, and I'm sure the jury is most curious by now, about the grounds on which Johnson's attorney moved to suppress Agnes Riordan's jewelry, which was found on Cletus Johnson after she was killed!" Ben demanded.

"Which will only require going into the manner in which Johnson was apprehended and searched!" Lengel protested, his irritation quite apparent now.

Ben paused, then in a voice that was soft but pointed and made everyone in the courtroom lean closer to hear him, he said, "Your Honor, we are dealing with a man's life. He is at least entitled to have all the evidence that pertains to his case heard by this jury before his fate is decided. The time for suppressing evidence is over. I demand an answer!"

Flushed in anger, Lengel made no further argument. Klein cleared his throat in a manner which forced Ben to turn to him. Klein beckoned. Ben started for the bench, joined by Lester Crewe.

In an angry whisper Klein warned, "Gordon, if you are jockeying for a plea bargain and this is your way of embarrassing this court, I can only offer you a plea if the District Attorney agrees." He glanced at Crewe to demand his cooperation in bringing this testimony to an end.

"I'll call the office," Lester Crewe said. "I'll talk to the Old Man."

"Don't bother!" Ben Gordon said. "We are not looking to make a deal. We intend to try this case to the bitter end!"

Klein and Crewe exchanged looks of surprised realization. For the first time they knew that Ben Gordon would not settle for anything less than the defense he had decided to pursue.

Judge Klein said, "Counselor, I think you have a moral obligation to confer with your client. After all, it's really his decision."

"My client wants to be tried for murder. He has told me that a number of times."

"I've noticed that when a case is on the verge of being submitted to the jury, defendants are no longer so brave. Talk to him again," Klein said with such emphasis that Ben was forced to concede.

He moved to the counsel table, shielded his face so the reporters could not read his lips. "Mr. Riordan, they are talking a possible lesser charge, and a shorter sentence. Provided I stop this examination. What do you say?"

"Kid, one year or twenty-five years is not going to matter to me. I want to know why the man who killed my Aggie was able to walk out of that courtroom a free man, without even a trial. So keep going. Put it to that arrogant bastard. I want to hear his answers!"

"Okay," Ben said.

Riordan reached out to grip Ben's bicep in a gesture

of support. Ben looked at the bench, shook his head firmly and returned to confront his witness.

"Sir, you were about to enlighten this jury as to the grounds on which Johnson's attorney asked that the evidence of that incriminating jewelry be suppressed. Would you continue?"

"It had to do with the manner of Johnson's arrest."

"In relation to the death of Agnes Riordan, when did that arrest take place?" Ben asked.

Lester Crewe shot to his feet. "Your Honor, we object to this line of questioning on several grounds. In the first place, the evidence in the Johnson case has already been ruled suppressed and that ruling was never challenged. In the second place . . ."

Ben intervened to protest. "Your Honor, that evidence was suppressed in the case of People versus Johnson because Judge Lengel felt Johnson's Fourth Amendment rights were being infringed. That is no longer true. Johnson is dead. His rights cannot be violated now. Therefore, there can be no further suppression of any evidence that relates to him!"

Klein was forced to nod, conceding that Ben's point was valid.

But Lester Crewe continued, "In addition, Your Honor, we are here to try the case of People versus Riordan. Under no conditions will we agree to retry the case of Cletus Johnson, which counsel obviously aimed to do from the start of this trial!"

"Your Honor," Ben replied, "if the manner in which the defendant formed his alleged intent to kill is not relevant to this trial, what is? We insist on continuing."

Judge Klein realized that Ben had very cleverly circumvented his two previous rulings preventing Cletus Johnson from becoming the main issue in this trial by adroitly introducing the same evidence in a different context, and for a different purpose. Though he was forced to admire Ben's shrewdness, he still felt a strong distaste for the grilling the young lawyer was giving Lengel. But since he could not immediately summon up any previous court decisions to counter Ben's argument, he felt compelled to overrule Lester Crewe's objection and permit Ben to continue. At the same time he scribbled a note to his niece, saying, "Find me some case, any case, in any jurisdiction, to close off this examination." He passed the note to the clerk, who left the courtroom at once.

"Continue, Counselor," Judge Klein ordered.

Ben turned back to Lengel. "Sir, you were about to tell us of the objection Johnson's attorney made to his arrest."

"As I recall the officer's testimony, Johnson was arrested an hour or so after the crime."

"That crime being the rape, robbery and murder of Agnes Riordan?" Ben prompted.

"Your Honor, must we have these interruptions?" Crewe beseeched the bench.

Ben turned on him. "I can play Mr. Riordan's confession again, if you'd rather!" When Crewe slipped back into his seat, Ben prodded, "Judge Lengel?"

"Yes," he conceded. "The crime was rape, robbery and murder. The officer's testimony as given at the suppression hearing was roughly as follows: He was in his squad car cruising along Mulberry Street when he spied a solitary black man walking down the street. Since that is a neighborhood inhabited almost exclusively by Italians, a solitary black man on that street at that late hour seemed to him to be suspicious."

"So he took him into custody?" Ben said.

"He stopped Johnson, questioned him and didn't like the evasive answers he was given. Also the fact that Johnson had scratches on his face. So he frisked him for weapons."

"Did he find any weapons?"

"He did not."

"Did he find any jewelry?" Ben pursued.

"The jewelry already mentioned. The watch and the gold chain and cross."

"Agnes Riordan's jewelry?"

"If you are fond of redundancy, yes!" Lengel replied sarcastically.

"At that time did the officer have any knowledge of the fact that only blocks away a girl had been raped, robbed and strangled to death?" Ben asked.

"He had heard such a report on his police radio," Lengel conceded.

"So that the officer had good reason to be concerned about any person he thought looked suspicious, and who was in an unaccustomed neighborhood," Ben concluded.

"No!" Judge Lengel disputed sharply. "And I'm surprised that as an attorney you don't know that!"

Ben did not respond, for he suspected that Lengel was about to aid his case, not hurt it.

"At the time of the arrest there was absolutely no clue as to the race of the murderer. So that the officer was not justified in concluding that because the lone man was black he was a logical suspect in the case."

"But the officer *was* aware of a murder in the vicinity," Ben reminded.

"Which in no way justified his stopping and searching the man just because he was black!" Lengel argued.

"And that was the ground on which Johnson's lawyer asked to suppress that jewelry as evidence?"

"He argued that stopping Cletus Johnson was an invasion of his Fourth Amendment rights, since there was no warrant issued, and no other immediate circumstances to justify his being stopped and searched."

"What sort of circumstances, sir?" Ben pursued.

"Well . . . uh . . . suppose a man were in the act of committing some other crime . . . or walking down the street carrying a weapon . . . or acting in a drunk and disorderly manner. Anything that would give an officer cause to believe that the law was being broken or about to be broken."

"But the fact that there had been a murder in the vicinity was not such a justification?" Ben asked.

"There was nothing in Johnson's behavior to justify connecting him with the murder!" Lengel argued.

Ben nodded thoughtfully before he framed his next question.

"Since, in your opinion, Johnson had been stopped and searched without legal justification, what happened to the evidence that was found on him?"

"Naturally I had to suppress all evidence that flowed from that arrest," Lengel said.

"Judge Lengel, is it true that at the time of the hearing the District Attorney also presented evidence that proved that hairs clutched in the hand of Agnes Riordan matched the hair of Cletus Johnson?"

"Yes, that is true," Lengel was forced to admit.

"Sir, you mentioned that the officer also found scratches on Johnson's face," Ben reminded him. "Is it true that at the time of the hearing it was proved that blood matching Johnson's blood was found under the nails of Agnes Riordan?"

"Yes, I believe so."

"*Believe*, Your Honor, or *know?*" Ben demanded. "Isn't it true that laboratory reports and hematologist's reports were quite definite and specific about that?"

"Yes," Lengel conceded.

Ben shifted his position so that he could study the jury to see what effect Lengel's testimony had on them up to this point. He could not tell. But from their intensity he knew he had at least commanded their concentration.

"Do you recall, sir, whether or not fingerprint analysis was presented to prove that the finger marks on Agnes Riordan's throat were those of Cletus Johnson?" Ben asked.

"Yes, I do recall," Lengel said. "Get on with it!"

But Ben could not allow himself to be hurried if his strategy was to succeed. So he pretended to search his pad for his next question, though he knew precisely what it was to be.

"Would you tell the jury if any other physical evidence was presented at the time of that hearing to suppress evidence?"

"I don't recall," Lengel said. "It's been many months. And I preside over a great many cases."

"Then may I refresh your recollection?" Ben continued. "Specimens of semen taken from the body of Agnes Riordan were matched with specimens found on the trousers of Cletus Johnson and proved to be the same. Do you recall that evidence being presented?"

"I do now. Yes," Lengel said.

"Sir, at the time of your ruling, did you know that there was in your courtroom a witness who could identify the jewelry found on Johnson as Agnes Riordan's jewelry?"

"Yes. Her father, who had made the original identification, was there," Lengel admitted, then added, "if you would not waste time on the details, we could get to the real issue involved!"

"Details, Your Honor?" Ben shot back. "By what means are crimes proved except by details? Blood matches! Semen matches! Fingerprints! Evidence connecting the accused with the victim!"

Klein banged his gavel and rebuked Ben. "Counselor,

you have a right to question the witness. But not to argue with him, badger him or hold debates! Confine yourself to proper questions or let the witness go!"

"Sorry, Your Honor, I beg the indulgence of the court since these are highly emotional issues for me." He turned to face Lengel and the jury. "Oh, yes, Mr. Riordan was in your courtroom at the time of the hearing waiting to testify about his daughter's jewelry, but your ruling prevented him from doing so. Am I right?"

"The *law* prevented him from testifying!" Lengel corrected. "Once Johnson was stopped and searched without proper provocation, all evidence found on him had to be ruled out. Suppressed. That is the law, young man. And you damn well know it!"

Lengel rose up in the witness box and addressed Klein directly. "Your Honor, we agreed that during this examination, which I believe to be highly irregular, I would not be called upon to justify my decision in the Johnson case!"

Lengel's outburst sent many of the reporters scurrying for the door, but Judge Klein froze them in place with a sharp rap of his gavel.

"We will not have people disturbing this court. Those of you who are on your feet will return to your seats at once!"

When quiet had been restored, Klein said, "Counsel will come to the bench!"

While Ben and Lester and the stenographer converged on the corner of the bench farthest from the jury, Lengel, still standing in the witness box, looked on.

Klein whispered angrily, "Gordon, how long do you intend to go on this way?"

"Until I've covered what took place in that hearing to suppress evidence," Ben replied.

"I think you've done that," Klein suggested strongly.

"There are still some questions I have to ask."

"How many?"

"Some."

"Relating to what?" Klein insisted.

"Relating to matters referred to in Mr. Riordan's confession," Ben said, for it was the only ground on which he could justify Lengel's testimony.

At that moment the court clerk came through the door behind the bench. He handed Klein a note.

> I find no cases on a judge being forced to testify under circumstances similar to these. Nor does any law clerk in the building. Do whatever you have to do to shut up Gordon and I'll invent some ground on which to justify it later. However, I still think Gordon is cute.
>
> Your loving niece, Esther.

Klein crumpled the note and said, "Gordon, I've given you a great deal of latitude and you've abused it. Confine yourself to pertinent questions, not arguments. On that basis I will allow you to continue. But at the first sign of badgering the witness, or trying to force him to justify his decision, I will rule out all further questions and excuse him!"

"Sir, if I may point out for the record, I only asked Judge Lengel questions concerning a hearing to which he was a witness. If he felt called on to explain, I can't be held responsible for that," Ben said respectfully.

Klein glared at him and would have responded angrily, but the presence of the stenographer inhibited him.

"Continue, but within reasonable limits," Klein finally said.

As Ben turned back to the witness, Judge Klein felt compelled to remind the jury, "These meetings at the bench have nothing to do with your duty as jurors. They are legal questions which judges and lawyers settle among themselves. You are concerned only with the facts."

Ben took up his place again, facing Lengel and the jury.

"Sir, I believe when questioning was interrupted, I had asked you why Dennis Riordan was prevented from identifying his daughter's jewelry. And you replied that the Fourth Amendment to the Constitution forbids such testimony. Is that correct, sir?"

"Yes!" Lengel replied, in a mixture of resentment and impatience.

"Now, sir, without in any way feeling required to justify your decision, can you tell us what went through your mind at the time?"

"I don't understand," Lengel replied, truly puzzled.

"Appearing before you was a man who by blood and semen tests, fingerprints and possession of stolen goods, was linked to the rape and murder of a young woman. Yet you felt it your duty to suppress all that evidence. How did you arrive at that conclusion?" Ben asked.

Klein intervened, "The question is improper. The witness need not answer.

Slowly Ben executed a turn that encompassed the entire courtroom until he finally faced the bench.

"Your Honor, once any witness has testified to his actions, an attorney has the right to inquire into his state of mind at the time. Or are the thoughts and mental processes of judges destined to remain a mystery to the public forever?"

"Counselor, I've already warned you not to try to force the judge to justify his decisions!" Klein shouted, his face red, his lips twitching.

Very softly Ben replied, "Your Honor, I've already reconciled myself to the fact that the decisions of judges are sometimes unjustifiable."

"Counselor!" Klein exploded. "I hereby hold you in contempt of this court. We will proceed to a punishment hearing as soon as this trial is over."

Immediately, Klein regretted his precipitous action. He beckoned Ben to the bench.

"Okay, you shrewd sonofabitch, you trapped me into committing reversible error by holding you in contempt in the presence of the jury. Now, let's sum up, go to the jury and get this over with!"

"Sorry, Your Honor, I insist that I be allowed to continue with Judge Lengel."

"Listen to me, young man. And believe me, your uncle Harry couldn't have given you better advice. If you humiliate Judge Lengel today, you'll pay for it every time you enter a courtroom in this city. We judges have our pride and we have long, long memories. Think about that. Now you have a chance to get a reversal on appeal and a new trial. Which is far more than I ever thought you'd get. Be satisfied. Excuse Lengel, sum up and let's give this case to the jury!"

A reversal, a new trial, Ben considered, he might have gladly settled for that once, but not now, not when he had succeeded in taking command of this trial and had the opportunity to do for Dennis Riordan what that simple but determined man deserved.

As for Judge Klein's need to invoke his uncle Harry, he was only confessing his own inability to silence Ben. Well, Ben decided, Uncle Harry might have taken the easier course of discretion. But Ben Gordon was no longer Harry's nephew. He was a bright, capable, innovative young lawyer on his own, not beholden to Uncle Harry or anyone. He was breaking new ground with this case, and he had not come this far only to compromise now.

"Your Honor," he said, "I insist on continuing with this witness!"

21

BEN RETURNED TO THE counsel table to pick up not only the questions he had prepared but also his notes on the cases he had read in preparation for his defense. As he arranged his papers, Riordan seized him by the arm.

"He's giving you a hard time, isn't he, kid? Well, don't get those judges mad at you because of me."

"Okay, Pop," Ben said, smiling.

"What does that mean?" Riordan asked.

"Unless you've got something better to do, stick around. We're in the ninth inning now."

As he shuffled his papers into the order in which he intended to use them, he glanced out at the courtroom. All the reporters' eyes were fixed on him, awaiting his next move. He saw Arlene in her customary place, leaning forward intently, urging him on, as if she knew what had transpired at the bench and she concurred in his resolve. He was ready to resume with the witness.

"Judge Lengel, when questioning was interrupted, I was inquiring into your state of mind at the time you threw out all the physical evidence in the Johnson case."

"Not threw out," Lengel corrected in his most severe judicial attitude. " 'Suppressed' is the proper term."

"Whatever the proper term, Your Honor, the fact is that before you was a man who by blood and semen tests, fingerprints and possession of stolen goods, was linked to a rape, robbery and murder, and you suppressed all that evidence and let him go."

"Once he had been illegally apprehended, no evidence found on him was admissible. As you well know."

"Which, sir, leads me to my next question. Let us suppose that instead of the officer stopping Cletus Johnson because he was a black man in an all-white neighborhood, he had found Johnson urinating against a corner lamppost on Mulberry Street. Would that have been sufficient ground on which to stop him, question him and search him?"

Lengel refrained from answering, glaring at Ben, who persisted, slowly and emphatically, "Your Honor, would that have been sufficient ground to stop Johnson?"

Finally, Lengel admitted, "Yes."

"And then all the evidence found on Johnson would have been admissible?"

"Yes," Lengel was forced to agree.

"How fortunate for Mr. Johnson that he had no urge to urinate at the time, but was only walking away from the rape, robbery and murder he had committed."

From the bench, Klein reprimanded him. "Counselor. The proper place for comments is in summation."

"Sorry, Your Honor," Ben said, but kept his eyes fixed on the jury as he asked Judge Lengel, "and, Your Honor, that is the law as interpreted by the Supreme Court of the United States?"

"For good reason!" Lengel shot back. "It is the only way to make sure that law officers obey the law!"

"I shall remember that every time I have the urge to urinate," Ben said.

"Counselor!" Klein started to warn, but before he would allow himself to be provoked into another judicial indiscretion, he ordered, "Remove the jury!" Once they had been sent out, he commanded, "Counselor! Stand before the bench!"

Ben took up his position, his back to the courtroom, facing Klein.

"Counselor, ordinarily I forgo punishment for contempt until a trial is over. But in this case, since you seem bent on continuing to evidence your contempt, I fine you two hundred dollars for your previous contempt. And now I find you in contempt for the last gratuitous remark you made, and fine you another two hundred dollars."

There was a visible reaction of protest from the press and the spectators.

Nevertheless, Klein continued, "Let that be a guide to your conduct during the remainder of this trial." He banged his gavel, turned to the clerk. "Return the jury."

Ben resumed his vantage point from which to address the witness while studying the jury's reactions.

"Judge Lengel, you have given us a clear and lucid explanation of what is called a Mapp hearing concerning the exclusion of physical evidence and, if I can gauge the jury's reaction, they suffered no serious aftereffects. Now, Your Honor, in your previous testimony you mentioned something called a Huntley hearing. Would you explain that to the jury?"

"It is a hearing to determine whether statements or confessions made by an accused are admissible into evidence at his trial."

For the benefit of the jury, Ben asked, "Statements being in a different category from physical evidence?"

"Of course!" Lengel said impatiently. "The Fourth Amendment protects a person from illegal search and seizure of physical evidence. But statements, admissions and confessions are protected by the Fifth Amendment."

"Which protects a person from what, sir?"

"The right of an accused not to testify against himself."

Lengel turned to the jury. "You've heard the expression, 'He took the Fifth,' meaning he refused to answer a question because it might incriminate him." Lengel turned back to Ben, challenging. "And now you can get to the question you've been trying to get to, young man!"

"Judge Lengel, I have here a typed record of the interview conducted in the police station on the night that Cletus Johnson was apprehended. Would you examine it and see if it is a copy of the same transcript that was presented to you during the suppression hearing?"

Lengel scanned the document and handed it back as Ben asked, "Judge Lengel, based on the questions and answers contained in this transcript, would you say that before making his confession Cletus Johnson had been apprised of his right to remain silent?"

"Yes. But that's not . . ."

Ben interrupted. "Please answer the question yes or no."

"There is an explanation required here. . . ."

Ben interrupted a second time by turning to the bench. "Your Honor, the witness was asked a question requiring a simple yes or no. Please instruct him to answer."

Since Ben's point was correct, Klein was forced to rule, "The witness will answer the question."

Lengel exhaled impatiently before conceding, "Yes. Johnson had been apprised of his right to remain silent."

Ben pursued. "Had he been warned of his right to have an attorney?"

"Yes," Lengel replied with impatient intolerance.

"Was he also apprised of the fact that any statement he made could be held against him?" When Lengel did not answer at once, Ben proffered the transcript. "Would you care to refresh your recollection, sir?"

"He was apprised of the fact that his statement could be held against him," Lengel finally conceded.

"Then, would you say that Johnson had been given all the Miranda warnings as prescribed by the Supreme Court of the United States?"

"Yes!"

"Now, sir, I show you another transcript, which I shall ask to have received in evidence for the further perusal by the jury if they so desire," Ben said.

He presented to Judge Klein a slim sheaf of papers. Lester Crewe came to the bench at once. Once Klein had scanned the document, he handed it to Crewe. Lester Crewe took one glance at it and said, "The People object to the admission of this document."

"On what ground?" Ben asked.

"It has not been properly authenticated," Crewe said, but Ben knew why Lester really objected so strongly.

"I can call in Detective Bridger and have him authenticate it," Ben threatened. "You know as well as I do how he must feel about the Johnson case slipping through his fingers."

Finally Lester relented. "We have no objection, Your Honor."

The document was marked in evidence, handed back to Ben and he presented it to Judge Lengel.

"Your Honor, will you inform the jury as to the nature of the document you now hold?" Ben asked.

"It purports to be . . ."

"Purports?" Ben challenged.

"It is," Lengel amended, "a copy of the confession made by Cletus Johnson admitting the robbery, rape and murder of Agnes Riordan."

"And is it the same confession Cletus Johnson made after he had been read his Miranda rights?"

"It is."

"Is it the same confession presented when you presided at the suppression hearing in People versus Cletus Johnson?" Ben asked.

"It is."

"Yet despite your statement that Johnson's Miranda rights were strictly observed, you ruled out this confession?"

"For very valid legal reasons," Lengel protested.

"I'm sure the jury is curious to know why."

Lengel looked at the bench, looked at Ben, then turned to the jury.

"Ladies and gentlemen, contrary to the false impression counsel is trying to give, it was not a capricious whim on my part. True, the warnings given Cletus Johnson conformed with the rule in the Miranda case. However, that alone did not satisfy the requirements laid down by the Court of Appeals of New York."

"In such cases as . . . ?" Ben asked, fingering his own copy of the decision.

"People versus Rogers."

"Please explain to the jury what the court held in that case."

"Counselor, it is a complicated legal point and I do not think the jury will be able to follow it," Lengel said.

"I'm willing to take that risk," Ben countered.

Having no alternative, Judge Lengel began, "I shall have to state the facts in People versus Rogers. The defendant, Rogers, while out on bail for one crime, was arrested for a second crime. While in custody, Rogers made a remark that directly implicated him in that second crime. At his trial the detective who overheard the remark was called on to testify. Rogers was convicted. But, on appeal, that detective's testimony was thrown out."

"Sir, had Rogers been advised of his Miranda rights?"

"Yes."

"Then on what possible ground could his admission be thrown out?"

"As I said, he was out on bail for a previous crime," Lengel explained.

"How could that help him in the second crime?" Ben asked, pretending ingenuousness. "Common sense would say a man out on bail should be held to stricter accountability, not less."

"Whatever you think common sense dictates, it is the rule in New York, and has been ever since the Rogers case, that if a suspect has an attorney in a pending criminal case, he is considered represented by that attorney in all subsequent arrests providing the police are aware of the pending criminal case or have reasonable cause to assume the suspect is represented by counsel. So, Rogers having an attorney in his pending case, any statement he made not in the presence of that attorney was inadmissible."

"Do you mean, sir, that even if Rogers did not ask to have the attorney present, he should still have been there?"

"So the Court of Appeals held."

"Meaning that, even if Rogers did not retain the attorney for the second offense, he was still to be considered his attorney in that second case?"

"The court held that an attorney would not forsake or desert a client who had gotten himself into further difficulty," Lengel declared.

"So the absence of an attorney the defendant did *not* ask for, who had *not* been retained, and who had *no* connection with the case under consideration, was the reason the court threw out the incriminating statement? Sir, I hope you will pardon me if I take a moment to absorb that."

Ben paused, but only for an instant, before remarking,

"I can see now why you thought the jury might have difficulty understanding that. It does baffle the mind."

"Counselor," Klein warned. "Confine yourself to questions, not comments."

"Sir, what is the connection between the Rogers case and the Johnson confession? Why did you rule to suppress it?" Ben asked softly, anticipating the effect of the reply.

"At the time Cletus Johnson was apprehended for robbing, raping and killing Agnes Riordan, he was out on bail."

'Knowing what Lengel's response would be, Ben asked, "Sir, do you happen to know the charge on which Cletus Johnson was out on bail at the time?"

"Yes," Lengel admitted.

"What was that charge, sir?" Ben asked.

"Rape."

As Ben expected, the outburst among the spectators and the press was instantaneous, loud and prolonged. Judge Klein had to gavel them quiet for fully two minutes before order could be restored.

"Any further such outbursts," he warned, "and I will have to clear this courtroom!" He turned to Ben. "Continue."

"Judge Lengel, you have just told us that Cletus Johnson was out on bail in another rape case at the time he raped and murdered Agnes Riordan. And that fact stood him in good stead at the hearing to suppress his confession. Can you explain to the jury why?"

Restraining his anger, Lengel replied, "Since a homicide was involved, the police who arrested Johnson didn't wait to get a BCI on him. They phoned downtown and discovered he was out on bail. At that moment, the police had reason to believe Johnson had an attorney. They had no legal right to take his confession without his attorney being present. Under the rule in the Rogers case, Johnson's confession was clearly inadmissible. It had to be thrown out."

"Are you telling this jury that if Johnson had had no previous arrest, was not out on bail, did not have an attorney, then that same confession would have been admissible?"

"Yes," Lengel was forced to agree.

"Then, sir, does it seem that the law is loaded in favor of habitual criminals?" Ben asked.

"Object!" Lester Crewe called out.

"Sustained!" Klein said.

"One more question," Ben said. "Judge Lengel, with all the evidence you had before you in the Johnson hearing, did you have any doubt in your own mind that he was guilty of the rape, robbery and murder of Agnes Riordan?"

"Object!" Lester Crewe shouted, rising to his feet. "Cletus Johnson is not on trial here. Therefore the question is completely irrelevant."

"Mr. Crewe's point is well taken. The question is irrelevant. The objection is sustained," Klein ruled firmly.

"But, Your Honor . . ." Ben tried to protest.

"Sustained," Klein ruled once more. However, the commotion created in the courtroom would not quiet down despite Klein's effort to gavel them to silence. It continued until Judge Lengel rose up from the witness chair.

Furious that he had been forced into this position by the pursuit of this intense and shrewd young lawyer, and feeling compelled to justify himself and his rigid attitude toward the law, Lengel exploded at the press and the spectators, with all the fury of a principled and misunderstood man, "Damn it, I know how all of you regard judges and courts. I read the newspapers. I listen to the TV news. I hear complaints. 'Judges are too lenient,' 'Judges are too liberal,' 'Judges are social reformers, bleeding hearts'! I've heard it all. But what you forget, or probably don't even know, is that a judge's hands are tied.

"How do you think I felt in this Johnson case? The District Attorney presented a solid case. Blood. Semen. Fingerprints. Stolen articles. And I had to rule all that out because the officer had made a mistake by stopping him on the street. They presented Johnson's confession. And I had to throw that out under the rule in the Rogers case.

"Did I want to? No! But I had to. It was my sworn duty under the law as decided by the higher courts. So, go ahead, Counselor, ask your question now. Did I think Cletus Johnson was guilty? There was never any doubt in my mind. He was guilty as hell!"

At those words, Dennis Riordan leaped to his feet. "That's what I had to hear, in some courtroom, from some judge. I owed it to Aggie. I owed it to Nedda."

Though Judge Klein banged his gavel, he could not silence Riordan until the man finally slumped back in his chair, weeping. Throughout Ben kept his eyes fixed on the jury. As Ben had intended, they appeared as stunned and outraged as Dennis Riordan had been when that killer walked out of Lengel's courtroom a free man.

Ben turned to the bench. "Your Honor, I offer in evidence this transcript of the opinions in the Rogers case."

Both Klein and Lester Crewe were surprised by the odd statement.

"Counselor, I don't see the purpose," Klein said.

"A vital part of this witness's testimony revolved around this decision, I would like it to be part of the trial record."

"If the People have no objection." Klein sought Lester Crewe's reaction.

Since Lester could see no value in it, he conceded, "No objection, Your Honor."

The document received and marked, Ben turned back
to the witness.

"I thank you, sir, for your frank and forthright statement. No further questions. Mr. Crewe?"

Slowly Lester Crewe rose in his place at the counsel
table. Despite his vigorous and violent objections
throughout this trial, Ben Gordon had finally succeeded in
putting not only Cletus Johnson but the law itself on trial.
Lester Crewe now had to reconsider his own strategy. He
decided that the one thing Ben had not been able to do
was obscure the facts in this case. He would rely on that
in his summation. He could accomplish nothing by sub-
jecting Lengel to further cross-examination.

"No questions," the young black prosecutor said.

As Judge Lengel stepped down, Judge Klein asked,
"Mr. Gordon, do you have any further witnesses?"

"No witnesses, the defense rests."

"Mr. Crewe?" Judge Klein asked.

"No rebuttal witnesses, Your Honor," Crewe replied.

"In that case, both sides will be prepared to sum up to
the jury tomorrow." Klein rapped his gavel to bring the
session to a close.

Ben Gordon, his damp shirt sticking to his bare chest
and back, slumped down into his chair at the counsel
table. He felt Dennis Riordan's strong hand grip his arm.

"Thanks, kid," Riordan said. "That's all I ever
wanted."

Ben patted Riordan's hand but pointed out, "It's not
over. Tomorrow we sum up. Then it's in the hands of the
jury."

"I know. I'm prepared," Riordan said.

The clerk approached Ben. "Judge Klein would like to
see you in chambers, Mr. Gordon."

Ben's first reaction was that Klein had decided on additional punishment now that all testimony was done. But the clerk had the same message for Lester Crewe.

By the time the two attorneys presented themselves, Klein's chamber was already heavy with a cloud of cigar smoke. The judge was busy signing orders which had piled up during his day on the bench. His law clerk, the plump, less-than-comely Esther, took each order from under his hand as he signed it and presented the next one, all the while glancing in Ben's direction. If Ben had been less concerned with the judge's purpose, he would have been embarrassed at being sized up so obviously. As it was, he was still recovering from the intense strain of questioning Judge Lengel.

"Well, now," Klein said as he looked up at the two young men standing before him, "if you have any requests as to matters you wish me to include in my charge to the jury, state them now. Or if you want to submit them in writing, have them on my desk before ten tomorrow."

Lester Crewe said, "The People have no requests. The charge, as we see it, should confine itself to the indictment. Murder in the Second Degree. As for the rest, what a judge normally includes in a charge to the jury is satisfactory."

"Gordon?" Klein asked.

"Your Honor, I have only one request. That now the jury be given the right to consider a lesser charge, in addition to Murder Two."

"Such as?" Klein challenged.

"Manslaughter in the First Degree," Ben urged.

"Gordon, you had your chance to make a deal, but your client turned it down!" Klein exploded. "As to including such a lesser charge at this time, sorry. You've had days to present proof of extreme emotional disturbance. You couldn't produce a single witness. Even his foreman, who God knows was trying to help him, even he said Riordan was nice and calm when he asked for time off to buy the gun and days off to track the victim. Show me one witness. One!"

"What if I show you twelve?" Ben Gordon asked.

Klein knocked the ash off the end of his cigar before he asked suspiciously, "All right, Gordon, what's the gimmick?"

"No gimmick, Your Honor," Ben said. "But I saw the faces of those twelve jurors when they heard Judge Lengel say that he was forced to set free a man he knew to be guilty of robbery, rape and murder. I tell you, in that moment that jury knew how Dennis Riordan felt. You won't have to lecture them on extreme emotional disturbance. I ask, sir, that you include that alternative in your charge."

"Gordon, no one commiserates with Riordan more than I do. I'm sorry I have to sit on this case. But the law does not allow me to include manslaughter in my charge. Not based on the evidence. The charge remains Murder Two!"

22

DAWN. THE RISING SUN was lighting up the sky to the east and casting its rays across the bay toward the Jersey shore.

Ben Gordon had fallen asleep in a chair in the living room, the pad in his hand, his pen on the floor at his feet.

Arlene called to him softly, "Ben? Darling?"

He woke with a start. "H'mm? What?" Then he realized where he was and said, "I guess I drifted off."

"Coffee? I just brewed some."

"Yes. Please." He stretched to work out the stiffness that had set in. He still felt a severe and painful tension cramp in his left shoulder. He extended his arm, rotated it, hoping the pain would dissipate. In such moments he always devoutly promised himself a regimen of physical exercise. He would join a gym. He would take up running. He would do what one of the men in the D.A.'s office used to do, get off the elevator four stops below his own floor and run up the stairs. He would do all those things, once this trial was over.

Arlene brought him the over-large cup which she had once bought as a joke. It had DAD inscribed on it. And he had bought a corresponding one for her.

She sat on an antique gold and white footstool, her red robe gathered about her, tucked under her legs. She looked up at him, studying the black rings under his eyes.

We'll have to get away when this is over, she thought, *a weekend somewhere, maybe even a week, though I can't take that much time off, after my days at the trial.* She was curious about his notes for his summation. She dared not ask. If he wanted to talk, he would, or else she would have to wait until she heard him in court.

He picked up his notes, scanned them, flipping the pages and muttering, "I wish I had better handwriting. Can't read my own notes in places."

She made him a substantial breakfast. He could eat none of it. While he showered, she laid out his dark blue suit, one of the white button-down shirts she had bought for his birthday, and the red and blue striped tie that was his favorite. When he came out of the shower, his shiny black hair was still wet and neatly combed in place, but she knew that when it dried it would become unruly again.

He was dressing when he remembered. "My mother didn't call last night. I wonder why? You think she ran out of advice?"

"You're too hard on her," Arlene said.

"I know. Soon as this trial is over we'll take her out to dinner." He had mistied his tie and had to start over. "Damn it, once this trial is over, maybe I'll learn how to tie a tie again."

"I'll do it," she volunteered.

He surrendered himself to her. While she worked deftly, he said, "It seems every thought I have starts with 'Once this trial is over.' Like, once this trial is over I'll be nicer to you. Once this trial is over I'll enjoy all those lovely gourmet dishes you cook. And once this trial is over I'll make love to you again."

He embraced her, kissed her, then released her. He looked at himself in the mirror. His red and blue tie was neat, a nice plump knot, just the right size for his collar spread. That girl had a way with all things. As he looked in the mirror, he said, "I have to compliment you."

"I used to do that for my father, long ago," she recalled sadly.

"I meant a whole hour and you haven't asked me what I'm going to say in my summation."

"If you want to tell me, you will."

"If I start to tell you, I won't stop, and that means I'll use it all up before I get there."

"It's okay," she said and kissed him, touched his hand and remarked to herself how cold it felt, a good sign.

He was ready to leave.

She asked, "Do you want me to go with you, or would you rather go alone?"

"I'd like to walk. Alone. To get my thoughts in line. Do you mind?"

"Of course not." She did, but she did not want to be a burden to him now.

The concerned look in her eyes made him say, "If it will make you feel better, pack me a lunch, hand me my books, kiss me and send me off to school."

"Don't, Ben. Don't joke about my feelings."

"Sorry. It's the pressure."

He kissed her.

He had reached the Brooklyn Bridge and was walking almost as fast as the stream of bumper-to-bumper cars that were pushing their way into Manhattan, the usual morning tide.

He had decided on, and discarded, four different openings to his summation. Finally, he resolved, *I've thought about it enough, I've got it all stored up, I'll just let it come out.*

It was not Uncle Harry's method. Harry always used

to go into court with his summation outlined like a battle plan.

Sorry, Harry, Ben apologized, *I have to do this my way.* He walked on, trying to think of anything but the trial. He glanced at his wristwatch. He had better pick up his pace if he wanted to be there in time.

He had left the main corridor and entered the narrow hall that led to the courtroom door. There was a line of spectators extending from the door all along the corridor wall. Two uniformed court attendants kept the people orderly, one of them announcing, "The courtroom's full. No one can be admitted until someone comes out!"

The other attendant stopped Ben at the door. "Hold it, Bud!"

"I'm the attorney," Ben identified himself.

"Oh, sorry, Counselor. Go right in."

As Ben started through the door he saw the woman first in line.

"Mom? What are you doing here?" he asked, startled. Then he realized. "Is this why you didn't call last night?"

She smiled in the sheepish way she generally admitted guilt for little transgressions. "I figured if I called and asked, you'd say no. So I didn't call. I didn't ask. And you didn't say no."

"I'm sorry, they say there's no room."

But the attendant had overheard the conversation and volunteered, "Counselor, if the lady's your mother we can manage to squeeze her in. Be my guest, Mom!"

They entered the courtroom. One look and Ben could see that today there was even more press and TV representation than before, added sketch artists, several new feature writers. *Why not,* he thought, *this was the World Series, the Superbowl.* As if courtrooms existed solely to provide material for headlines and newscasts.

He spied Arlene in her accustomed place on the first bench. *And, wouldn't you know,* Ben realized, *Victor Coles alongside her.* Ben reached her and leaned over to whisper, "She's here."

"Who?" Arlene asked.

"Mom."

"Then be good," she said. "Be very good." She smiled, pressed his hand encouragingly to send him on his way into the pit of the courtroom.

Ben reached his counsel table. Lester Crewe was already at his place, his summation before him, neatly typed and waiting. Ben estimated two pages, three at the most. Evidently Lester was planning on a short summation. *Why not,* Ben thought, *my examination of Judge Zengel might have fulfilled Riordan's demands, but there were still the facts in the murder of Cletus Johnson. That's what the jury will be pondering in a few hours. And the facts were clear and undisputed.*

The door to the other side of the bench opened. The clerk led the jury in. Ben studied their faces. They all appeared grim with the knowledge of their impending responsibility as the trial drew to a close.

He had no way of knowing what had happened to them since their obvious outrage of yesterday.

Elihu Prouty had left the courtroom the previous day deeply disturbed. Did the law really set guilty men free like that? And Johnson was a black man. Shame! He thought of Abigail, his daughter, an assistant professor of English. Abby could have been Agnes Riordan or could be tomorrow.

He had stopped at his tailor shop to do the one emergency job he had promised a customer, to let out his tuxedo so he could wear it to his daughter's wedding. Then Prouty had closed up and gone home.

He had turned on the ball game while he made himself some supper. Tuna fish, the salvation of live-aloners. But he had not enough appetite to prepare it. He ate it out of the can while he stared at the television set without seeing the game. Finally, he turned it off.

In bed he had come to the root of his torment. However much sympathy he felt for Riordan based on what he had heard, he knew his duty was to vote the man guilty.

Violet Tolliver had struggled with a long memorandum that her tax attorneys had delivered that afternoon and on which they needed an immediate answer.

As she tried to eat the roast beef sandwich she had picked up on her way home, she scanned the memo. It involved a trip she had made to Paris, Geneva and St. Moritz. The IRS was willing to grant as legitimate deductions expenses directly attributed to the commercials she shot in St. Moritz. But they were claiming that the rest of the time, in Paris and Geneva, was vacation and not deductible as a business expense.

Ordinarily she would have been incensed and willing to fight the government, not only in a hearing but in tax court as well. Tonight, that seemed inconsequential compared with what would confront her tomorrow morning.

She wrote across the memo in her bold hand, *Pay the damn tax!* If that meant thousands of dollars in additional taxes, it was trivial compared to the life of a man like Dennis Riordan.

Walter Grove had also spent a restless night. In his mind he had replayed the evidence in the case as if editing a work of his own. The writer in him protested, *God if I could only rewrite the Riordan script! Let it build the way it built: the rape, the murder, the hearing, Johnson going free, even laughing. Then Riordan buys the gun*

*drives to Harlem, finds Johnson. But at the last moment
Riordan discovers that he can't commit murder. He just
drops the gun and turns away. Or he kills Johnson, goes
home, realizes what he did, goes to the priest to confess
and then kills himself. Or else . . . or else . . .*

Until Walter Grove realized that, in a selfish way, he
would have wanted Dennis Riordan to do anything but
what he did, which was to go on trial and have as one of
his jurors, Walter Grove.

Just as Dennis Riordan was now involved in a fate from
which he could not extricate himself, so was Walter
Grove. He did not relish the duty he would have to perform once the attorneys were done summing up. But
there was no avoiding that now.

Judge Aaron Klein entered the courtroom as the clerk
intoned, "All rise!" Klein's puffy cheeks were flushed, his
lips tightly set. He had taken a great deal of flak from his
wife last night.

All during dinner she had berated him. "Aaron, do you
know what they're saying? Especially that nice young TV
fellow on the five o'clock news, the one with the cute
smile and the curly blond hair, he said, and I can give it
to you verbatim, 'Today in the case of People versus Riordan, Judge Klein found the defendant's attorney guilty of
contempt of court. It was obvious the judge was using that
to intimidate Attorney Gordon, but the courageous young
lawyer refused to be intimidated.'

"That's what he said," Berenice continued. "How does
that look, picking on a young man like that? Personally,
he looks like a very nice young man. I wish my niece,
Esther, had the good luck to meet such a young man. But
that's beside the point. A judge is supposed to be impartial. And when you're not, it's doubly important to look

like you are. Tomorrow, be careful. Don't lose your temper!"

Klein had sighed, thinking, *Television will be the death of the judicial system yet*. His determination not to lose his temper showed very clearly in his attitude this morning as he entered the courtroom. He took his place on the bench and turned in the direction of the jury. "Ladies and gentlemen, we come now to the final stages of the legal process. The attorneys will make their summations, I will deliver my charge and you will take this case into your own hands. It is both the duty and the privilege of a citizen in a free society."

He turned to the counsel table. But before he could invite the first summation, he noticed that the defendant was not present.

"Mr. Gordon, is your client ill?"

"Not to my knowledge," Ben responded, rising.

"Then where is he?"

"I've been expecting he would be delivered here as usual."

The judge looked in the direction of the door to his left, which opened and a uniformed guard entered, approached the bench and whispered to Klein, who beckoned Gordon to approach. When Lester Crewe rose Klein motioned him back down.

"Counselor, your client wants to talk to you before he comes in."

"Of course," Ben agreed.

He found Dennis Riordan in the small holding pen where prisoners were kept before entry into the courtroom.

"Mr. Riordan?" Ben asked. "Something wrong?"

For the first time during the trial Riordan seemed grim. "I've been thinking about this all night. Couldn't sleep."

Oh, God, Ben thought, *don't tell me that now, when it's too late, he's decided to cooperate. With proper coaching, I could have put him on the stand. Maybe I still can, if the judge allows me to reopen my case.*

"Yes, Mr. Riordan? What is it?"

"When you make that speech of yours, that summation, say a few nice words, about Aggie, and about Nedda. It's the last time anyone'll ever have a chance to hear 'bout them."

"Okay, sure, Mr. Riordan," Ben promised.

"And, kid, don't make any big plea for me. Just tell them why I did it. Warn them, warn the people, warn the judges."

"I'll do that. Is that all?" Ben asked.

"That's all. Except don't blame yourself. You're a good lawyer. A very good lawyer. And, in time, you'll forget 'bout this case and you'll win some big ones. In fact, things about you remind me of Dennis Junior. You have that same conviction, that same determination."

Ben felt moved to ask, "Mr. Riordan, why didn't he come up for the trial?"

"I know Father Nelson told him. And Denny wrote me he wanted to come. But I wrote back and said, 'Stay with your people, son, where you can do some good.' You see, kid, Jesus says in the Gospel, 'He who loves father or mother more than me is not worthy of me ... and he that does not take up his cross and follow me is not worthy of me.' Well, my Denny has taken up his cross. He's got to stay with it. Whatever he can do for those poor people down there is more than he could have done for me."

"I understand," Ben said softly. "They're waiting in here."

"Sure," Dennis Riordan said, squeezed Ben's arm and preceded him into the courtroom.

23

THERE WAS A hush of great anticipation in the courtroom as Judge Aaron Klein looked down at Ben and asked, "Mr Gordon, are you ready?"

Ben gathered up a handful of yellow note pages and started toward the jury box. The grim, strained atmosphere that he had created yesterday during his cross-examination of Judge Lengel still prevailed. He could see it in the eyes of the jurors. He could feel it in the silence in this crowded room.

He glanced in Arlene's direction, saw, out of the corner of his eye, his mother hunched forward, her fingers pressed against her lips as if to stifle an outcry of support. He turned to the jury.

"Ladies and gentlemen of the jury, I want to thank you for your patience. If at times I have seemed difficult, even irreverent toward the bench, it is only because I feel that I am fighting in a good cause. I wish I had been able to give my client a better defense. Because he is a decent man, a good man.

"So one thing I would like to dispel at the outset. My client is not a racist. The man who introduced the question of race into this case was not my client, but Cletus Johnson. No one picked him. He picked Agnes Riordan.

"That young woman, a fine, decent young woman

hard-working, intelligent, with dreams and constructive ambitions, was on her way home from night school where, ironically, she was studying law. Without a word of warning, she was seized, dragged into the shadows, her clothes torn off. She was robbed, raped, and, when she struggled, she was strangled to death by strong hands.

"That they happened to be black hands was not her choice. That she happened to be white had nothing to do with it. Because the previous rape for which Cletus Johnson was out on bail when he attacked Agnes Riordan was that of a fifteen-year-old girl who is black!"

The jurors stared at Ben in shock and surprise. He allowed that fact to settle in their minds, then continued:

"So I ask you to banish from your minds any question of racial prejudice, or any prejudice you yourselves may harbor. You cannot expect any father, black or white, to accept the rape of a daughter without feeling anger, fury!

"But in this sad chain of events, rape was not the end. For after rape there was murder. And what had been an earnest, conscientious young law student at nine o'clock one night was, by nine o'clock the next morning, an unidentified body until they called Dennis Riordan to make the identification.

"You heard him in his confession relate how they showed him into a small room with a glass-covered opening. They raised a body into view for him to look at and say, 'Yes, this is my daughter, Agnes, my dear, dear Aggie.' Her hair was disheveled, and this father, torn by grief but remembering how neat his Aggie was in life, wanted to reach out and straighten her hair, but that glass was in the way. So all he could say was, 'Yes, this is my daughter.' And turn away.

"But there was more. Days and nights when he would sit and watch his wife Nedda cry. Trying to retrieve from an irreversible fate the daughter she loved so well, of whom she was so proud.

"How do you hang on after a shattering blow like that? How do you keep your sanity? You find ways. One was the police had caught the man who did it. And this time, different from some cases, there was no question. For Dennis Riordan himself had gone down to identify the jewelry they found on him. So, when his trial came up, Dennis would get on the stand, identify that jewelry and seal the fate of that killer!

"Revenge? Yes. That would be only natural. But one thing more important, Dennis Riordan would make sure that for the rest of Cletus Johnson's life, he would not be free to do to any other woman, young or old, black or white, what he had done to Aggie! That was important to Dennis Riordan. As a father, as a citizen, as a God-fearing man, who asked to see his priest before he saw a lawyer.

"That was what sustained Dennis and Nedda Riordan during the months after their tragedy. For the law is a slow process. But they were patient. They would wait and attend the trial. Dennis would testify. The police experts and Detective Bridger would testify. That was the way the system worked, wasn't it? In the movies. On television.

"But then Dennis and Nedda Riordan made a shocking discovery. The same discovery you twelve ladies and gentlemen made yesterday. That is *not* the way the law works. There was no trial of Cletus Johnson. There was only a hearing. And for what purpose? Judge Lengel, who presided at that hearing, told you yesterday. *A hearing to suppress evidence!*

"That phrase by itself is shocking. Evidence is the testimony, facts, tests, which taken together are the materials from which a jury extracts the truth to arrive at a verdict. Yet we hold hearings to suppress the very thing juries need to know to arrive at an honest and fair verdict. They might better call it by its rightful name, a hearing to suppress the truth!"

Ben paused, studied the faces of jurors as he let that phrase sink in. Then he continued.

"Yesterday, in that witness box, a judge, an intelligent man, a reasonable man, a man of principle, in full possession of his senses, testified to the righteousness of suppressing the truth. He mentioned the Fourth Amendment and the Fifth Amendment, all worthy guarantees of our rights.

"Yet all the while he was testifying, I kept thinking of blood tests, semen tests, fingerprint experts, jewelry, a confession, any one of which would have convicted Cletus Johnson, and all of which together made Judge Lengel say, 'Did I think Cletus Johnson was guilty? There was never any doubt in my mind. He was guilty as hell!'

"You recall that. You will never forget it! I know I won't. Because while he was testifying I was tormented by a strange bit of history I learned in school. Back in the Middle Ages, church philosophers used to argue with great seriousness, how many angels could stand on the head of a pin.

"How ridiculous that seems to us today. How superior we feel to those poor benighted philosophers. Yet today we are witnessing a similar spectacle. Judges sit on court benches, or meet in paneled conference rooms in the Supreme Court in Washington, or in our highest state courts, and argue how many protections and defenses for the accused can we invent? How can we protect a man who is obviously guilty from being found guilty, from going to jail?"

Judge Klein, whose face had been growing redder as his anger increased, interrupted. "Counselor, you are straying from proper summation."

"With all deference, Your Honor, I think that I am not.
And if you want to hold me in contempt again, get it over
with, because I have a lot more to say before I'm
through!"

"Counselor, for your sake, I will ask the stenographer
to strike that last outburst," Klein replied. "But I will not
sit by and listen to you degrade and demean the judicial
system of this state and this nation. Now you may proceed
but confine yourself to commenting on the evidence."

Ben turned back to the jury.

"Ladies and gentlemen, I will conform to His Honor's
ruling and confine my comments to the evidence you
heard during the course of this trial. You heard Judge
Lengel say that he was forced to let Cletus Johnson go free
because, mind you, *because* Johnson was out on bail for
another rape! In your presence Judge Lengel admitted
that if Johnson had not been out on bail for a previous
rape, his confession would have been admissible. By God,
what have we come to, when a man's criminal record is
his best defense?

"How many angels can stand on the head of a pin
seems a great deal more logical than what we are engaged
in now. We have reduced justice to a game. A game
played by arbitrary rules. No longer do judges ask, is the
accused guilty? But can you *prove* him guilty by these
very arbitrary rules? Guilt or innocence go out the window. Only the rules are sacred. Not the lives of innocent
people. To hell with the people! Save the rules!"

Ben paused only long enough to toss aside his notes
and, inflamed by his cause, he continued, leaning on the
railing that flanked the jury box to stare into the eyes of
the jurors.

"What is the result of these decisions to protect criminals' rights? They have turned loose guilty men like
Cletus Johnson to continue to rob, rape and murder!

Why? One reason they give us is this: We will force the police to adhere to the law by punishing them when they bring in faultily obtained physical evidence. How? You recall Judge Lengel testifying that he threw out all the evidence against Cletus Johnson because the officer stopped him without good cause. Remember, if Johnson had been urinating against a lamppost all that evidence would have been admitted. But what did Lengel do? Threw it out. Did he punish the officer? No. He punished *you*. He punished *me*. He turned loose on us, the public, a guilty murderer, and that was supposed to teach the officer a lesson.

"Ladies and gentlemen, that is madness. Because, except for the action of my client, who knows how many more women, white and black, would have been raped by Cletus Johnson? How many would have been murdered to teach the officer a lesson'? Yet that is the logic of our courts. Well, there has to be a better way to reprimand the police than turning killers loose to kill.

"But the logic behind throwing out Johnson's confession is far more tortured than that. Yesterday, in that witness chair, Judge Lengel referred to the Rogers case in which our highest court held that when a defendant has an attorney in a pending criminal case, he is deemed to have that same attorney for all subsequent arrests. That is a pure fiction, invented by the court. The fact that a man has an attorney for one case does not mean that he would select that same attorney for another case. The odds are if he still owed that attorney a good-sized fee he would most likely choose another one.

"Now, what is the effect of this far-fetched, judicially concocted fiction? It forced Judge Lengel to throw out Cletus Johnson's confession and turn him loose. Why? Because the attorney who got him out on bail for another rape was not present!

"Now, before you become totally disillusioned with al
judges, let me point out something Judge Lengel did no
tell you yesterday. Not all the judges in the Rogers case
agreed. There were two of the seven who dissented from
the Rogers decision. Judge Jasen and Judge Gabrielli
Now, I would like to read you a few words from Judge
Jasen's dissenting opinion. Speaking of the incriminating
statement in the Rogers case, Judge Jasen said:

> '. . . to prevent the officer from divulging incriminat-
> ing statements made to him by defendant Rogers
> would stretch the comprehension of the average citi-
> zen to the breaking point.'

Lester Crewe rose, saying at the same time, "You
Honor, we object!"

Ben turned to the bench swiftly. "Your Honor, the
Rogers opinions are a defense exhibit. Therefore, I an
merely commenting on the evidence, which I have every
right to do in summation."

Klein glanced at Lester Crewe. Both men realized
why Ben had offered the Rogers decisions in evidence. A
unfortunate blunder, Lester admitted to himself, he
should never have allowed it. But too late now. He sank
back down into his chair.

"Continue, Counselor," Klein said, but his tone wa
one of admonishment more than permission.

"Ladies and gentlemen, Judge Jasen's statement is
very significant one. So let me repeat, 'Would stretch th
comprehension of the average citizen to the breaking
point!'

"But he went beyond that. He said:

> 'Judges' decisions must appear to be rational, fair
> as well as practical, if the courts are to retain the
> respect of the people!'

"Ladies and gentlemen, that is not Ben Gordon speaking. That is a judge of the highest court of this state. I wonder, if Judge Jasen said that in this courtroom today, would he have been held guilty of contempt?"

"Counselor!" Judge Klein warned.

"Sorry, Your Honor." Then Ben resumed. "Judge Jasen concludes his opinion by quoting the words of another judge, Benjamin Cardozo, now long dead:

'Justice, though due to the accused, is due to the accuser also. The concept of fairness must not be strained till it is narrowed to a filament.'

"And that brings us now to Dennis Riordan. And to the events he lived through, from the night his innocent daughter was murdered until the day her guilty murderer walked out of that courtroom free. In that case, the concept of fairness was not only strained until it was narrowed to a filament, that filament was snapped. There was not even a filament of fairness left!

"And you know that. I saw it on your faces and in your eyes yesterday when Judge Lengel stood in that witness box and said, 'I knew Johnson was guilty as hell, but I had to let him go free.' Outrage. That's what you felt. Well, if you felt outrage yesterday, put yourself in Dennis Riordan's place. Think of how much greater outrage he must have felt.

"Yes, put yourself in his place. Work for fifty-one years of your life. Abide by the law. Pay taxes. Marry. Raise three children. Give one to your country, to die in a far-off place. Send another son, a priest, to serve the poor in another far-off land. But you still have Aggie. Your dear Aggie. Until that dreadful night, after which this man's life could never be the same again.

"What did he discover as a result of that night? When innocent Agnes Riordan needed protection, the courts did not protect her. But they did protect her murderer by making justice into a game and turning the murderer loose on a defenseless public.

"Having been forced to witness that, this defendant's 'comprehension' was indeed 'strained to the breaking point.' As yours would be. As any fair-minded person would be.

"Outrage, ladies and gentlemen! Outrage is what he felt!

"Now, in his summation, the District Attorney will lay great stress on intent. It is one of the key elements in the crime of murder. He will claim that Dennis Riordan had the intent to kill Cletus Johnson.

"I say to you, Dennis Riordan's intent was not to kill. His intent was to do what our system of law has rendered itself powerless to do in cases like Cletus Johnson's. That is, to administer a reasonable measure of justice that conforms to the concept of fairness. So that the people will retain some respect for our courts.

"You will not accomplish that by sending my client to prison. By doing so, you will only support the courts that set rapist and murderer Cletus Johnson free, but would now condemn father, husband, decent human being Dennis Riordan.

"This trial is not the trial of Dennis Riordan. If that were all, we would have had this over with in a single day.

"What is on trial here is our system of justice!"

In the same instant, Lester Crewe rose to object and Judge Klein banged his gavel rhythmically like a church bell tolling.

"Object!" Lester Crewe shouted.

"Sustained!" Klein agreed so quickly that he drowned out the objection. "Counselor, that is improper comment for summation!"

"I am commenting on the evidence, Your Honor, and I have that right," Ben protested.

"You will not put the legal system on trial in my courtroom," Klein shouted.

"Why? Because this jury might rise up and say to the judges, *our* patience has been strained to the breaking point? *We* demand to be protected. We want to be safe in our homes, on our streets."

"Your Honor," Lester Crewe shouted, trying to interrupt Ben Gordon.

Klein banged his gavel, but Ben continued, determined not to stop even if the judge attempted to have him forcibly ejected from the courtroom.

"Because this jury might say, we will no longer accept from the courts tortured, twisted decisions that are neither fair nor rational. Is that what you're afraid of?"

Judge Klein continued to bang his gavel as loudly and continuously as he could until finally Ben Gordon was forced into silence. Then, summoning all his judicial self-restraint, Klein confined himself to a controlled admonition. "The jury will disregard the argumentative outbursts of counsel, which are neither proper nor justified. And counsel will join me inside. This court will stand in recess for ten minutes!"

"Gordon, never before in my years on the bench have I had to interrupt an attorney during his summation so I could find him in contempt. But I am doing that now. And I not only fine you two hundred dollars for this offense, in addition to the four hundred I have already fined you, but since money fines seem to make no impression on you, I hereby sentence you to five days in confinement to begin at the end of this trial. And I warn that there will be more if at any time another such incident occurs. Understood?"

"Yes, Your Honor," Ben Gordon said.

"Now, go out there and finish your summation within reasonable bounds."

"Yes, sir!"

The courtroom had been restored to quiet as Ben Gordon approached the jury to finish his summation.

"Ladies and gentlemen, in this state the law does not provide capital punishment in such a case as this. Yet any finding of guilty against my client, a man sixty-six years old, will in effect be a sentence of death."

"Object," Lester Crewe called out. "The jury is not concerned with sentence. Only with guilt or innocence."

"Sustained," Klein ruled crisply.

Ben Gordon had no alternative but to conclude as quickly as possible.

"Now as I close I must confess to you that in all my meetings with my client, all my discussions with him about this trial, he has never asked to be set free. To the end, a simple, God-fearing man, he is willing to pay for what the State considers his crime. But I ask you to set him free. Not for his sake. But for your sake, for the sake of us all. Thank you."

Brushing away the sweat oozing down into his eyes, Ben Gordon turned from the jury and walked toward the counsel table. He found Dennis Riordan weeping silently.

From the rear of the courtroom someone burst into applause, but Judge Klein stifled all public reaction with his determined gavel.

"This court will stand in recess for fifteen minutes!"

The jury filed out. The shuffling behind Ben told him that the reporters had rushed out to report. He left his chair and started to where Arlene was sitting.

When he reached Arlene, she said nothing. She mopped his damp face with her handkerchief, brushed back his unruly hair, reached for his hand. She could not warm it because her own hands were even colder. She offered no opinion, no prediction. But he found in her eyes the approval which comforted him.

Two reporters approached him, but he refused to answer their questions, even with a "No comment." He was silent, drained and greatly worried.

For he knew better than anyone that the outcome of this trial hung not on what he had said, but on what Lester Crewe would say, and even more on Judge Klein's charge to the jury.

The only consolation Ben Gordon had was that he had done his best for Dennis Riordan.

24

THE JURY HAD RETURNED, as grim and sober as when they had filed out. Judge Klein reappeared, stood at his large high-backed chair and surveyed the courtroom, stilling the last whisper among the spectators by his glare. Then he seated himself, leaned forward and ordered, "Mr. Crewe."

Lester Crewe rose, a few pages of typed notes in hand. He nervously readjusted his thick-framed glasses and faced the jury.

"Defense counsel has made an eloquent plea on behalf of this client. And I am sure he was deeply moved and completely honest when he urged you to cast aside the law and overturn the judges. But I wish to point out to you that the law in this case has been fair and impartial. The same law, the same courts, that protected the rights of Cletus Johnson have also protected the rights of Dennis Riordan. From the first moment he had contact with the law, he was informed of his rights. His confession was taken legally. He was assigned an attorney. The State has gone to great lengths to ensure him a fair trial. You, his jurors, have given of your time and your patience to hear all the witnesses. You will, I am sure, carefully debate his fate. As with Cletus Johnson, Dennis Riordan has been given every consideration the law allows. We cannot now say the law applies to some people and not to others. We cannot have selective justice. Nor is it the right of juries to rewrite the law. So I say to you, no matter how touching the plea by defense counsel, you must lay aside all emotions.

"In the course of your deliberations, I ask you to keep in mind only the testimony you heard here. The man who sold the gun to Riordan and the false statements Riordan made to him. The eyewitness who actually saw Riordan fire the fatal shots. The police sergeant to whom he surrendered. The confession he made to me in which he stated his intent to kill Cletus Johnson. The Medical Examiner's findings as to the cause of Johnson's death. Every element of proof required by the law has been presented to you. And it is that proof which must determine your verdict.

"I am sure we all feel sorry for this defendant. We would not wish on any father what has befallen Dennis Riordan. We can commiserate with him. We can even weep for him. We can say, 'The world has done you a terrible injustice.' And so it has.

"But the one thing we cannot do is say to Dennis Riordan, and to the society at large, we sanction murder! We cannot say, you have a right to kill another man with our approval and blessing. For if you do that, then our entire structure falls apart. We must deal with all criminals as criminals.

"It does not matter what Dennis Riordan was for the previous sixty-six years of his life. Once Dennis Riordan pulled that trigger, he became a criminal. A murderer! And that is the only basis on which we must deal with him.

"Else what would happen if we granted the family of every victim a hunting license to go out and kill the killer? Shall we say to Cletus Johnson's kin, you are now free to kill Dennis Riordan? Where does it stop?

"Well, the law demands that it stop right here! It is your obligation, unhappy as that may be, to see that justice is carried out. Else our whole structure of law falls and each person becomes his own policeman, his own judge, his own jury and his own executioner. We can't let that happen. You can't let it happen.

"Defendant's attorney has tried to divert you from your duty by appealing to your passions. By arguing that because justice was misguided in the case of Agnes Riordan, you must remedy that situation by your verdict. Bear in mind the cornerstone of our system of justice: 'Better ten guilty men go free, than that one innocent man be condemned.' That is the reason why we have all the constitutional safeguards with which we surround every person accused of a crime. Without those safeguards, what protection would you have if ever you were accused of a crime?

"In the case before you now, this is no innocent man you are judging. Your duty is hard, but clear. Judge him by his actions. By the testimony you heard. By his own confession. And you must bring back a verdict of guilty!"

There was total silence in the courtroom when Lester Crewe returned to his chair. In the jury box fourteen people sat silent and motionless. Violet Tolliver dared to stare at Dennis Riordan, who stared back through blue eyes which were strong and clear in his ruddy, freckled face. She looked down to study her fingers, which were twisted into a tight, tense knot. Walter Grove noticed and appreciated her dilemma, which faced them all.

Judge Klein commenced his charge.

"Ladies and gentlemen, the indictment in this case charges the defendant with the commission of Murder in the Second Degree. The vital elements in that crime are, first, that the act was committed with the intent to kill; second, that the defendant did indeed shoot his victim with a gun as charged; third, that the action of the defendant caused the death of the victim, Cletus Johnson.

"Your job is to arrive at the facts, based on the evidence, and to determine by unanimous verdict if those facts sustain all the elements of the People's indictment beyond a reasonable doubt.

"The phrase 'reasonable doubt' is sometimes clouded in mystery, not only in the minds of lay people but sometimes in the minds of judges as well. Reasonable doubt does not mean beyond all doubt. It does not mean beyond a mathematical doubt. It means a doubt that can be substantiated by a reason. If such a doubt does exist, then you must find the defendant innocent of the crime charged. If not, then it is your duty to convict.

"Finally, it is not your job to interpret or reinterpret the law. Or to correct what you may deem deficiencies in the law or the manner in which it functions. Your job, your only job, is to decide, did Dennis Riordan commit the acts with which he is charged, did he do so with intent to cause the death of another man?

"If, during your deliberations, you have any questions as to testimony you heard, exhibits which were introduced or questions of law, you will send me a note. I will have the testimony read back for you or answer your questions myself.

"Now, the two alternates who have been kind enough to bear with us during this trial are excused. The twelve remaining jurors will file into the jury room and commence your deliberations. I will add only one thing more. Since it is customary for the first juror selected to be the foreman, I hereby appoint Mr. Prouty to that responsibility."

The full courtroom watched in silence as the twelve people entrusted with the fate of Dennis Riordan filed out of the jury box and through the door on their way to the jury room.

Once that door closed, the courtroom exploded into activity. Newspaper people rushed for the phones. Television reporters raced to the lobby of the courthouse, where camera crews were waiting to record them. Public interest in the fate of Dennis Riordan had reached such intensity that all the media felt compelled to report not only fully but often. Some TV channels were alerted to interrupt regular programing with any important breaks in the case.

Those newspeople whose jobs consisted of commenting on events rather than reporting them crowded at the barrier to ply Ben Gordon and Lester Crewe with questions as to strategy and predictions. Aware of the unpredictability of juries, neither man ventured any guesses or felt free to make any comments.

Each man started shoving notes, memoranda and other trial aids into his briefcase. They glanced at each other.

"Want some coffee, Ben?" Lester asked. "Or even a good stiff drink?"

"Arlene is here."

"Bring her along. Hortense wanted to come. But there was a knifing up at her school yesterday. She figured her students would need her today."

They left their bulging briefcases in the custody of the clerk and started out. Arlene met them at the barrier.

"Well?" Ben asked. "What do you think?"

"I'm glad I'm not a juror," was all she said.

"Me, too," Lester Crewe agreed.

When they reached the corridor, Ben found his mother waiting, her eyelids trembling with tears. "I don't know what will happen. But if Uncle Harry was here he would have been very proud." She kissed him and clung to him for a moment.

"Mom, it isn't over yet."

"But you did your best. A very good best. Listen, Ben, next week come to supper. And bring Arlene. At least I can talk to her. She is the nicest thing that ever happened to you."

She kissed Arlene on the cheek, kissed Ben once more and decided. "Better than Uncle Harry." She started away.

Ben touched the damp place on his cheek. Lester urged, "Are we going to get that drink?"

"Shhh," Arlene cautioned. "He has just received the Uncle Harry Award for Aspiring Young Lawyers, and he's enjoying it."

25

CONFRONTED BY SUCH unaccustomed and grave responsibility, his lean, wrinkled, light brown face glistening with nervous perspiration, Elihu Prouty confessed, "I never been on a jury before, no less being a foreman, so I don't know how this works. But I think it would be a good idea to find out right away where we stand. So, Miss Tolliver, if you don't mind, would you please pass out these sheets and pencils? Then everybody mark down how you would vote. We don't need no names. Sort of a secret ballot like on election day."

Violet passed out the sheets and pencils. Each juror glanced about the long table, trying to fathom the disposition of the others before venturing a vote. Walter Grove was the first to shroud his paper with his left hand and mark his ballot. Following his example, the rest voted in like manner.

When all twelve folded ballots had been returned, Violet opened them and passed them one by one to Prouty, who intoned the results:

"*Guilty. Not guilty. Not guilty. G.*—I guess that means guilty. Blank. *Guilty. Guilty.* Another *G. Not Guilty.* Blank. *Innocent.* Another blank. That's five guilty, four not guilty. And three didn't vote."

Walter Grove spoke up. "Mr. Foreman, we're here to

arrive at a verdict. And the judge said it has to be unanimous. If we differ, we can argue among ourselves and try to reach a decision. But if there are three people who won't even vote, well, I think we have a right to know who those three are."

"Good point, Mr. Grove," Prouty said. "I hope you three won't mind, but would you raise your hands, please?"

No one stirred. Finally, Harold Markowitz, foreman of a plumbing supply warehouse, raised his right hand and in the same instant dug his left hand into his pocket to clutch the reserve package of Tums he always carried for moments of stress. Then, timidly, young Eudora Barnes raised her hand, followed by Luther Banks, the commercial artist, who sat opposite her.

Prouty looked at Harold Markowitz. "Could you tell us why?"

Markowitz chewed furiously on his chalky tablet, but found it difficult to generate enough saliva to swallow the elusive white bits that stuck in his throat like fishhooks. It took a large glass of water to enable him to speak.

"Well, I'll tell you, Mr. Prouty, all through this trial I sit there listening and thinking, in the beginning, the judge said, don't make up our mind until we heard all the evidence. So I kept thinking till that time comes I'm not supposed to make up my mind. Now the time has come and I still can't make up my mind."

He paused to take another tablet.

"What I mean is, it's like this. What that young black District Attorney said is true. But what that defense attorney said is also true. Now, which one is truer than the other, I don't know.

"Did Riordan do what they said? Sure he did. But as the father of three daughters, I am not going to vote against that man. In other words, I know what I should do, but I don't want to do it!"

Prouty looked to Eudora Barnes, the young bank teller and student. The slight black girl was tense, gripping the edge of the table as she spoke, her voice low and her lips tremulous.

"I don't think it's fair. I am not trained for this kind of thing. I mean, who am I to have an opinion about another person's freedom? I wanted to stand up in that jury box and say, 'Judge, I'm scared. I don't want to do this.' I didn't even want to come into this jury room. I didn't . . ."

Eudora Barnes hid her face in her hands and wept. Veronica Connell, the lay teacher in the parochial school, who sat beside Eudora, put an arm around her and whispered, "Easy. You'll be all right."

"I just want to go back to work and back to school. I have exams every night next week," the girl sobbed.

"Shhh. I know how it is. I'm a teacher."

That established a reassuring bond between them, and Eudora sniffled to a gasping silence. Veronica Connell produced a packet of Kleenex. "Dry your eyes. Blow your nose. And you'll feel better."

Elihu Prouty looked at Luther Banks, who hesitated before answering. He stared at his delicate, nimble, creative hands. Then finally, he looked the length of the table toward the foreman.

"Mr. Prouty, in my own way I feel like Miss Barnes. Show me a sketch, a design, a work of art, I will not only have a firm opinion, I will not hesitate to express it. But to dispose of another man's life, that's different. Far different. Sitting in that jury box I wondered about that. And finally I realized why.

"Because I am black!"

His statement was met by reactions of anger from several white members of the jury.

Deborah Rosenstone openly accused, "If you're going to defend the likes of a rapist and murderer like Johnson just because he's black!"

Prouty intervened. "Mrs. Rosenstone, please, let him have his say first."

"I don't know if it would do any good to address myself to a closed mind like Mr. Banks's!" she retorted.

Prouty beseeched, gently, "Mrs. Rosenstone? Please?"

She exhaled in combined anger and disgust, then became silent but poised in a tense attitude that threatened another explosion.

"I'm sorry if I upset anyone," Banks continued. "Now, I would like to say what I started out to say. And it has not to do with Cletus Johnson. I wish that bastard had never been born. I wish even more that he had never been born black. That's not what I'm talking about at all.

"When I was a little kid, I used to trail my grandmother around the kitchen, watch her cook, mainly listen to her complain. Most of all I remember her saying, 'Going to come a time when people will stop disposing of other people's lives. All my days,' she would say, 'white folks have been disposing of colored people's lives. Well, that time got to soon be over.'

"She died before the civil rights movement really got going. So she never lived to see the changes. But I remember her great resentment against people disposing of other people's lives. Now the time has come for me to dispose of another man's life. And I find I can't do that."

"But is your duty," Armando Aguilar, the Puerto Rican building superintendent, interrupted.

"I wish someone could convince me," Luther Banks said. "Right now, no."

Prouty nodded soberly and prodded. "Before this is over, Mr. Banks, disposing or not, you are going to have to vote. As Mr. Aguilar says, it's your duty."

"I know, I know," Banks agreed sadly.

"Now," Prouty continued, "anyone else want to explain their vote? It might help us all."

Deborah Rosenstone raised her hand so sharply as to constitute an act of protest.

"I voted not guilty and I'm proud of it!" she announced. Anticipating some rebuttal, she continued, "I am sick to death of how the courts and the judges are endangering our safety! We need strict law enforcement! And if the judges continue to play revolving door justice, we are all in danger!"

Veronica Connell stared across at her and said, "Mrs. Rosenstone, didn't you hear the judge's charge? We've only got one job. To decide on the evidence if Riordan did what they accused him of doing."

"Miss Connell, you may be a schoolteacher, but don't try to teach me! I am a citizen! I have rights! And one of my rights is to vote however I choose at this time!"

"Ladies, ladies, please," Mr. Prouty intervened. "I don't know if I got a duty as foreman, but I like to point out Miss Connell is correct. We got to do what we took an oath to do. Remember when we were sworn in? Something like, 'Try this case in an impartial manner . . .'"

Walter Grove assisted. "'In a just and impartial manner to the best of your judgment and render a verdict according to the law and the evidence.'"

Hesitantly, Violet Tolliver raised her hand. "I would like to make a confession. When we were being questioned on the *voir dire* examination, I had several chances to be excused from serving, because, frankly, I felt I really didn't have the time. But finally I said to myself, I feel sorry for Dennis Riordan so I am going to stick it out and make the sacrifice because that poor man is going to need a friend on this jury. I know that was against the oath we took. And it was wrong. But then as I listened to the witnesses, as I heard the lawyers argue and heard Judge Klein's charge, I realized what I had sworn to do. And now, much as I dislike it, I had to do it. I voted guilty."

"I am not voting against that man!" Harold Markowitz maintained in an angry, determined whisper.

"Anyone else?" Prouty asked. When no hands were raised he continued, "Would you each say how you voted?"

Veronica Connell announced simply, "Based on the evidence, guilty."

Armando Aguilar said, "Is a lousy job we got, and a lousy law, but I got to say guilty."

"Not guilty!" Anthony Mascarella, the produce manager, said, volunteering, "we got to do something to keep the animals in check!"

"Guilty," Aurora Devins said.

"Not guilty," Mildred Ennis, the black X-ray technician, announced.

"Not guilty," Walter Grove declared, aware of the reaction of surprise from Violet Tolliver who sat opposite him.

Eleven having identified their votes, all eyes turned to Elihu Prouty. "Vengeance is mine, saith the Lord. No man can take that upon himself. Guilty."

He stared at his colleagues and remarked, "Well, ladies and gentlemen, five against four and three not voting. Seems like we got a long way to go."

26

FIVE HOURS AND seven ballots later, the three reluctant jurors having been convinced to vote, and after a dinner of sandwiches and coffee, the score stood: Guilty, nine. Not guilty, three. At that point, Foreman Prouty summoned the attendant to inform the judge that no verdict seemed attainable tonight. The jurors were tired and would welcome a night's sleep.

Judge Klein ordered them transported by police department van to a midtown hotel, where accommodations had been arranged.

Ben Gordon, Les Crewe and Arlene, who had waited out the jury's deliberations, left the courthouse, stood on the broad steps and stared up at the dark sky, and all three breathed deeply of the night air. Foley Square, an area devoted to courthouses and official federal, state and city buildings, was utterly deserted after business hours. The daytime rush of traffic, the screeching of cars coming to abrupt life-saving stops no longer shattered the air.

Lester Crewe inhaled deeply, exhaled tiredly and said, "I didn't think it would go this long."

"Neither did I," Ben admitted.

"I wish I knew what they are debating," Lester said.

"As long as they're debating," Ben replied, for it was more than he had anticipated.

"See you in the morning." Lester started away, heading in the direction of the East Side subway.

"Let's walk a little," Arlene suggested. "You need it."

Slowly they started down the courthouse steps, waited for a green light, crossed the street, felt the tremor of a subway train as it rumbled by under their feet. They turned south and were at City Hall Park. They paused, then entered that tiny green oasis amid ancient buildings and new, tall glass skyscrapers. They reached the steps of City Hall, famous as the setting for greeting sports and world celebrities, heroes of the age of flight—from Lindberg to the first astronauts to walk on the moon. On a quixotic impulse, Ben raced up the broad steps and, with only Arlene Robbins for an audience, in mock defiance raised his clenched fist and shouted, "All you courts and all you judges, I'll beat you yet!"

Arlene laughed and called up to him, "Ben, you're insane."

"And my prognosis is even worse, unless you agree to marry me!" he shouted back.

By that time a police prowl car had stopped, mounted the sidewalk and reached the steps. Both uniformed policemen emerged hastily, their pistols drawn.

"What the hell are you doing up there, Mister?" one of the officers challenged.

"Just taking a walk with my girl friend," Ben said as he came down the steps.

The policeman studied Ben suspiciously, looked at Arlene. "Lady, are you with this man, or is he bothering you?"

"I'm with this man all the way," she declared.

"What was he doing up there?"

"Proposing," Arlene replied.

"Proposing what?"

"Marriage."

"Oh? Yeah?" The policeman was doubtful but his accusatory attitude softened. "Well, he could have picked a better place. A safer place. You know a girl was killed in this park about a year ago."

"Yes, yes, I know," Arlene said. "We both know."

"My advice is get moving," the officer said. "And you, Mister, find some other place to do your proposing." He started back to the patrol car, stood in the beams of its headlights, turned, studied Arlene and said to Ben, "I don't blame you."

"Let's go home," Ben said.

When they arrived at the apartment, the phone was ringing. Arlene answered it because she knew that Ben would not.

"For you. Victor Coles," she announced, holding out the phone.

He hesitated. She insisted, thrusting the phone at him. He finally took it.

"Coles? Hi."

"Ben, to prove what I've been saying, I took a little liberty. Booked you on the *Today* show!" he announced proudly.

"Booked me . . ." Ben protested angrily. "I have to be in court all day tomorrow. We never know when the jury is coming in."

"Don't get excited, Ben. I provided for that. The booking is for the day after the verdict, no matter when that is. They'll bump some other celebrity to make room for you."

"Look, I don't know if I can do that kind of thing," Ben protested.

"After that summation you made today, you can do anything! Now, listen good, and I'll tell you what I told the *Today* people. I said, this was the greatest summation since Darrow defended Leopold and Loeb! How do you like that for billing?" Coles gloated.

"Comparing me to Clarence Darrow? Are you crazy?"

"The point is, it worked!" Coles shot back, insulted that his strategy was not being greeted with the enthusiasm he felt it deserved. "Look, Ben, get one thing through your head. For the rest of your life, people are going to be divided into two classes: Those who are *on* TV. And those who only *watch* TV. If you're not on, you might as well not exist. This is your chance to get on. And when you go on make the first announcement of our book on the *Today* show. After that, I got a little bonus in mind."

"Yeah?" Ben asked skeptically.

"A regular feature. Say two or three times a week on the *Today* show or *Good Morning, America*—Ben Gordon, now famous young attorney, deals with the legal problems people phone in. Phone-ins are big these days. Phil Donahue does it and it works great. There's money in it. Big money. And exposure. That's the thing in these times. You'll get more cases than you can handle!"

"Yeah," Ben said, too tired to argue.

"So, think up some terrific things to say, controversial things, things people will talk about afterward. If you like, represent a very funny comedy writer who could write you some one-liners. He used to write for the President," Coles said, then added in what he considered a subtle way, "of course, to make everything legally correct, you should have Riordan sign that agreement first. After all, you wouldn't want to be in the position of announcing a book that isn't even signed yet and let someone else steal it. How would that look for a smart young lawyer?"

"Not good," Ben agreed, thinking, *that's the best reason in the world not to announce a book and not to go on the* Today *show either.* But he would fight that war when he was less tired. He hung up.

* * *

The hotel in which the jurors had been sequestered boasted only two refreshment facilities open at this late hour: the Elizabethan Taverne, a small, dark bar masquerading as an English inn in the time of Sir Walter Raleigh, and a coffee shop called the Tropicana Room, which pretended to be a South Seas paradise and abounded in green and orange plastic vegetation.

Walter Grove selected the Elizabethan Taverne, where the waitresses were adorned in costumes so tightly bodiced that they threatened to pop their breasts at any moment. Too tired to be entranced by feminine wiles, Walter Grove felt the need of a drink before he could sleep, for he was far too agitated by the fear that this jury was going to doom Dennis Riordan to jail for the rest of his natural life. It violated Grove's sense of justice and outraged his concern for a good and decent man. Feeling that way, he knew he would not fall asleep without some help. He was on his second glass of assistance when he noticed, across the lobby, Violet Tolliver enter the Tropicana Room. Glass in hand, Walter Grove deserted the Taverne and crossed the lobby.

Violet was scanning the menu for a dish that would satisfy her late-night hunger without risking some greasy food that had been warming in a steam table all day. Though it was almost midnight, she settled on breakfast. After she had given her order to the waitress, Walter Grove appeared.

"May I?" he asked.

"Of course."

"Would you like a drink? I can get you one from the bar."

"What I would like right now, really like, is some of that terrific Chinese food."

"Do you realize, Miss Tolliver, that after tomorrow there won't be any terrific Chinese lunches?"

"I've thought about that," she confessed. "But I also thought you weren't calling me Miss Tolliver anymore."

"The minute you walk out of that courtroom for the last time you'll go back to being the celebrity you are. So, after tomorrow, it'll be Miss Tolliver again."

"Why?"

"You couldn't live my way. It would bore you to death. And I couldn't live your way. The continuous excitement would bore me to death."

For the first time she realized the degree of serious thought Walter Grove had given to their brief relationship. She studied his intense gray eyes and found them frank and unashamedly revealing. If she had not had fantasies of her own about him, she would have resorted to one of the many glib and amusing evasions she had accumulated over the years for exactly such remarks. But this was not the usual ploy to which she was frequently exposed. This was an honest revelation and out of respect for that she remained silent.

Soon the waitress arrived with a large plate of scrambled eggs, crisp bacon, home-fried potatoes, along with toast, marmalade and a pot of coffee. Embarrassed by so much food, Violet apologized sheepishly. "I told you once, I have a tremendous appetite."

"I know," he recalled, "and it drives all your friends crazy how you still keep your fabulous figure."

"Metabolism, I guess. Wouldn't you like something?"

"No thanks. Go on. Dig in!" Once she started, he said, "You must think I'm a stubborn fool."

She stopped eating to look across at him. "Why would I think that?"

"Because I'm holding out for acquittal."

"If that's the way you feel, that's the way you have to

vote." She tried to resume eating, but instead felt compelled to add, "Though I must admit I'm quite puzzled . . ." She stopped precipitously. "Sorry, I didn't mean to say that."

"Why not? If that's the way you feel?" he echoed.

She confessed, "Because most arguments I ever had with both my husbands used to start that way. I'd say something like, 'I must admit I'm puzzled by your resentment of my friends.' Or, 'I must admit I was embarrassed by your conduct at the party tonight.' Always it was, 'I must admit something or other.' Somehow that phrase leads me into saying something I later regret."

"What were you going to say about me and then regret?" Grove asked. When she failed to respond, he urged, "Tell me. At least it can't lead to a divorce."

"All right." She put down her fork and knife, looked directly into his eyes and said, "I must admit that for an intelligent man, which you are, a very sensitive man, which I discovered you also are, you are totally incapable of accepting reality."

"Oh, am I?" he exploded, far more resentful than he had anticipated.

"We took an oath as jurors that we would abide by the evidence. The evidence is very clear. The defense attorney, a bright young man, and highly capable, could not rebut one bit of proof the prosecutor presented. Yet now, despite that, you, that very verbose Rosenstone woman and that plumbing supply man, what's his name . . ."

"Markowitz, Harold Markowitz."

"The three of you keep holding out. Believe me, no one can feel sorrier for Dennis Riordan than I do. But he did kill Johnson. And it's our duty, our unfortunate duty, to find him guilty."

"Why?" Grove demanded.

"Because the law demands it!"

"Your eggs are getting cold." He rudely disposed of her argument.

"Don't you dare say that to me!" she protested angrily. "My first husband always used to do that."

"Do what?" Grove demanded, adding his own heat to the conflict.

"Whenever we got into an argument on any important subject, he would always try to shut me up with some non sequitur. As if it was beneath his dignity to discuss anything seriously with a woman. 'Your eggs are getting cold' is just such a put-down. Well, to hell with the eggs! I would like one rational argument from you to support your unreasonable stubbornness!" she demanded.

"Okay," he said, not agreeing but rising to her challenge. "Answer me one question . . ." He stopped abruptly. "Are we allowed to discuss this?"

"The case has been entrusted to us. We're allowed to discuss it now," she stated firmly, but then added a hesitant, qualifying "I think."

"Just the two of us? Shouldn't we discuss it with all twelve jurors present?"

"You're saying that because you can't give me a single logical reason for your very *il*logical attitude," she accused.

"Logical reason? Okay! Take all the evidence you heard about Cletus Johnson having raped, robbed and murdered Agnes Riordan. Take all the proof the police had. Blood tests, semen, fingerprints, jewelry, his confession. Far more evidence than they have against Dennis Riordan. Your 'logical' law set Cletus Johnson free. Yet now you are willing to convict Dennis Riordan. Well, that violates *my* sense of logic, fairness and justice!"

"But we're not called on to judge Cletus Johnson, only Dennis Riordan!" she argued.

"Without Johnson and what he did, there would never

have been a Dennis Riordan case!" he shot back, his voice now so loud that other customers in the coffee shop were staring in their direction.

In a lower, guarded voice, Violet countered, "That does not relieve us of the duty to vote on the evidence. Don't you think I'd like to see Riordan go free? But our system of justice demands a guilty verdict!"

"And I think there's too damn much *in*justice in our system of justice," he maintained in a low, hoarse voice. "I'm just sorry that *you* are too insensitive to understand that!"

She resumed eating, her eyes directed down at her food, which had indeed grown cold. After a long silence, he spoke again.

"Didn't it trouble you when the judge shut Gordon up as soon as he got onto that Rogers decision?"

"I was curious to know what he intended to say but that would not have changed my vote."

"I guess not. Sorry I intruded on you. *Bon appetit!*" he said sarcastically as he departed.

27

ON THE TRIP DOWNTOWN in the police bus, the jurors studiously avoided discussing the case. Their conversation was cautiously confined to the hotel and their accommodations.

"I should have remembered to ask for a bed board," Harold Markowitz moaned. "With my back, even one night in a soft bed is torture. If we're still at it, tonight I'll ask for one."

"Tonight," Anthony Mascarella said, "I would like to eat supper in my own home and sleep in my own bed. So tomorrow I can go back to work nice and fresh."

"Right!" Markowitz agreed.

Veronica Connell accused Markowitz, "You're one of the three who are prolonging this procedure!"

Elihu Prouty felt it his duty as foreman to intervene. "I think we better wait till we're back in the jury room before we get to arguing."

Once the door was closed, Foreman Prouty suggested, "Let's have another ballot. Maybe some minds got changed overnight."

Violet Tolliver passed the slips down the table. They were marked and returned, and, as had become routine by now, Prouty tabulated the votes and announce "Guilty, ten. Not guilty, two."

Evidently one mind had been changed. But no on except Harold Markowitz, knew whose mind that was. H had arrived at that decision after much pondering durin his sleepless night. *It's a losing battle,* he had reasone *nine to three, no matter how sorry I feel for Riordan u ain't got a chance.*

That was only a rationalization. For though hours argument and logic failed to convince him, one night torment from his painful back had succeeded in changin his vote. He would do anything to avoid another night agony.

"Well," Prouty remarked, "at least we're gettin closer."

"But not close enough," Veronica Connell said. " there's a single good reason for voting not guilty based o the evidence, I'd like to hear it."

"I, too!" Violet Tolliver said, directing her remar across the table directly at Walter Grove.

But it was Deborah Rosenstone who took up the cha lenge. "I would think, Miss Connell, that of all of us, yo would have some sympathy for that very nice Irish Cath lic gentleman who, God knows, has suffered more tha enough for one lifetime!"

"If I wanted to express sympathy I wouldn't serve o a jury. I would send a Hallmark card!" Veronica Conne replied. "The evidence against Riordan has nothing to d with his being Irish or Catholic. It has to do with buyin a gun and killing another man. And of that he is guilty She might as well have been lecturing her ten-year-ol boys in parochial school.

"Unfortunate, but true!" Violet Tolliver agreed.

Walter Grove studied her beautiful and famous fac now strong and determined. He was about to respon heatedly, but feeling considerable guilt for his insults of last night, he moderated his voice and his attitude.

Quite thoughtfully, he said, "Before another vote is taken I would like to do what Judge Klein said we could. Examine the evidence. I would like to see the opinion in that Rogers case that Gordon talked about. Mr. Prouty, will you request it?"

There was a stir in the corridors outside the courtroom when word spread that a note had come from the jury room. Newspeople, who had been standing by anxiously, thought it might presage a verdict. More experienced courtroom hands knew it did not, though it might yield a clue to which way the jury was leaning.

Still hastily pulling on his black judicial robe, Judge Klein ascended the bench, as Ben Gordon and Lester Crewe assembled at their counsel tables. Klein slipped on his reading glasses, scanned the jury's note, reacted with some irritation, then said, "They wish to see defendant's exhibit, the opinion in the Rogers case."

Lester Crewe asked, "Not the transcript of Judge Lengel's testimony about the Rogers case?"

"This note says the decision itself. Since it's in evidence, I have no ground on which to deny it. Any objection?"

"No, sir," Lester Crewe finally had to concede.

"No, sir," Ben Gordon said, as puzzled as his opponent by this strange request.

While Walter Grove studied the text of the Rogers decision, his colleagues passed the time nervously doodling on scratch pads, making up shopping lists and notes reminding themselves to call the dentist or the doctor for appointments now that jury duty would be coming to an end.

Twice Harold Markowitz lit up cigars only to have Veronica Connell protest, "Mr. Prouty! Must we permit our lungs to be contaminated because he likes to smoke smelly cigars?"

"Mr. Markowitz, please?" the benign but harried fore man requested.

"Let's get this over with so I can have a decent smoke!" Markowitz exploded, grinding out his cigar. He turned to Walter Grove. "What's taking so long?"

But Walter Grove persisted in his silent study of the Rogers opinions.

Markowitz grumbled, "I think we ought to tell the judge we have one stubborn juror who's holding up the works."

"*Two* stubborn jurors!" Deborah Rosenstone correct ed proudly.

Harold Markowitz did not respond but chewed anoth er Tum and felt it crunch between his teeth like ground glass. After this, he thought, the M & R Plumbing Supply Warehouse will seem like heaven.

Anthony Mascarella, also hoping to convince Grove to finish his study of the decision, remarked, "If we could reach a verdict, I could be back at my market before it closes. After all, I am not a writer who has nothing to do but sit around reading judges' opinions."

Grove did not react.

Violet Tolliver said nothing but continued to glare at him, silently accusing him of being intransigent beyond all reason. *But then,* she concluded, *what could you expect from a man with such a strong, craggy face.*

Finally, Grove placed the transcript on the table. The simple act brought them all to attention.

"Well, Mr. Grove?" Foreman Prouty asked, anxious to progress matters.

"I want to say right off, I am not a lawyer," Grove began.

"We knew that before you started to read," Anthony Mascarella interrupted.

"I am not a lawyer," Grove reiterated, "but I do understand the English language. And when I read this, I see clearly what Gordon was trying to tell us. The Judge Jasen he referred to did not agree with the other judges. He said they are wrong in the way they interpreted the law."

"But they were the majority," Violet Tolliver pointed out, "and they are therefore correct!"

"Before you concede that so willingly, just listen to this example Judge Jasen gives in his opinion." Picking up the transcript, Grove continued, "He says, suppose a man is arrested on a drunk-driving charge and retains a lawyer to defend him. Then later the same man witnesses a brutal murder. Under the Rogers decision, the police would not be allowed to question that man about the murder he witnessed unless his lawyer on the drunk-driving charge was present. Mind you, there is no relationship whatsoever between the drunk-driving charge and the murder he witnessed, still he couldn't testify about it without the lawyer being there. And so a brutal murderer might get away scot-free. Now that is insane. And we would be insane to accept that. Right, *Miss Tolliver?*"

Violet did not answer, just glared at Walter Grove as he continued.

"Now, Gordon was trying to tell us that to throw out Cletus Johnson's confession was just as insane. That the decisions of courts should be as Judge Jasen says in here, 'Rational and fair if the courts are to retain the respect of the people.'"

"We are not judges, we are only jurors," Violet reminded him.

"Hear me out!" Grove said, intense and on the verge

of anger. "Then Judge Jasen repeats Judge Cardozo's warning, 'Justice though due to the accused is due to the accuser also.' Meaning, yes, be fair to the defendant, but be fair to the public as well. Now, listen to Cardozo's words carefully. 'The concept of fairness must not be strained till it is narrowed to a filament.'"

"Gordon said that before, so what?" Harold Markowitz challenged.

"And Gordon was right! When Judge Lengel threw out Johnson's confession, he not only narrowed fairness to a filament, he ripped it to shreds."

Foreman Prouty intervened. "What are you getting at, Mr. Grove?"

"Just think," Grove said to his fellow jurors, "if Johnson's confession had not been thrown out, Riordan wouldn't be here. *We* wouldn't be here!"

With an air of impatient condescension, Violet Tolliver pointed out, "*Mr.* Grove, Johnson's confession *was* thrown out. And we *are* here. With a duty to perform. Now, let's get to it."

"Duty? What duty?" Walter Grove challenged.

"We are jurors! We have to vote guilty or innocent on evidence that all points to only one conclusion. Believe me, I regret that as much as anyone," Violet confessed.

"Do you? Then do something about it," Grove challenged.

"Do? What can we do?" she asked.

Grove paused until he had secured their complete concentration, then slowly he said, "I am ready to do what Gordon was suggesting when Judge Klein shut him up."

"And that is?" Violet Tolliver asked.

"I am ready to say to the courts and the judges, damn it, we've had enough! Our patience *has* been strained to the breaking point. The public does have rights, as well as the criminals!"

"It's one thing to feel that way," Violet Tolliver said, "but what can we twelve do about it?"

"Judges are not infallible. They're human beings like us. When they're wrong, we ought to tell them they're wrong!" Grove declared.

Less argumentative and more curious, Violet Tolliver asked, "Just what are you suggesting?"

"If judges are going to punish the police by setting criminals free so they can victimize us, why can't we rebuke the judges by setting Dennis Riordan free as a sign of our indignation?"

"Dare we do that?" Violet asked softly. "After all, the evidence . . ."

Anthony Mascarella picked up on it. "Right! I'm for the man, it's the evidence that's against him."

"Evidence?" Grove challenged. "One thing we learned during this trial. Evidence is only what the judges allow. And how do they do that? Lengel gave us a perfect example. He ruled out Johnson's confession because he was out on bail for a previous rape and his attorney in that case wasn't present. What a tortured, twisted technicality on which to let a murderer go."

"Unfortunately," Veronica Connell pointed out, "Riordan does not have such a technicality in his favor."

"Wait," Walter Grove said. "Maybe he does."

All eleven of his colleagues sat up straighter and more intent.

"Remember what Judge Klein said in his charge? One of the vital elements the prosecution must prove to get a verdict of guilty of Murder in the Second Degree is *intent*," Grove pointed out.

"I hate to argue against Riordan," Violet Tolliver retorted, "but the clerk testified that he bought that gun days before he killed Johnson. I think that indicates intent."

"It's obvious to me that he intended to kill Johnson all along," Veronica Connell said.

"Besides, he also openly admitted that," Violet said.

"When?" Grove asked.

"You heard him. In his confession!" Violet declared, now evidencing signs of impatience.

"Exactly!" Grove shot back. "*In his confession.* But suppose we decide to throw out his confession, where is proof of intent? As Gordon brought out on cross-examination, Riordan never told the store clerk he intended to kill Johnson. The store clerk admitted he never suspected such an intent. Riordan never told his boss. Never told anyone. The only admission of intent Riordan ever made was in his confession. Now, if we were to throw out Riordan's confession, just as Lengel threw out Johnson's confession, where is proof of intent? There isn't any. Thus, we are missing one vital element that Judge Klein said we had to have to convict for murder."

A sudden and thoughtful silence settled on the room. Foreman Prouty felt it incumbent on him to say something, but Grove's proposal was so startling that he was at a loss for the proper words.

"Gee, I don't know," Eudora Barnes said timidly, admitting that she was tempted to consider Grove's suggestion but was frightened by the consequences.

Veronica Connell mused softly, as if unwilling to admit openly what she was thinking, "It would be a bold thing to do . . . revolutionary, almost."

"I don't think we have that right," Violet Tolliver whispered.

"It's the only way for outraged citizens to make their voices heard in the courts," Walter Grove pointed out. "And remember, in this case we would not be turning loose a man who might commit other crimes."

Foreman Prouty said, "Maybe we ought to have another vote. Miss Tolliver?"

Violet began to fold and tear the sheets into ballot-size slips and pass them out. Once each of the twelve had a slip, but before they had the opportunity to mark them, she asked, "What would happen . . . I mean, what would Judge Klein do?"

"There is nothing he can do!" Walter Grove declared. "Once a jury acquits, that's final. No court, no judge can reverse a verdict of not guilty."

"I don't know," Violet said. "It frightens me."

"Why? Because we are overwhelmed by this august, official-looking building? Because we are in awe of a man in a black robe who sits up on that high bench? What are we afraid of? Our own government? Remember, that government is us. And if we think it's wrong, it's not only our right but our duty to say so. Yes, our duty to apply Judge Jasen's rule, to make our verdict 'rational, fair, as well as practical' . . . to help our courts 'retain the respect of the people.' "

He looked around the long table, studied the eleven other jurors, most of whom either did not share his view or were overcome by the gravity of what he had suggested.

Deborah Rosenstone was first to inscribe her ballot, doing so with a defiance which made no secret of her decision. But Walter Grove did not count that a victory, for she had been on Riordan's side all along.

He was more curious about Veronica Connell, a strong-minded, exacting young woman. And Harold Markowitz, Anthony Mascarella, timid Eudora Barnes and Elihu Prouty, a righteous man who voted his religious conviction. Mainly, Grove was curious about Violet Tolliver's response.

She took up her pencil, shielded her ballot from the

others and marked it. She folded it but instead of passing it to Foreman Prouty, she suddenly tore it up.

"I tried to vote not guilty," she confessed, "but I keep thinking of what Mr. Crewe said about granting the family of every victim a license to kill. I can't vote for that."

"Nor I," Veronica Connell said, turning over her ballot which was clearly marked *Guilty.* "That's going back to frontier justice."

"Miss Connell," Walter Grove replied, "may I point out that we are once again living on the frontier. Our cities and towns have become the frontier. And only the law can save us. But if our courts have turned the law into such an impotent instrument as to cause a decent, law-abiding man like Dennis Riordan to go out, buy a gun and kill, then perhaps our courts have to be made aware of our anger, our frustration. This case has put into our hands the chance to do that. I ask you, all of you, to tear up your ballots, think about that, then vote."

Eudora Barnes timidly pointed out, "Judge Lengel said those constitutional safeguards are not for the benefit of criminals but to protect our rights."

"However," Deborah Rosenstone said, taking up the fight, "Judge Lengel also said that guilty as he knew Johnson to be, he had set him free! Did he want to do that? He did not. You know, when Lengel said that, I actually felt sorry for him. The Johnson case wasn't easy for him, just as this case isn't easy for most of you. But I'm with Mr Grove. This is the only chance any of us may ever have to stand up and say, 'Enough! We want safety in our streets and in our homes. Stop finding so many ways to protect the guilty that you endanger all the innocent.'"

"That's a nice speech, lady," Armando Aguilar said "but the evidence, the gun, the witnesses, everything. tell you the truth, I would like to see the man go free. Bu the evidence . ."

"The evidence," Grove replied, "mountains of it, said Johnson was guilty. But he went free on technicalities. I ask, let's create our own technicality. If Lengel felt compelled to turn free a confirmed criminal to kill again, I think we can take the same liberty for Dennis Riordan who never committed a crime before in his whole life and never will again. Can any of you deny that?"

No one rebutted him.

"At the same time, by our verdict we can make our voices heard in the press and in the courts. We will be saying, the people want reason restored to justice once again. Vote on that basis. Vote your outrage!"

Since there was no answering argument, Foreman Prouty said, "Miss Tolliver, more ballots, please?"

After the ballots were marked and counted, the vote stood: *Guilty,* seven. *Not guilty,* five.

It was going to be a long and arduous day.

FOUR HOURS AND seventeen minutes later, after considerable argument and eleven more ballots, word was sent to Judge Klein's chambers. He ground out his cigar, seized his robe and, as he started out, called to his law clerk, "Tell them to return Riordan to the courtroom. Find Crewe. Find Gordon. There's a verdict!"

From all over the building, people converged on the courtroom. Ben Gordon, Lester Crewe and Arlene Robbins had been having coffee in the restaurant across the street when the clerk found them. Ben and Lester looked at each other.

"This is it," Lester said.

"Look, Les, I want to say again how sorry I am about what I said that day."

"Forget it," Lester said. "Let's go!"

When they arrived at the courtroom door, they were besieged by cameras, lights and microphones, bombarded by requests for predictions. Ben and Lester waved them aside and pushed through the door. From just inside the door, Ben saw Dennis Riordan being led into the courtroom to the counsel table. He squeezed Arlene's hand, then went forward to greet his client.

"Mr. Riordan . . ." Ben greeted him sympathetically.

"Well, kid. I guess we get the bad news now."

"I guess."

"Listen, you did your best. Just last night I wrote Father Dennis a letter . . ." Riordan smiled. "Never get used to calling my own son Father. But I told him what a fight you put up. How you battled with the judges for my sake. What's the judge going to do to you?"

"Nothing much," Ben said, not wanting to upset the old man.

Judge Klein ascended the bench and signaled to the clerk to return the jury. Once they were in place and seated, he addressed Prouty, "Mr. Foreman, I have been notified that the jury has reached a verdict."

"Yes, Your Honor."

"Will the defendant please rise?" Klein ordered.

Both Dennis Riordan and Ben Gordon rose in place.

"Face the jury." Once Riordan had complied, Klein asked, "Mr. Foreman, what is the jury's verdict?"

Elihu Prouty wet his lips nervously, then proceeded to read from a written statement, "We, the jury, find a verdict of guilty . . ."

He was interrupted by a loud outburst from the spectators and the press, but Judge Klein gaveled them to silence. "This is not a football stadium but a court of law!" He turned in Prouty's direction. "Your finding then is guilty?"

"I'm sorry, Your Honor, I was interrupted."

"Continue!"

"We, the jury, find a verdict of guilty insofar as the justice system is concerned. As for the defendant, Dennis Riordan, we find him not guilty!"

There was a moment of hushed silence, until Judge Klein said, "Mr. Foreman, you obviously have a written verdict. I would like to see it." The clerk took it and handed it to the judge, who glared at it and finally muttered, "Clearly against the evidence!" Then he added regretfully, "But bound to happen one day. Bound to happen. We do the best we can, but the people refuse to understand." He folded the note and determined to keep it among his more significant possessions. *That writer fellow, Grove, he must have written this,* Klein decided bitterly. He looked at Dennis Riordan.

"Mr. Riordan, you heard the jury's verdict. You are free to go."

Then, without the usual thanks and commendation accorded to juries, Klein declared, "This jury is dismissed!"

He banged his gavel for the last time in this trial.

Before the media could engulf them, Dennis Riordan and Ben Gordon went to the jury box to shake hands with each juror. Violet Tolliver could not resist. She kissed Dennis Riordan on the cheek as she pressed his hand.

"I'm so relieved we found a way to do it," she said. "You can thank Mr. Grove for that."

"Mr. Gordon," Grove insisted. "Thank Mr. Gordon."

The jury felt suddenly bereft and empty. What had so totally dominated their lives for days had abruptly come to an end. There were handshakes and polite good-byes as they departed to resume their normal lives.

On this final day when Violet Tolliver asked Walter Grove if she could give him a lift uptown, he accepted quickly, adding, "Especially if I can apologize for some of the insulting things I said last night. Say, over lunch? I happen to know a good Chinese restaurant uptown."

"I wish I could," Violet said, "but there's the office decisions, complaints. I've been away for days."

"Don't you ever do anything but go to your office appear in commercials and attend parties that always end up in the gossip columns?"

"Yes."

"Such as?"

"Quiet Sunday mornings are private time, all mine. This city's at its best then. So I go for long walks alone."

"Ever make exceptions?"

She hesitated before saying, "Sometimes."

"Like next Sunday morning?"

"I start early," she warned. "Eight o'clock."

"By eight o'clock I've done ten pages of my novel." He said, "Pick you up."

With Dennis Riordan between them, Ben and Arlene came down the courthouse steps. They were immediately surrounded by cameras and microphones. One question, repeated over and over, emerged out of the babble.

"Mr. Riordan, how does it feel to be free again?"

A simple man, and shy, Dennis Riordan replied, "I don't know yet. You see, I never thought I would be free. It was only thanks to Ben . . . he's a terrific kid . . . I mean he's a terrific attorney, my counselor." He sheepishly glanced at Ben seeking approval for having finally said it properly. "Thanks to him I have my freedom again. Now I have to figure out what to do with it."

"Mr. Riordan, if you had your life to live over, would you have done the same thing?" one woman reporter asked.

Riordan considered thoughtfully. "If I had my life to live over I would want Aggie to be alive, Nedda to be alive and this whole thing never to have happened."

His eyes misted. As the photographers closed in, Ben intervened. "Please! Mr. Riordan is entitled to his personal feelings and his privacy!"

"Thanks, Ben," Riordan said, gripping Ben's arm and drawing him close so he could whisper, "I'll be seeing you again, kid, won't I?"

"Sure," Ben promised. "Soon as all the publicity calms down, I'll come out to visit."

"And bring your girl. She's very nice. You two ought to get married."

With that remark, Dennis Riordan pushed through the crowd of reporters and cameramen, ignoring their remaining questions. They turned to besiege Ben and Arlene.

"Mr. Gordon, did you hear what District Attorney Crewe said?"

"No," Ben replied.

"He said he didn't regret the verdict going the way it did. Was he being a gracious loser or trying to minimize a tough defeat?"

"Neither," Ben said. "He was saying what all conscientious prosecutors in this country will be saying tomorrow. From now on maybe our courts will be more concerned with the basic question of guilt or innocence so we can convict the habitual criminals who menace our society. And you can thank one man for that."

Ben pointed in the direction of Dennis Riordan, who was stolidly making his way toward the subway which would take him back to his home, his garden and the remains of his shattered life.

Ben and Arlene finally broke away from the reporters and were crossing City Hall Park when she asked, "That moment when Riordan grabbed your arm and whispered to you, what did he say?"

"He said we ought to get married. That you're letting an early childhood experience overshadow your whole life. That Ben Gordon is not the same kind of man your father was. That Ben Gordon is a nice kid and a very good lawyer who will make you a loving and devoted husband."

"He said all that in just a few seconds?" Arlene asked, her voice incredulous.

"Well, actually," Ben replied, "he just said we ought to get married. The rest of it was my summation. Based on the evidence, of course."

> "FAST-PACED, EXCITING... BRUTAL AND BLOODY."
> BESTSELLERS

RICHARD A.

SOL YURICK

In this explosive thriller, a young electronics genius taps the phone of his love, and gains unexpected access to the nation's top security lines. Soon the CIA, the KGB, a cartel of business kingpins, and the President of the United States are involved in the ultimate confrontation. What begins as the reaction of a jilted suitor quickly becomes a dangerous and deadly game—a game which Richard A. must master if he is to save his life. 62430-3/$3.50

> "A constantly surprising thriller... Pulsing with energy... Sharp explosions of action."
> Philadelphia Inquirer

> "On the LeCarre turf... an engrossing and scary political thriller." The New York Times Book Review

> "Hums with tension... one of the cleverest and most chilling espionage thrillers yet."
> Publishers Weekly

An **AVON** Paperback

Available wherever paperbacks are sold or directly from the publisher. Include 50¢ per copy for postage and handling: allow 6-8 weeks for delivery. Avon Books, Mail Order Dept., 224 West 57th St., N.Y., N.Y. 10019

Richard A. 2-83